SABOTAGE

kristin harte

SABOTAGE: A VIGILANTE JUSTICE NOVEL
Copyright © 2019 by Kristin Harte

Paperback ISBN: 978-1-944336-71-4
EBook ISBN: 978-1-944336-70-7
Large Print Hardcover ISBN: 978-1-954702-07-3

This is a work of fiction. Names, places, businesses, characters and incidents are either the product of the author's imagination or are used in a fictitious manner. Any resemblance to actual persons living or dead, actual events or locales is purely coincidental.

Edited by Silently Correcting Your Grammar, LLC

Cover by Kinship Press

For inquiries, contact Kristin@KristinHarte.com

SABOTAGE

kristin harte

$$Chapter\ One$$

PARRIS

Text messages were both a blessing and a curse in my world. Two text messages over the past few months had sent my life spinning smack into Justice, Colorado, and it was another that made me want to leave the town for good.

I'm in Sterling. Meet me in an hour, or I come to Justice.

Nothing more needed, not when Cartel, the warlord of the Black Angels national club, was the one doing the summoning. The man had as much power as the big prez, instilled more fear, and was running my fucking life. Even at butt-crack-of-dawn o'clock.

"Gotta go." I rolled out of the strange bed, grabbing my jeans from the floor and pulling them on. The chick who'd taken me home with her lay on the mattress—naked, sleepy, and obviously growing cranky at my quick exit.

"You're not staying?"

"Can't." I grabbed my jacket from the top of her chest of drawers—that hadn't been tossed like the jeans. My colors, my club designation and nomad patch, were far too important for that. I'd busted my ass and paid my dues to be a Black Angel, and though the thrill of the life had dulled over the years, I still respected the sign of my ties to them.

The girl—with a name I couldn't remember—sat up, letting the sheet fall around her hips. "I was hoping for some more time with you."

Translation—she was hoping for a little more of the drugs she'd been given when she'd been pawned off on me. "Sorry, babe. I'm all out of snow and have no time to get you more."

She huffed as I headed for the front door, which didn't exactly endear her to me. She'd been both a responsibility and a necessary evil. A chick who'd needed babysitting so Edge, the Las Vegas Black Angel club president, could focus his attention elsewhere, and a tool to help me get off. She'd used me and I'd used her right back, so this clingy shit was just that. Shit. She wasn't anyone to me, and I wasn't anyone at all.

But she wasn't giving up easily. "How will I reach you?"

"I'll track you down."

She yelled something about arrogant pricks as I walked outside, but I didn't stick around to hear it. I had a warlord hounding my ass who would likely be taking a piece of it before our meeting was over. I didn't need some trick's bullshit added on to that. Besides, I had text messages making my life go sideways. Again.

It had been a text message that had brought me to Justice, Colorado, for the first time. A short one, at that—a friend I knew from my days in the Marines wanting to know if I could help a guy out with some information on motorcycle clubs. Simple, or so I'd thought.

It had been another message that had gotten me to come back to the Rocky Mountain Front town—not simple, that one. A note in the middle of the night saying Gage was shot and there'd been an explosion. Those two facts hadn't gotten to me, though. I'd known who Gage was—a heavy machinery mechanic from Justice, former Navy SEAL, and one of Alder Kennard's guard dogs. I'd met him, and while I had no ties to him, I'd been surprised the town's battle with the Soul Suckers motorcycle club had escalated so quickly. Still, not my problem, and yet...

That message had haunted me.

Not the fact that Gage had been shot. Not the explosion. It had been the word hurry at the end, all in caps, that had stuck with me. That word written in that manner on a group text had led me to believe it had been a woman who'd sent it. A woman who cared about Gage. One thing with the Justice men—they were whipped over their women. Not a bad situation unless you were about to go to war against an enemy who would use anything and everything against you. Which they were. I'd seen guys in their position—rolling into battle with something precious putting a huge fucking target on your back. They always lost...big-time. The fact that the guys in Justice could lose as well hadn't sat right with me.

That text and how it had seemed to be following a path I'd already trod had refused to let me go, not that I'd thought there was anything I could really do to help. I'd been dealing with my own shit.

Fate was a cruel mistress, though. One mistake on my part— and a huge overreach on the part of my so-called brothers in the Vegas Black Angels—had shoved me right back into the town that seemed to need me. And it looked like I'd be staying for a while.

I rode out of Rock Falls and headed east, passing through Justice on my way to Sterling, Colorado. If I were the settling-down type, Justice would be the sort of place I'd want to plant my roots. Small, quiet, good people, lots of opportunities to be outdoors, and very little in the way of bullshit. Alder Kennard ran the town like a military base, something that definitely appealed. But I wasn't settling any time soon—I'd been working for too many years to accomplish my goal, had spent the last two in a hell I hadn't been prepared for but was finding my way through, and I wasn't stopping until I got the answers I'd been hunting. Not even for the fucking reaper himself.

My bike practically growled underneath me, soothing a little bit of the nervous buzz that seemed to have become my default state. Maybe nervous was the wrong word—hyperaware. There was a lot coming at me lately, a bunch of moving pieces with sharp edges and deadly consequences if I didn't work them just right. It'd been too many years of this shit—nine years in the club, five spent behind bars, and two being a turncoat to one particular crew. Something about the Vegas Black Angels joining forces with the Soul Suckers to terrorize Justice had brought all of that down on my shoulders, adding weight to an already impossible load.

There was no way to end the war without bloodshed—mine, my friends', my brothers' from the club. Maybe all of us. And it all started with this fucking warlord. Just like last time.

Sterling sat higher in the mountains than Justice—a small town without much going on, it lay quiet and still as I rolled through. No sign of life except for a single open sign at a diner on the side of the highway. That had to be the place. I pulled in and parked my bike among the pickup trucks and SUVs scattered about in the gravel lot. Snow would be returning to the region soon—it might be time for me to think about buying a cage. A nice, used truck to cart my ass around these mountains. One with luxuries like heat.

"Too old for this shit." I tucked my keys into my coat pocket and headed for the door, prepping myself to come face-to-face with the man who controlled my fate on a daily basis.

Cartel sat at a back table with a cup of coffee in front of him, looking to all the world like another trucker on a long haul through town. I knew better, though—the man had eyes as sharp as blades and a tongue that could steal your breath. He was not to be trusted.

"What's up, boss?"

Cartel turned those dark tunnels of death my way, as if he hadn't known the second I'd pulled into the lot. "Parris. Getting comfortable in Rock Falls?"

The town where the Vegas Black Angels chapter had set up camp...at a literal camp. "Nothing to complain about yet."

When the waitress came by, Cartel smiled her way and asked for a warmer before ordering me a cup of coffee and some toast. Not that I was hungry in the least.

"So," Cartel said once the coffee and food arrived and the waitress left us alone. "How are things really going with the crew?"

But I knew Cartel—had been doing his dirty work for two long years. He wasn't there to shoot the shit, and neither was I.

"Pull them out."

Cartel's lip twitched as if trying to smile. Or not to. "You know I can't do that."

"You can, but you don't want to."

The smile broke free, slicing across his face in a look only a pirate could pull off. "Sounds about right."

"These guys in Justice—they're not rolling over for the Soul Suckers. That crew is losing men left and right, and our guys are now in the mix here. They don't deserve to be slaughtered all because Edge decided we should be backing up his dealers."

"True, but he's the boss. The rest of the men need to follow their leader."

"You asked for my opinion, and I gave it—"

"And I'm dismissing it. The crew stays."

I really wasn't in the mood for his bullshit. "You put me in the Las Vegas crew, told me to keep an eye on things. I've done that. For two years, I've done that. It was messed up before, but I'm telling you, Edge running things is a shitshow and a disaster waiting to happen. Especially since you've got him calling the shots for other houses as well. I've been with the Vegas group every day. I know how twisted he is."

"The crew picked him for prez."

"The crew didn't know the whole story. Besides, he's not working for the crew. He's in this for himself."

Cartel sat back, eyeing me hard. "Aren't we all, though?"

Because I was in it for one thing and one thing only—the head of the man who'd murdered my sister. And Cartel knew it. "Edge has got good men under him. They deserve better."

"Perhaps, but men stupid enough to elect a sadistic narcissist for a leader deserve what they get, don't you agree?" He took a sip of his coffee, not really wanting or waiting for an answer. "We stay. I want you keeping tabs on them, though. They make a single move, I want to know about it. This working with the Soul Suckers has the possibility of bringing the entire organization down, and I don't like it."

But he'd force his men to stay anyway, which made no sense. Nothing ever did with Cartel. "I'll watch, but this is getting to be too much. If Edge finds out I'm keeping an eye on him for you, they'll kill me."

"Then don't get found out." Cartel took one last sip from his mug then stood, grabbing his jacket from the seat and slipping it on. "Stay warm out there, Parris. I'd hate to see you frozen in a ditch on the side of the road somewhere."

Motherfucker. The words he didn't say were *like Ashley*. My sister and old lady to a fellow Black Angel, who'd been murdered during a club war the bastard had started. She'd been found half frozen in a bank of snow on the side of the road, her husband having been shot by a rival club. Cartel knew that history, which made his comment an intentional kick to the balls. One that hit just as hard as the warlord wanted it to. While I hadn't known the girl well because of a substantial age difference, she was still kin. Blood family and club family. It was my responsibility to avenge her death, and I had yet to accomplish that feat. Cartel knew that too. Likely, my failure was his fault. Not that he'd ever admit it.

I couldn't even respond to the bastard, could only sit and stare after him as he walked out the door. Could only do my best to calm my racing heart and not charge the man down and give him a bullet to the back of the head. He deserved to die, but taking him out might sign my own death certificate. And I had shit to do before I let that happen.

"Too damn old for this shit," I whispered, assuming I was talking to myself. I'd missed the waitress walking up, apparently.

"Oh, hun. Aren't we all?" The woman smiled down at me, her brow puckering. Likely seeing something in my face that set off her instincts. Smart woman. I wasn't someone she needed to be around, but she didn't seem like one not to do her job. "You need more coffee?"

"I'm good, thanks." I was far from good, no matter how you

wanted to apply that word to me, but she didn't need my sob story.

She strolled off without another word, leaving me to stew in the bullshit swirling through my head. Ashley and Jinx...two very different women, two different responsibilities. Ashley hadn't really ever been mine to worry about. My dad had remarried later in life and ended up with a second family, one I hadn't spent a lot of time with. Ashley had gotten married right out of high school to a Black Angel named Gunner, the two settling down in Reno where I'd been living. They'd enjoyed club life, and I'd enjoyed getting to know the girl a little better.

Then Cartel had stirred up trouble with other clubs in the region, and things had gotten hot. Too hot. He'd started a club war in Nevada, one that had cost us far too many men. Had cost me my sister, too. And had left me in the position of being the vengeance seeker for her death. He'd gotten me my nomad patch so I wouldn't be tied to one club and sent me out on my mission —kill those who'd killed our men and women. I'd managed to knock out three of the four men responsible for Gunner's and Ashley's deaths, leaving only one left walking this earth. A Soul Sucker by the name of Wolf. I'd track him down eventually, though, and when I did...lord, I might just die myself. Wasn't like I could retire—that particular luxury wasn't available to me.

And fuck, before I could think of doing anything, I needed to deal with the Jinx situation. Get her safe and settled somewhere that Edge couldn't put his hands on her. Or his blades. I owed her because I'd failed her mom. I'd failed her mom because I'd been hunting Wolf.

My world had become one big carousel of suck. A ride I could never seem to get off, no matter how badly I might want to.

Once I finished my coffee and dropped a twenty on the table, I followed in the footsteps of Cartel and hustled out of the diner.

To my surprise, the man hadn't left yet. Instead, he sat inside a beast of a truck, one that towered over my bike—purposely, I was sure. The man was nothing if not a showman, and having a truck that big was definitely for show.

"By the way," he said through the open passenger side window even as his driver revved the engine. "I sent a few guys on a mission to check things out in that town you seem so fond of. Figured your crew could do a ride-through and give the residents of Justice a show."

Fuck me, Alder would have my balls if he tied this to me. "How many guys?"

"Enough to get the job done. You'd better hurry if you're going to try to play the white knight in this story. We both know that's not your strongest skill, or so I understand. What's the girl's name again—Curse? Witch? No...Jinx. The daughter whose mother you couldn't save. A mother and a sister. Good thing you don't have a wife, or she'd be in the cemetery for sure."

Cartel roared off, leaving me stewing in the cold as the sun began to shine down on me. The guy was a fucker, but he knew me well enough to hit hard in all those sensitive spots. The ones that never seemed to heal quite right. Two shots, and I might as well have been down for the count.

Two women dead, all my fault.

And if Edge got his hands on Jinx, it'd be three for sure.

I raced for my bike, knowing I needed to haul ass back to Justice. Tearing out of the parking lot and speeding back down the mountain.

I was halfway there when a text came, the robotic voice of my phone reading it to me through my helmet speakers.

Text from Finn Kennard. Trouble in town. Meet me at the hardware store on Main Street.

"No shit." I hit a red light at an intersection, yanking out my phone and tapping a quick reply of *already on my way* before pocketing it again. The light turned green, and I took off, racing toward town. It didn't take me too long to get there, though time was a relative sort of thing considering the situation. Had the Black Angels done as they'd been told and simply rolled through town, no time at all. Had they broken orders and snagged someone to play a little cat-and-mouse game with, I'd taken far too long. Totally depended on what was going on.

Main Street seemed quiet as I rolled up to the hardware store that sat on the corner. Bell's Hardware, *Mercy Bell, Store Manager*, the sign above the door read. Which likely meant whoever needed help was a woman. Just what I needed—some damsel in distress.

I dismounted my bike and sauntered toward the door where another sign proclaimed the shop closed. Inside, the lights remained off, the space seemingly empty, door locked when I tried it. I knocked, peering inside but seeing nothing. No movement, no sign of life. I was about to leave, to walk back to my bike and wait for Finn, when something caught my attention. A shadow sliding across the floor. I crept to my left, walking along the length of the front window with my hand on the gun in my shoulder harness. Ready to draw. Ready to fire if need be.

But the only person getting shot was me. Not with a bullet, but with gorgeous blue eyes and the most perfect, beautiful face I'd ever seen. Even through the glass window, even with an expression of total distrust in place, she nearly knocked me to my knees. I could feel the weight of her stare, sense the chemistry between us. One look, and I was a goner.

Had I said fate was a cruel mistress? I was wrong.

She was a bitch on wheels, and she'd just run me over.

Chapter Two

MERCY

I should have been a dental hygienist.

"Great job, buddy." I grabbed Beckett's toothbrush before he could put it down—still covered in toothpaste, of course—and gave him my best mom smile. "How about I go over your teeth one last time, just to make sure they're sparkling clean?"

My little boy—all three feet and thirty-four pounds of him—gave me a foamy grin. "That way the tooth fairy will bring me extra toys, right?"

A little white lie never hurt anyone. "Right. Now, give me a big smile."

He did as he was told, letting me scrub those baby teeth one last time before he could spit and use his rinse. At five years old, he'd already lost one tooth and had a couple wiggly ones ready to go. And he was super excited about more visits from the tooth fairy.

"I wonder if this one will fall out before my birthday tomorrow."

Six. He would be six in a matter of hours. Where did the time go?

"I doubt it. And hey, how about we keep our hands out of our mouths, okay? That's how you catch colds."

"But they're clean." Beckett held up two tiny little hands, showing me his palms. "I washed them."

"I know, but still. Hands away from your face. I don't want you to get sick." I followed him to his room, taking a seat on the bed to watch as he picked out his clothes. Nothing would match, of course, but I let him handle this part of his day. He was clean, well fed, and happy—I wasn't about to let the fact that he couldn't figure out what color sweat pants to wear with his favorite flannel shirts bother me.

He yanked off his pajamas, babbling away about something to do with some cartoon. I was too mesmerized by the little human standing before me. Skinny legs and even skinnier arms, rib cage showing—the child was bony as all get-out, and I loved every inch of him. He'd been my buddy since the day he was born, but he had stolen my heart long before that. He'd come into the world on an unusually cold Saturday, screaming and flailing until he was set on my chest. So tiny then. And now... Well, now he was old enough to go to school and pick out his own clothes. Seriously, where did the time *go*?

"Ready for school." He held up his arms and shot me a smile before running for the kitchen. Red plaid today paired with gray sweat pants and bright yellow socks. Sure. Why not?

After a quick breakfast, I bundled Beckett up—"But it's not *that cold, Mom.*"—and brought him downstairs to the hardware store. Late start day meant we got to sleep in a little, but we still had to get our butts out the door if we were going to make it to his elementary school halfway across the county. Most kids from Justice—not that there were many anymore—attended schools in Rock Falls. I'd wanted him to have more than a basic public education in Nowhere, Colorado, could offer, so I paid tuition at a private school. It was tough to make ends meet sometimes, and I had to work a lot of hours to keep paying the bills, but the juice would eventually be worth the squeeze. I wanted Beckett to have more opportunities before him than I'd had. I wanted him to have better.

Better cost money.

"Got your folder in your bag?" I asked. Beckett nodded, looking ready to go. "Okay. Let's—"

Before I could finish my sentence, a rumble disrupted the quiet of the morning. For a moment, I thought maybe some of the men who worked at the mill were rolling through town on their heavy equipment. But I'd grown up in Justice; I knew the sound of those engines. This was different, and different likely meant dangerous.

"Get behind the counter, honey." I slipped to the front of the store, peeking around a shelving fixture to get a better look. Bikers. Lots of them. I counted ten turning onto Main Street before I even thought to reach for my phone. Bikers meant trouble, and trouble meant I needed a Kennard. We had no police force in Justice—no firemen or EMTs either. What we did have was a family who took care of those of us who lived there, and that family was run by one Alder Kennard, former Special Forces soldier in the Army and current boss of the mill that employed most of the town.

A man who was apparently too busy to answer his phone.

"Shit," I hissed when Alder's voice mail picked up.

"You said a bad word."

"I did, buddy. I'm sorry." I dialed the next Kennard in line—

Bishop, former Navy SEAL—but he didn't answer either. Not surprising—the man had been spending most of his time with his girlfriend in Vegas lately. That left me one Kennard sibling in town, the only one I really didn't want to call. The one who avoided me at every turn. Finn Kennard—ex-boyfriend, ex-addict, ex-con. Lots of exes going on

"You'd think we'd all be over high school by now," I said to myself as I pulled up Finn's information.

"I haven't even gone to high school yet." Beckett snuck in beside me, wrapping his arms around my hips. "Uncle Gage said if I saw bikers, I was to run home or to the restaurant."

"Then it's a good thing we're home. We don't have to run anywhere."

He tugged me tighter and whispered, "I'm scared."

So was I. "It's okay to be scared, but you can't let it stop you. We're just going to call for help."

"Are you calling Uncle Alder?"

Because everyone was either aunt or uncle in this town. "No. His brother, Finn."

I finally found the number I was looking for and pressed send, suddenly thinking I should have sent Katie a text to warn her. Ever since she'd moved back to town and opened a restaurant a few doors down, we'd been rekindling a friendship that had grown distant. She'd even lived in the second apartment over my store for a while. She'd definitely be at her restaurant down the street by now and likely unable to hear the engines if she was cooking. Of course, she had Gage with her. The big, beastly man never left her alone and would keep her safe. It was just Beckett and me in the hardware store, and hopefully soon, a Kennard.

Speaking of which—

"What's up, Mercy?"

"Hey, Finn. I hate to bother you, but I can't reach either of your brothers, and I wasn't sure who else to call."

"No problem. What is it you need?"

"Are you anywhere close to town? I think there's trouble over here, and I can't go check because I've got Beckett with me."

"I'm about six minutes out. Stay put—I'll be there."

"Okay. Hurry."

I hustled Beckett into the back room and shot a quick text to Katie.

Bikers rolling through.

There. Conscience cleared.

"Mom?"

"Yeah, buddy?"

"Is someone coming to help us?"

God willing. "Uncle Finn is. We're just going to hide back here until he gets here."

And then, we waited. I wasn't worried about one of the bikers breaking in to the store—not really. The doors were still locked from the night before, after all. I was more worried about what those nasty bikers were doing here. Some motorcycle club had been causing trouble for months, had even set a fire that had killed a woman. They weren't welcome in town. Not that something as simple as our attitude would stop them.

Some days, I regretted moving back home. Not many, but some. Like today.

"It's okay, Mom," Beckett said, patting my leg and hanging on tight. "We'll be okay."

Oh, my Beckett. I hugged him and kissed the top of his head, praying hard he was right.

"You are my favorite Beckett in the whole wide world. Did you know that?"

He giggled. "Yeah. Because you tell me all the time."

"Well, it's true."

Beckett had always been an easy child to love—a good boy, so sweet and kind—very much like his father. At least, how he'd been before he'd decided he wasn't ready to be a grown-up and left me and Beckett without a backward glance. Those had been a rough few months—being a new mom and all alone—but we'd made it. Somehow.

A couple of years into diapers and day care and sleepless nights, my dad had called, saying he needed to retire. He'd offered to give me the family business and the apartment over the store if I just brought the baby home. I hadn't wanted to at first—small towns like Justice weren't exactly great places to find opportunities for education and social development like I wanted for Beckett, but I'd eventually packed everything up and headed back to the place where I'd grown up. My dad had needed me, and I'd never let him down.

Thankfully, he'd stuck to his word. The business was mine along with an apartment I didn't need to pay rent on. Dad complained sometimes about my deviations from a true hardware store, but he never stood in my way. I needed money to take care of Beckett, and I'd get it no matter what. Even if that meant no longer just selling nails, hammers, and plumbing supplies.

Minutes passed with the two of us hiding out in the back room, silent. Too many minutes. I was about to sneak back into the store to grab the shotgun from under the counter when someone knocked on the front door. Heart pounding, I pushed Beckett behind the table I used as a shipping counter.

"Stay here, okay?"

His lip trembled but he nodded, my brave boy. I kissed the top of his head then snuck in to the store, staying low and keeping away from the main aisle so whoever was outside wouldn't see me. My plan would have worked, too, if the guy had stayed by the door. But of course, he walked along the front windows and happened across my path just as I was attempting to move into a different section. Tall and thick with cropped light hair and heavy features, the man was an imposing sight. And his eyes—so deep and striking, pinning me in place with a look. Devouring me with that blue stare. I'd never seen eyes like those, never felt trapped by a glance before either. The rest of him didn't make him seem any less dangerous either. Black work boots, jeans, black jacket—he looked like some sort of goth kid all grown up. Mature—older than me for sure. A dangerous man. But then he moved, and the patches on his jacket caught my eye. One in particular.

Black Angels.

Not a Soul Sucker, but still... Biker.

"We're closed," I yelled, glaring hard. Not that it mattered. The guy crooked a finger at me, beckoning. *As if.* "Not happening, dude."

His lips twitched, one corner escaping and rising just enough to give him a lopsided sort of smile. "Finn sent me."

That caught me off guard. The bikers might have known of Alder, but Finn? I doubted anyone would know much about him. He wasn't like the rest of the Kennards—wasn't super successful or former military. He was just...Finn. Lots of exes Finn.

"How do you know Finn?"

"How do *you* know Finn?"

"You can't answer a question with a question—that's just rude."

The guy raised an eyebrow—just one—and tapped his phone against the glass, looking ready to laugh. "I'm staying at The Jury Room motel and working with Deacon."

The Jury Room—the bar Deacon owned and Finn worked at. Okay, this was getting more believable. I hurried toward the door, looking behind the guy just in case. No sign of the other bikers, so his motorcycle stood in stark contrast to the now-empty street. Just one guy...I could likely take care of one if I needed to.

"Don't try anything funny," I said as I opened the door for him.

He gave me a once-over from my head to my toes, then turned a megawatt grin my way. "I usually try to keep those sorts of activities serious instead of funny, but I'm down for whatever your preference is. What exactly did you have in mind?"

My internal groan would have been a seismic 4.0 had I released it. "Just what I need—a cocky biker trying to woo me."

He followed me as I headed for the counter, his footsteps loud against the shiny tiled floor. "You think I'm trying to woo you? You looking to be my princess, beauty? And who the fuck says woo anymore?"

I spun, advancing on him and lowering my voice. "You're certainly no prince, so I'll skip that, thanks. And yes, I said woo. I think you're trying to get in my pants, but there's a little boy in the back room who would wonder what that meant. I'm not in the mood for that particular conversation, so I'm going with woo. Can you deal with that?"

His smile grew. The asshole.

"Yes, ma'am."

Polite asshole...but still an asshole.

"Then we're good." I hurried the rest of the way to the counter, my heart pounding and my breath coming faster even once I was able to put the hulking piece of furniture between us. Who was this guy, and why did I get the feeling he was hitting on me with just a look?

"How about you tell me what happened today?"

I shrugged. "Bikers rolled through town. I tried calling Alder and Bishop, but they didn't answer. So I called Finn."

"Alder and Bishop have pussy on the brain."

My entire body felt as if it had gone up in flames. "Can you not with the language, please? Seriously...little pitchers have big handles."

He blinked. "Huh?"

"Kids. Little kids...they overhear stuff."

"What does that have to do with pitchers?"

I didn't really have an answer for him. That pitchers-handles thing was something my grandmother had always said when she had wanted people to remember there were children present. It had never occurred to me to question the meaning.

Not that I had time for this particular discussion. "Look, I appreciate your coming by, but I think we're okay to wait here until Finn arrives. You can just...go."

He leaned over the counter, looking way too much like a predator pinning his prey in place. "I'm not leaving, beauty. I'm on guard duty."

"No thanks. I think we can handle this."

"I'm sure you can handle anything coming your way, but you might as well get used to me being around. Consider me your personal hero. I plan to remain all up in your space."

How did he make that sound so dirty? "I don't know you."

"Well, you'd better get to know me, sweetheart. Think of me like the local cop—you have trouble, I'm your 9-1-1."

"The Kennards are my emergency number. That's who I called." I looked up as the bell rang, spotting Finn coming my way. A little on the thinner side with haunting gray eyes and cheekbones most people would pay money for, he looked a lot rougher than his brothers. Tattoos aside, he carried an air of danger about him. A quiet sort of confidence that tended to throw the locals off. And I had never been happier to see him in my life, even if feeling like a complete idiot for leaving the door unlocked. That asshole had truly messed with my head.

"What's going on here?" Finn asked, stopping right beside biker guy. "I figured you'd wait outside for me."

"Thought I'd jump right in, but beauty here doesn't seem to want my help."

That nickname was getting old really fast. "The name is Mercy."

The biker leaned over the counter again, dropping his voice as he practically growled, "Be thankful I'm not calling you Beast."

What the... "Are you saying I'm ugly?"

"Hold up," Finn said before the douchenozzle at his side could answer me. "Before we fall down the rabbit hole of name-calling and fairy tales, can we talk about what's going on? What did you see that made you call me?"

I darted a glance at the guy's leather jacket with the patches—one said Parris, which must have been his road name. Not that it mattered. "Bikers. Lots of trashy bikers in town."

"Aw, beauty," Parris said, placing one hand over his heart in some exaggerated pose. "You're breaking my heart, calling me trashy."

"If the boot fits—"

"Okay," Finn snapped before taking a deep breath. "So, you saw a group of bikers. How many? And where?"

Right. The reason I'd called. "Ten, maybe twelve. They drove down Main Street this morning heading toward the highway."

"You see Gage this morning?"

"Not yet, but I'm sure he and Katie are at the restaurant. You know he won't let her open that place alone."

Finn's brow furrowed, his eyes holding mine. "Was it just you and Beckett this morning?"

I hated the undercurrent of that question. Just what I wanted to talk about. My nonexistent love life. "Yeah. Just us."

"And the bikers—they didn't come in here?"

"No, they just rode past. I would have followed them to see where they went, but it's late start day so Beckett's still here and —" I shot a glare at Parris "—I don't trust bikers around my son."

Finn nodded once and turned to Parris. "We should head over to The Baker's Cottage. See if Katie and Gage had any trouble. We can loop through town on the way back to be sure they're all gone."

Parris, meanwhile, refused to look away from me, staring me down like a dog on the hunt. "Sounds good."

I nodded, focusing on Finn and doing my best to ignore the way the other man's stare made my blood pump. "Thanks, Finn. I appreciate your coming so quickly."

"Anytime. You can call me whenever you need to."

"Or me," Parris said, practically smirking. "Like I said before, I'm your personal hero."

I couldn't hold back my grimace. "More like my personal zero."

"You wound me, beauty. You really do." He knocked on the counter once, making me jump. "You'll change your mind eventually."

"Why don't you hold your breath and wait for that moment?"

"But then I'd miss breathing in that pretty perfume you wear." The man inched closer, sniffing me. Literally *sniffing* me.

His deep-blue eyes practically devoured me. There was no other way to describe the way they absorbed the light and took me in. Trapping me. Holding me hostage. How did he do that?

He might have said something, or he might have simply moved his lips in some sort of ancient dance. I had no idea because those eyes—they wouldn't let me go.

"Back off, Parris," Finn said, startling me out of whatever spell the biker had put me under.

Heart pounding, face hot, I crossed my arms over my chest and stepped away from the counter. It was time for that man to leave. "You are insane. Finn, he is insane."

"Nah, I'm just a man who knows what he wants." Parris moved away, backing toward the door even as his mouth kept moving. "I'd say see you later tonight, my beauty, but I've got plans already."

"I'd say this playboy attitude is overcompensating for what you lack, you presumptuous asshole, but I prefer to be unique and not follow the trend of every woman you've ever met."

His laugh filled the store, chipping away at my confidence. "You'll give in eventually."

The hell I would. "Never going to happen."

"We'll see."

"You can just keep on looking because the only thing you'll see is my middle finger." I showed him that particular digit, shooting him an eyebrow arch simply because I could. The one my mom had always said was the physical representation of the phrase *Try me.*

Parris apparently didn't get the message. "Do you not want me to leave, or are you just the type of woman who has to get the last word?"

I...had nothing to say to that. I clenched my teeth and held my tongue as I counted to five in my head, then turned to the other man in the room. "It's good to see you, Finn. Tell Katie to pop over if she needs anything. And try to keep your guard dogs chained up, would you?"

I turned on my heel and strode into the storage room, too pissed off and on edge to stand still but not wanting to give Parris any more ammunition against me. Who did he think he was anyway? This was my store, my town, and he had no right to come in and—

"Mom?"

I froze, closing my eyes and giving myself three glorious seconds to shove my temper deep down inside myself before turning to Beckett. "Yeah, baby?"

"Are we going to school now?"

Because, of course, he still had school. And I still had work. And there were still bikers to deal with. Ones not named Parris.

This day was going to need a lot of wine.

"Sure are, buddy. Come on—let's go grab your bag."

Chapter Three

PARRIS

Tale as old as time..."

I sang the stupid song for the millionth time as I made my way back to Justice. Beauty...Mercy. One and the same, and I was definitely a beast to her. That chick had grabbed hold of my balls the second her eyes had met mine, and she'd refused to let me go. Sure, she was hot and curvy, just the way I liked my women. But she was strong, too. Feisty. The woman had a backbone and a smart mouth—those characteristics appealed to me in a way I hadn't experienced before. I wanted to know more about her, to learn everything I could. To discover all her secrets. I hadn't been able to stop thinking about her all day, which might have been why I'd taken my bike out for one last spin around town even though my hands were about ready to fall off from hypothermia.

A day on my bike had once been a dream, but the cold of October in Colorado was seriously cutting into my enjoyment. Still, even after so many hours of riding, I wasn't cranky enough not to lean into the curve heading off the highway and toward Main Street in Justice. It helped that I was on my way to spy on that sweet-ass little woman at the hardware store and that my day had been somewhat productive—I'd had lunch with Finn after making sure the town was clear—not that I'd been worried anyone had hung around. If Cartel had told them to handle the morning as a drive-by mission, that's what the guys would have done—drive by. And then leave.

After lunch, I'd coordinated with the Black Angels on a guard schedule for Rock Falls, did a little recon on the Soul Suckers with Deacon, and hadn't killed anyone. All in all, a good day. The best part—after meeting my beauty—had been talking to Finn. The kid had been to prison, something I hadn't expected to learn, and he had a hard-on for a Soul Sucker named Coyote. One I was pretty sure I'd be able to find as I'd met the dude a few times over the years. Finn would owe me for that, and a blanket favor owed from a Kennard might as well have been gold in my world. I needed to work all the angles of that particular task. And I would because I wanted that open-ended favor. If I ever got a lead on Wolf, I'd need backup, and this town had a fuckton of it.

Finn was also chasing Jinx's tail, which could solve another problem I had—what to do with the girl to keep her safe. If Finn was anything like his brother Alder, he'd be busting his ass to protect hers in no time. That worked in my favor. It also freed me up to chase a little tail myself, one belonging to a woman who likely hated me. Not that I was too worried about that—I'd change her mind.

I was about to pass the corner where Bell's Hardware sat when I noticed a couple of shadows working away under the awning. Mercy and the little boy who must have been her son— Beckett, if I remembered right—stood outside the front of the store. Mercy on a ladder and Beckett holding what looked like lightbulbs.

Time to show my beauty I wasn't just some dumb beast.

I pulled into a spot in front of the store and climbed off my bike, removing my helmet as I did. "You two look like you could use a little help."

Mercy didn't even bother to shoot me a glare. "Funny. I think we look like we're handling things just fine."

And she was...sort of. That ladder wasn't quite tall enough for her, so she was stretched onto the balls of her feet and reaching for the burned-out bulb. Nice view for me, certainly, but that couldn't be safe.

I grabbed her hip and tugged slightly, making her drop her weight back into her heels. "I've got at least a foot on you. Why don't you let me get up there?"

Those light eyes of hers—blue and icy cold—practically sliced through me. "I can change a light bulb."

So much fire, this girl. "I'm sure you can, and with a taller ladder, I bet you'd already be done. But you looked like you were struggling as I drove by, so I'm here to help."

"At what cost?"

"Pardon?"

"Guys like you don't do anything for free."

"I'm not going to charge you to change a light bulb."

She cocked her head, her dark blond hair falling over her shoulder. "And I'm not going to think you're some sort of nice guy because you stepped in when I didn't need you to."

Oh. She thought I was trying to get in her pants again. Not that I wouldn't mind taking a trip between those shapely legs, but that hadn't been my goal. Not yet, at least.

"I swear, there's no payment of any sort required here." I

stepped back as she descended the ladder, giving her room to move out of the way.

She never once even came close to smiling. "Fine. I think the base of the bulb has rusted a bit. I couldn't get it to turn."

"No problem." Hustling up the ladder, I inspected the fixture. Damn thing looked older than I was, which was saying something. "You know how to turn off the power to these? Not just the switch—the breakers?"

"Yeah. Why?"

I grabbed the bulb, using my other hand to hold the socket in place. "In case I break this thing."

"Ah, well, that's an easy fix, then—just don't break it."

I chuckled and shook my head, muttering "ballbuster" under my breath as I braced myself. As I twisted the delicate glass slowly, keeping a firm grip. Thankfully, the bulb eventually spun without anything breaking. "Got it."

"Really?" Mercy leaned in close, setting her hand on my thigh as she craned her neck to look up. Fuck me. That put her pretty face so damn close to my cock. The reaction in my body was immediate, the blood rushing south and my thoughts turning decidedly not G-rated. Those lips *right there?* Yeah. I was going to be jerking it to that image later for sure. Maybe more than once.

But first, I had a job to do, which meant I needed to not act like an animal. "You got a new bulb for me?"

Her eyes met mine, and she jolted back, her cheeks flushing. As if she'd only just realized our positions. Not surprising because that was the same moment I remembered there was a little boy five feet away watching our every move.

"Beckett, right?" I said, nodding his way. "Are those the new bulbs?"

"Yeah," he said, far more wary than anyone his size should have been. He stepped closer, holding out a bulb. Walking right between his mom and me. "Uncle Gage told me bikers are bad and to run home if any show up."

Of course he had. And there I was on my hog with my club colors bright as day. "Not all bikers are bad."

Mercy huffed a sarcastic-sounding laugh. "Is that like that not all men talk bullshit? Because, seriously—you'll have to do more than vomit some cheap words to convince me you're not like those Soul Suckers."

I stared after her as she headed toward the garbage can at the far side of the sidewalk, unable not to look at the way her hips swung and those jeans hugged her ass. That attitude and those curves might as well have been catnip for me, and I was the biggest tomcat around.

At least until a little voice filled with anger said, "That's my mom."

I glanced at Beckett, almost withering under the glare of the kid. "I know that."

"Stop looking at her like that."

I stepped off the ladder, holding his gaze. The kid didn't back down for a second, didn't even waver. I had to respect that, so I offered him my knuckles for a bump. "Sorry, little man. It won't happen again."

"What won't happen?" Mercy asked as she joined us.

Beckett didn't say a word, so I took the lead on that answer. "Just a moment between men, beauty."

She huffed again, adding in an eye roll this time. "Are you done being a thorn in my side? Beckett and I have plans."

"It's my birthday tomorrow," Beckett said. "We need to bake the cake tonight."

"You bake?"

He shrugged as if that should have been a given. "Yeah. Don't you?"

"No." Had I been with the guys from the club, I'd have said I didn't bake because it was too girlie or some shit. That wasn't really the truth, though, and the kid deserved honesty. So I dropped down into a crouch, putting me at eye level with the little man, and I gave it to him. "I don't know how."

"Your mom didn't teach you?"

I shook my head. "I didn't have a mom—it was just my dad and me growing up."

"Oh." Beckett looked at his own mom, his brain obviously spinning. And then he nodded his head once. Decision made. "Come on, then."

"Come where?"

"Upstairs with us. My mom taught me—she can teach you, too."

Mercy suddenly looked awfully pale. "Oh no. I'm sure Mister Par—"

"Thanks. I'd love to learn." I grinned at the woman, loving this particular development. Fuck yeah, I'd bake with the kid if it meant getting a little time to show my beauty I wasn't the big, bad wolf she assumed I was. Plus, the little guy seemed cool as hell. Total bonus for me.

Mercy looked pissed, but she didn't argue with her son. Instead, she huffed and headed for the back of the store, glaring at me when I took the ladder from her. Sassy woman. We entered the building via a door in the alley. The back room was what you would expect—concrete and bland with boxes stacked on metal shelving units and products for the store in bins.

"The ladder goes over here." Mercy led the way to the far wall, leaving Beckett to stand by the stairs leading up. Once we were out of earshot, her attack began. "You can just go."

"Maybe I don't want to."

"Maybe I would rather you did."

"Beckett invited me."

"Yeah, well..." She sighed. "He's too nice for his own good."

I set down the ladder and turned to face her. "If you really want me to go, I'll be the bad guy and tell Beckett I can't come bake with him. But he invited me, and I'd actually like to stay. No assumptions, no games—just a baking lesson I should have gotten a few decades ago."

Her frown deepened, and her lips tightened. "I'm not afraid to call a Kennard and have you tossed out of my house."

"And I'm not stupid enough to give you a reason to do that."

Her silence hung heavy, her face devoid of any emotion other than irritation for a long pause. But then she huffed. "Fine."

Jackpot. "I promise to behave."

"Why do I doubt you can live up to that?"

I didn't answer her, instead, following her across the floor. Breaking my promise to Beckett and watching his mom's ass as the three of us climbed the back stairs. Couldn't help myself. It was a spank-worthy, bitable piece of art that deserved to be worshiped and admired. And I certainly spent some time admiring it. I could look and behave at the same time.

"What's your favorite cake flavor?" Beckett asked as soon as we'd crossed the threshold into their apartment, taking my attention from something bitable to something...edible. Cake.

"Chocolate. For sure." I did my best not to look as if I were casing the place, but I couldn't stop myself. I needed to know more about Mercy and Beckett, wanted to discover any shortcut to her attention. The apartment didn't give away much other than that they certainly didn't live an extravagant lifestyle. The place was neat and clean but plain. Simple. The two deserved to be spoiled, and it certainly didn't appear as if anyone was doing that for them.

"Wash your hands," Mercy said, directing her words to

Beckett but giving me a look that said *you as well.* I knew when to follow orders, so I stepped in front of her and turned on the water in the kitchen sink, scrubbing my hands. A towel appeared at my elbow along with a toothy grin. Well, mostly toothy.

"You've got a hole in your smile."

Beckett grinned even wider. "Yup. Lost that tooth forever ago. I have more wiggly ones too."

I knelt down, looking him square in the eye as I leaned forward and quietly asked, "Did the tooth fairy show up here?"

Beckett's eyes grew larger, and his mouth fell open. "She *did.*"

I nodded, catching Mercy's eye over his shoulder. Winking at her when I thought I could get away with it. "And did she bring you a present for that tooth?"

Beckett took off like a shot, running past me and down the hallway. Mercy laughed.

"What did I do?"

She shook her head as she moved to the refrigerator, pulling out eggs and butter. "He won't tell you—he'll want to show you."

I nodded and took a spot next to the counter where I figured I'd be out of the way. "Was it a good present?"

"I did what I could."

Honest answer. "I never had a visit from the tooth fairy."

"No?"

"No. Grew up on a military base, and my dad didn't believe in fostering childish things. No Santa, no Easter Bunny, no tooth fairy."

She frowned as she measured sugar into the bowl of a big, blue mixer. "That sounds sad."

"Nah, just forthright."

The thunder of little feet on wood floors sounded through

the kitchen, and Beckett appeared from the hall at a full run. "This. I got this."

He held up what looked like a block of plastic—square, green, and...I had no idea what. "And what is that?"

"It's a creeper."

I looked at Mercy, hoping for a little help but not receiving any. "What's a creeper?"

"It's from a video game he plays," Mercy said before focusing in on the stand mixer in front of her. "Okay, so this bowl is for the wet ingredients—you always mix your wet stuff first. Beckett, are you going to help me crack the eggs?"

"Yeah!"

And with that, the creepy green guy was forgotten and Beckett took his spot on a stool next to his mom. The two worked together to crack a ridiculous number of eggs, then poured something from a dark bottle into the bowl. Mercy kept a running commentary on what she was doing—teaching me, apparently—but I couldn't focus on her words. Too caught up in the feeling of rightness being in this place with these two brought me. The sense of home I'd never once experienced before.

"Ready to mix," Mercy said when she had everything liquid in the bowl. And sugar, though she'd specifically said you started with your wet ingredients. Why sugar was with the wet, I had no idea.

Beckett was the one who got to turn on the machine. The look of excitement on his face, the obvious thrill of something so simple, called to my heart. As did the gentle smile on Mercy's face as she watched her son. The moment almost froze, the view cementing itself in my mind as my heart fucking lurched.

This.

This moment right here was what life was all about. Not stuff or outside world bullshit. This sort of quiet, calm, everyday shit. I wanted it. Wanted it so bad, I knew right then I'd walk through fire for these two. I'd barely met them, knew very little about them, but this was it. They were mine.

The buzzing of my cell phone in my pocket shattered that moment, bringing me back to the reality of my life. No way was that a friendly *What's up* or *How you doing* text. It would be for the crew or for the protection of Justice, and there was no way I couldn't answer it.

"Nice and slow," Mercy said, helping Beckett add the white, flour mixture to the bowl. I kept my eyes on them as long as I could, kept the dread of having to leave this warm little bubble shoved down in my gut until the last possible second. And then I read the screen.

Get your ass to the camp now.

Fucking Edge. The asshole was likely still hunting down Jinx, or he'd figured out where she was and wanted me to bring her to him. Not that I would. I technically couldn't hide Jinx from them, but I certainly wasn't plopping her into their laps.

On my way.

As unfortunate as that was. "I'm sorry to break up this party, but I've got to go."

Beckett looked up, frowning. "You're leaving?"

"Sorry, Mr. Beckett. I need to go to work."

He glanced at his mom, who was decidedly not looking at me. "What kind of work do you do?"

And wasn't that a hard question to answer? I'd been a soldier most of my adult life, had gone to prison for avenging someone's death, and was still battling my way through the big bads...just from the wrong side of the field, it seemed. "I fight for people who can't fight for themselves."

His eyes went wide. "Like on the *A-Team*."

"You watch the *A-Team*?"

Mercy finally caught my eye. "He loves it. Drives me crazy."

Court-martialed soldiers running from the law and hiring themselves out as soldiers of fortune? Fitting. "It's a good show. And yeah, sort of like the *A-Team*, man. But cooler."

"Can I go to work with you?"

Mercy and I said *no* at the same time, making the kid drop his smile in an instant. I wasn't happy about that look, but there was nothing I could do about that.

I shot a smile at Mercy, making sure she knew I wasn't about to take her son on some crime spree. "No worries, beauty. I know where that particular line is. But the weather's supposed to warm up—maybe this weekend we can bust out your bike and go for a ride together."

That might have been overstepping—assuming I'd be allowed back into the little bubble of their life—but fuck it. I wanted to be here, and if Mercy had a problem with it, she'd just have to adjust.

"I don't have a bike."

Those words from Beckett's mouth pulled me up short. "No bike?"

Mercy's face tightened. "He had one but outgrew it, and I was going to buy him a new one, but with the Soul Suckers hanging around..."

She didn't have to finish that sentence. With the Soul Suckers around, it would be too dangerous for Beckett to be riding around outside. Even if he only rode down the block, that would be too far for her to get to him if someone came riding up.

But while the Soul Suckers were definitely dangerous, I had

one up on them. From my perspective, I was the most dangerous man in town. And I'd prove it to keep that little boy and his mom safe.

My phone buzzed again, and Mercy's eyes darted to where it sat in my hand. "Time to go?"

I nodded, not even needing to look at the screen. "Yeah."

She nodded, that frown back in place. Killing me with a look. "Say goodnight, Beckett."

"Goodnight, Mister Parris."

Fuck, I hated that name on his lips. I hadn't gone by my true name in too many years, though.

Maybe someday...

"Goodnight, little man. Be good."

He grinned. "I am good."

Of course he was. Mercy followed me to the door, crossing her arms and leaning against the wall to watch me leave. "Thanks for being kind to him."

As if I wouldn't. "Thanks for letting me stay."

"I don't remember *letting* you do anything." Harsh words, but she tempered them with a soft tone and a slight smile. I'd take that.

"He's a great kid."

Her smile grew, making her look like the proud mother I knew she would be. "He is."

"Tomorrow really his birthday?"

"Yup. He's the big six."

"Good to know." I opened the door, pausing before crossing the threshold to shoot her a smirk. "Do I get a kiss goodnight, beauty?"

"Over my dead body."

The words were meant as an exaggeration, but still...my gut dropped. No fucking way. Never.

"Not happening," I said, my voice a low growl even to my own ears. She locked eyes with me, that frown back in place. As if she knew where my thoughts had gone. Soul Suckers. Black Angels. Death.

No way. I reached into my inner coat pocket and grabbed the pen and notebook I kept there, writing down my details. Knowing it wouldn't be enough but needing to do something to keep her safe.

She eyed me as I handed her the paper. "What's this?"

"My number. Call me if you see trouble again."

"I'll be calling the Kennards."

As if they could do a better job than me. Though, at the end of the day, I wasn't the hero of her story. I was the villain. And maybe I should have kept that in mind instead of pursuing her. Maybe I should have walked away to protect her and Beckett. I'd sooner cut off my own hand, though.

No way should I fall for her. Any more than I already had. Too bad I was shit at doing the right thing.

"The Kennards can't handle what's coming, but I can. Remember that." I leaned closer, making her breath catch. Raising my voice as I spoke over her shoulder. "Night, little man. Thanks for letting me help bake."

"Good night, Mister Parris. Come by tomorrow for my birthday dinner."

Mercy glared at me, her cheeks flushed. Faking her dislike so hard.

I grinned, ignoring her and answering Beckett instead. "It's a date."

Chapter Four

MERCY

I'd never been the type of woman to let a handsome smile and a tight pair of jeans get to me. Never fallen for the wrong guy with intention. Beckett's dad had been a *good* guy—stable and sure with solid roots and well-practiced manners. He'd been just about perfect...on paper. Of course, he'd ended up an asshole who'd abandoned us, but he hadn't started out that way. I wouldn't have dated him if I'd have ever thought he'd turn out so wrong for me. Parris? He was a bad boy from the start, a man obviously a little too old and too hardened for a woman like me, who was nothing *but* wrong. I shouldn't have been lusting after him.

But I was. I *so* was.

All night after Beckett had gone to bed, I'd thought about that man. About the gruffness of his voice and words, dreaming of how that would translate to his hands. I'd have put money on the fact that he had strong, callused hands, and I wanted to feel them all over me. I wanted to know the weight of him, the smell. The heat of his body against mine. I wanted the exact thing I shouldn't have. Him.

The man was dangerous from the start—to me, to Beckett, and to our stability in Justice. I shouldn't want him around, but I did. To the point that I had to go reaching for my favorite toy in the middle of the night to break the tension. Something I rarely did as time alone was a true commodity with a five-year-old in the house.

Six. Good lord, my baby was six. And if the sound of a herd of rhinoceros coming down the hall meant what I thought it did, he was also currently running my way.

"Mommy," Beckett said as he jumped on the bed. "It's morning."

It was. Way too early in the morning after a sleepless night, but I couldn't blame him for being excited.

"Happy birthday, buddy." I snuggled him close, loving the way his little arms wrapped around my neck. The way he still wanted those snuggles from me. I wasn't an idiot—I knew that would stop someday. His friends would tell him it wasn't cool to love on your mom anymore, and my affectionate little boy would back off. I had to enjoy every second.

"I'm six, mom."

"Yes, you are. Do you feel different?"

"Yeah. Can I open my presents?"

I laughed as I rolled us out of bed, setting him on his feet. "Not yet. You have school this morning. Then tonight, we'll have dinner at Auntie Katie's and open them there."

His pout matched the whine of his voice as he said, "But that's so far away."

"I had to wait nine months to hug you. You can wait a few

hours for your presents." I pushed him out the door and into the hallway, ready to get our day started.

Beckett practically skipped on the way to the kitchen, impatience forgotten. His normal sunny disposition back in place. "Was I a good present?"

A *good* present? Not even close. I pulled him to a stop, leaning down to give him a smacking kiss. Hugging him close as my heart practically beat its way out of my chest.

"You were the best present I ever could have asked for." I had to swallow down the tightness in my throat, the emotion trying to tug me under. There were no words to explain my love for that little boy. No way to quantify the feelings he brought out of me. All I could do was love him and snuggle him and try my hardest to give him a happy life. Starting right then. "Come on, buddy. Let's have cake for breakfast."

Two small pieces of cake, a yogurt, and a big glass of milk later, we were ready to get the day truly started. Beckett dressed himself—blue-and-green plaid flannel with a gray undershirt and mustard-yellow sweat pants—while I packed his lunch and hurried through my own morning routine. Once ready to go, I loaded him into my SUV and headed to his school. I was extra careful on the drive, looking out for any sign of motorcycles around me. More worried than usual after the events of yesterday. And if I sort of hoped to see one biker in particular in my rearview mirror, that was only because Beckett liked the guy so much. Not because I actually hoped to see the bastard.

I made it through the chaos of the drop-off lane at the school and was back on the road in practically no time, my mind already thinking ahead to the work I needed to accomplish. Dealing with local artisans and selling their products on the store's website had been a huge boon for us, one I needed to feed and grow. Emails, shipments, SEO updates, marketing ads—all details I touched every day. I'd had to teach myself photography, coding, and tax law, had to work hard to build a business that might someday give Beckett and me the security I craved.

Justice sat as quiet as ever when I rolled through town. Just in case, I double-checked that the alley was clear before heading inside to work, shooting a text to Katie to let her know I'd be in the store if she needed me. Lights on, music playing softly, I dove into my day. Invoicing customers, updating product details on the website, adding new finds, and reaching out to more local artisans with offers to host their goods on my site. Stats, sales, packaging, shipping—it all fell on me alone. I was a jill-of-all-trades, and I would keep my family business relevant in the new market. Even if that meant never selling another hammer again.

I had just finished an early lunch—my favorite tomato soup from Katie's and a grilled cheese sandwich—when an email I'd been waiting for popped up. Sam Elliott, a local glassblower and one of my favorite artists to work with, had a couple new pieces for me. The pictures he sent didn't do them justice, and I knew they'd sell within hours of being on the site. I checked the time and grabbed my keys, typing a response to let Sam know I was on my way before I even hit the door. I had enough time to get up the hill, grab the pieces, and come back before I needed to go pick up Beckett. Plenty, really. This would be a piece of cake. An easy task that came with a view of late fall in Justice.

The mountains burned in the afternoon light, the snow that had already fallen glistening in the distant peaks. Soon enough, we'd be covered with it again. Not yet, though. The weather had turned warmer lately, early snow giving way to an Indian summer sort of pattern. Perfect for getting outside for one last adventure before the chill of winter set in completely.

The idea of the snow and ice that would be coming made me think of Parris and wonder what he would do when the weather turned. Not that it was something I should be worried about. Not that I should care one iota what a biker did when they couldn't ride their motorcycle. But I did...I thought about it. About him straddling more than just a piece of machinery during the cold winter months ahead. About ways I could help him warm up after a long ride.

"You are such a hussy," I said to myself, shaking my head as if the motion would clear the man from my thoughts. It didn't. At all. But pulling up to Sam's house and seeing the doors to the barn he'd converted into a workshop did. Time to get to work.

"Well, hey there, sunshine," Sam said, smiling my way as soon as I walked in the door. "I didn't mean to interrupt whatever you had going on today."

I shrugged, already eyeing the pieces he had ready to sell. They'd move fast for sure and would bring a nice profit. If I could buy them for a decent price, I might even be able to set aside Christmas-present money. Maybe buy Beckett that bike, after all. There were a ton of empty businesses on Main Street. Alder would certainly let me use one so Beckett could ride inside of it.

"You know how much I love your work," I said, smiling at Sam. "These are stunning."

"I figured you'd like them." He strolled over, wiping his hands on a rag. "The early snowfall we had put me in a creative mood. I finished them all in the last week."

That piqued my interest. Sam usually labored over his pieces, taking days on end to make a single one. If these had less time put into them, I might be able to haggle him down on his price a little. Bonus.

"What were you hoping to sell them for?"

He frowned, looking over the glass vases and orbs for several long seconds. "I was hoping a hundred a piece."

Yeah, I could probably sell them for that. My profit would

come from that, though—meaning Sam wouldn't get that full hundred. Something I always made sure my clients understood so there were no hard feelings later.

"If I put them at a hundred retail, that means you'll walk away with seventy-five after my cut. Are you okay with that?"

He waited just long enough for me to begin worrying he wouldn't sell them to me at all before he shrugged. "Yeah. That seems fair enough."

I held out my hand, shaking his before reaching for my phone. "Great. I'll send you a receipt for my acquisition of these right now. I expect them to sell quite quickly, so you should have your money in a few days."

"That fast?"

"I can't keep your stuff on the site. People love it." I gave the blown-glass sculptures another look, capivated by the gracefulness and colors he'd used. "I might even try to set the price a little higher on these. See if the market will support it. They're truly unique."

"And if they pay more, we both make more."

"Exactly."

Sam grunted his approval to that thought. "Well, perhaps I'll try to spend a little more time in the workshop now that summer's ending. Give you more stock to sell."

I boxed up one piece, wrapping it in bubble wrap to keep it safe on the ride back down the mountain. "You make them, I'll sell them. But don't work yourself to death."

Sam laughed, carrying a couple boxes toward my SUV as I followed him. "I'm technically retired. This is fun for me."

"Good. Then have lots of fun this winter so we can make a little extra cash. Just text me when you have more to sell."

"I'll email," he said, his response firm. I almost laughed. We'd started our relationship with phone calls, then I'd slowly moved him to email. He still preferred to call and actually speak on the phone, which wasn't my thing. Texting might have been too far outside of Sam's comfort zone to ever expect, but I'd keep pushing.

We finished wrapping and loading all the pieces—eight in total, which would definitely earn me enough to get Beckett a decent mountain bike. Score one for mom. Sam strapped everything into place for me, securing the boxes as best he could before slamming the lift gate closed. Transaction complete.

"You be careful on that mountain now," Sam said just as the rumble of engines coming closer broke the more natural sounds of mountain life. We both turned, staring toward the head of the driveway. Dread made my gut tighten, the sound far too familiar at this point. Did Sam even know the trouble brewing in Justice? He wasn't a resident, so perhaps not, though he had to know about the fires. About Leah's death.

If he didn't know, it was too late to tell him because six motorcycles crested the hill and headed our way. Six men in black coats and heavy boots, a wall of danger moving closer. Crap.

"Sam—"

"Stay calm, Mercy. I can handle this."

But I had my doubts. Not many men could handle six bikers alone. A picture of Parris popped into my head—the idea that he likely could settling over me—but there was no way to alert him. No way to call for help without the trespassers seeing. I was stuck with Sam, who certainly didn't have the same skills as Parris.

"Afternoon," one of the bikers yelled as soon as they had all shut off their engines. "Nice day for a ride."

He looked me up and down as he said ride, his gaze telling me he wasn't talking about riding motorcycles. The feeling of being exposed—of danger—made my heart thump loudly in my chest, but I didn't flinch. Didn't move a single step. I figured I should treat those bikers like the stray dogs they were—show no fear.

Even though fear was quickly making my stomach turn.

"You lost?" Sam asked, pulling that ever-present rag from his back pocket and twisting it between his hands. "We don't get many visitors up this way."

"Not lost, no. Just checking out our neighbors. Got friends bunking down in Rock Falls at the campground." He peered past Sam, lifting his chin toward the view over the ridge. "Thought maybe you'd seen them setting up down there."

Sam shook his head, glancing over his shoulder toward the city of Rock Falls. "Trees are too deep up here to see much of anything. I hadn't even realized anyone had been using the old campground."

The biker didn't look convinced, though he did smile. The expression of a predator knowing he had his prey cornered. "Funny. Our friend said he could see the lights of your house from down there."

"Nah, that's probably the workshop." Sam edged in front of me, walking slowly toward the bikers. "My boss here was just leaving, so I've got a little time. Why don't you come down to the barn with me? I can show you the view."

The biker leered at me, that dangerous smile firmly in place. "Boss, huh? I've never been one to let a bitch tell me what to do, but I might with someone who looks the way you do in a pair of jeans."

So gross. "I'm not hiring."

The bikers chuckled, three of them dismounting their rides as they did.

"My loss," the one said. "I'll take you up on that tour, though, sir."

"Name's Sam." He turned my way, giving me a serious look

that spoke volumes. "Why don't you head on out of here? You've got things to do."

"You're not staying, beautiful?" one of the bikers hollered.

I shook my head, clutching my keys and looking from the biker to Sam and back. "I need to get some work done. You sure you're okay, Sam?"

He flinched, the only tell I could spot of his lie as he said, "I'll be fine. Now, get."

He was not going to be fine. I knew that to the very depths of my soul. I hated leaving him, hated knowing that I was running from danger and forcing him to face it alone, but I had Beckett to worry about. I needed to get off that mountain. Needed to make it back to Justice to keep my boy safe.

This was not the hill I was going to die on.

"I'll call you when I get back to the office," I said, raising my voice enough so everyone could hear me. "Oh, and Alder had said something about coming up this way this afternoon, so I'd expect him within the hour."

Sam nodded, likely understanding the lie was more for the bikers than for him. Hopefully getting what I was trying to say— *I'll call for help. I'll send backup. Just hang on.*

"Drive safe," Sam said, and the realization that he hadn't said my name the entire time the bikers were there slammed into me. Sam was protecting me the only way he could—getting me off the mountain and keeping my identity a secret. I owed that man hugely.

No one stopped me from climbing into my truck. No one blocked my path as I headed down the driveway and back onto the mountain road. Not a single bike followed me down the mountain, and still, I couldn't stop shaking. Couldn't get my hands to hold still. Tremors racked my body, and my stomach twisted to the point that I felt I might be sick all over myself.

Didn't matter. No way was I stopping until I made it back to Justice. But the thought of Sam up there alone ate at me, and the knowledge that whoever I called would be going up against six bikers had me pulling a slip of paper from my bag. Had me typing in a number I had saved but assumed I'd never use.

Had me sending a text to the one man who might just be more dangerous than the six on that hill.

Chapter Five

PARRIS

Ravel of the Black Angels might have been the most sadistic bastard I'd ever met, which was saying something, considering how long I'd been dealing with Edge.

"She needs to be taught a lesson."

Yeah, Ravel was talking about Jinx. As he had been all fucking night and morning. I hadn't slept yet, hadn't even taken a break from the drug-fueled party Edge and Ravel were throwing. The women they'd brought—all ten of them—lay scattered throughout the trailer. Some piled on top of others, some camping out on the floor. All of them bloodied and bruised. And high. So very high.

"She's at that fucking motel in Justice," Ravel said, snorting what had to be the tenth line of coke I'd seen him consume. "Just go get her."

Edge had become the voice of reason, definitely an odd turn

of events. "I'm not going to do shit. She'll come back. And when she does, I'll make her pay for this shit."

I nodded, making a mental note to tell Deacon to keep a tighter rein on Jinx. Just in case. "You gotta make her want to come back. Otherwise, she'll keep running."

The words were what I needed to say, what the guys needed to hear, but they still brought bile up the back of my throat. If they ever got their hands on Jinx again, they'd kill her. No doubt in my mind. Just as they'd killed her mom right under my nose. I couldn't save Jinx without blowing my cover, and I couldn't stop them from obsessing over her either. I'd tried with her mom, but I'd failed. Miserably.

And that was something I refused to live through again.

"Fucking Zed," Edge said, reaching for one of the women passed out on the couch next to him and groping her ass. "He never should have played her in that game."

The card game where we'd lost ownership of Jinx to the Soul Suckers. The impetus that had led to us coming to Colorado to back up that crew on their ridiculous Justice mission.

The thing that had brought me to Mercy and Beckett.

Two people I definitely shouldn't be thinking about right then.

"I took care of it," Ravel said before taking a long swig of some sort of dark whiskey.

"Taking his colors was a good punishment," I said. "Losing his brothers will stick with him."

Ravel slammed the bottle down and wiped his mouth with the back of his hand, giving me a look that spoke volumes. "Right. That."

And just like that, I knew he'd killed Zed. Something I hadn't been aware of. Something the national president likely knew nothing about. Cartel might, though. The man had informants all over—probably more than one in our Vegas chapter. He might have been playing the game from different angles, looking for ways to gain information I couldn't give him.

And likely setting up for my disposal should things go south.

Not that I blamed them for killing Zed. Hell, I would have done so once my mission for Cartel ended for sure. If my mission ended with me alive.

One of the women reached up and grabbed my thigh, likely still high as fuck and looking for something I wasn't willing to give. Not anymore. Past-me might have taken part—gotten my dick wet just to kill the time. Since meeting Mercy? No fucking way.

I stood and walked toward the back of the trailer, trying hard not to show how much I didn't want her touching me. Didn't want to see all the naked flesh around me. All the human meat ready for slaughter. Edge had a decent hold on his obsession with blood, it seemed, but I had no idea how long he'd hang on to it. Eventually, these women would be replaced by new ones, never to be seen again. Some would leave, some would hook up with other bikers and work their way through the circuit. And some...well, some wouldn't be breathing once Edge was done with them.

A fact that needed to be dealt with once Cartel pulled his head out of his ass.

"Leaving us?" Edge said, his voice rough. He had his hand between a chick's thighs, drawing moans from her as she lay there with her eyes hazy and unfocused. Fuck, I wished I could have left.

"Nah, just gotta piss."

I locked myself in the closet of a bathroom and took a deep breath, leaning over the tiny sink and avoiding looking in the mirror. Tired. I was bone-tired. Exhausted from lack of sleep but also drained. Two years of this shit—of being undercover for a club I'd never wanted to join in the first place—had left me feeling empty. Weak, almost. Not that I could be. I needed to keep my wits about me, keep my back protected, and power through this mission. Then and only then could I even begin thinking about getting back to what I truly wanted—hunting down the man they called Wolf and giving him the long, slow death he deserved. Avenging my sister once and for all. And if I ended up back in prison for it, I'd serve every fucking second with a smile on my face knowing I'd done what I needed to.

A picture of Beckett—all big grin and missing tooth—flashed in my head just before another one of Mercy. A reminder of the tease I'd gotten last night. Of the life I could have had if I hadn't gotten messed up in the Black Angels in the first place.

Maybe. Just maybe. Someday. But certainly not today.

I finally looked up. Hating the face in the mirror. The age and wrinkles showing there. The obvious exhaustion. I would have to be better if I wanted a shot at them. At that life.

My phone buzzed in my pocket, drawing my attention from the old man staring back at me. I grabbed it and swiped the screen without thought, assuming the text was from one of the guys in my crew.

I was so damn wrong.

Bikers at a customer of mine's place. I'm away, but I'm worried for him. Should I call the Kennards?

The number didn't come up as one in my contacts, but it didn't have to. That could only be Mercy. And she was in trouble. I was running through the trailer before I even started to respond, ignoring Edge's and Ravel's yells without a second thought. Fuck them and fuck this club. My girl needed me.

Where?

Another ping came through as I reached my bike. She'd sent a pin for a spot close by, likely up in the hills overlooking the campground. Smart girl. I tapped to get directions then started the bike, turning on the Bluetooth in my helmet so I could hear the instructions the GPS would lay out for me. Taking the time to send her a response before rolling out.

Give me fifteen minutes. You see one bike, you drive like hell for the store.

But as I hit the road outside of the campground, I slowed to a stop and grabbed my phone again. Needing to send one more message. To Deacon Manns.

Need backup—Mercy Bell in trouble.

When his response came in, the robotic voice of my phone read it to me.

Out of town with Alder. I can send Gage—where?

Fuck. I pulled over again, heart racing and irritation high. Definitely needed to buy a cage. Texting and driving might have been dangerous, but less so than trying to steer a bike and send a message.

Tell him to start here and keep an eye out for her truck.

I forwarded him the pin and tucked my phone away, roaring toward the destination once more. I was about halfway there when an SUV came barreling down the highway toward me. The face staring back at me through the windshield was my beauty, and she looked scared as fuck. I raised my hand, hoping she'd understand it was me, and did a one-eighty right there on the highway to follow her. She pulled over, hopping out of the vehicle and walking toward me with her arms crossed. Looking scared and small.

I'd never dismounted my bike and run so fast in my life.

"Are you okay?" I asked before I even reached her.

"Yeah, Sam might not be, though. I felt bad leaving him, but—"

"Don't." I grabbed her, unable not to. Needing to hug her and stop the trembles I could see shaking her body. Needing to know she was safe. "Never feel bad for putting yourself and your son first. Never."

Her broken sob gutted me, and the way she clung to my shoulders only made the guilt worse. This girl had exploded into my life, taking up space in my heart I hadn't even known existed. I was the most dangerous thing to her, but I was also the only one who'd give his life for her.

And right then, I needed her to be okay.

"Go on home," I said, even though the words tasted like a lie. I didn't want her to leave my side, didn't want to let her out of my sight. But the safest place for her—other than right the fuck next to me—was in Justice. She needed to get home, and I apparently needed to lay down some fucking rules for whoever had scared her. "I'll head up there and check things out."

"What if they follow me?"

I'd kill every last one of them. "Gage's already on his way. He'll follow you home."

"Will you be okay?"

Oh, that voice. That concern. It made my balls hang heavy and my cock hard as stone. Mercy Bell was worried about me—I couldn't remember the last time anyone had given a single fuck on my behalf.

"I'll be fine," I said, tucking her hair behind her ear and wishing like hell that I could taste those plump lips just once. Knowing now was the worst possible time to even think such a thing.

Deal with bikers first. Kiss the fuck out of her later.

"Go," I said, directing her toward her truck. "It's birthday dinner night."

She nodded, her arms dropping to hold herself together. Turning her back on me as she walked away. Before she reached her truck, though, she stopped. "Birthday dinner will be at The Baker's Cottage at six. If you happen to be free."

Well, fuck me. I hadn't been expecting that. And even though the invite was likely under duress—some sort of misguided appreciation for me jumping in to help her friend—I wasn't too noble to take advantage. "I told Beckett I'll be there, so I will."

She nodded, looking almost lost. "Okay. See you later, then."

I sure as hell hoped so.

I watched as she pulled out onto the road, not turning for my bike until she'd passed over the next hill and disappeared from sight. Gage had better be on the road to meet her. If she got hurt along the way, if she ran into more bikers...

If she ran into guys like me, she'd be in trouble.

But I had to trust in Gage—had to put faith in my teammate. I might not have known him for long, but the guy was solid. A true soldier. He'd protect Mercy until I could get back to her.

Not really good enough, but it would have to do.

I rode up the rest of the way to the little cabin in the woods that overlooked the campground. No wonder the guys had come up here—anyone who might see their antics would be considered a threat. I could understand the logic, but I certainly wouldn't let them screw with the guy. He was Mercy's friend, and that meant he deserved my protection.

But as I came to a stop in the driveway and six bikers walked out of the barn with an older man behind them, the error of my thinking became clear. They weren't Black Angels—they were Soul Suckers. All of them. And at least one I'd already had a run-in with the night Jinx had stupidly decided to go to the truck stop for ice cream with Finn Kennard.

Motherfucker.

"What's going on, boys?"

One of the Soul Suckers—a guy with the road name Goose on his cut—lifted his chin at me. "Got a problem?"

I shrugged and held out my hands, still straddling my bike. "Not at all, just wondering what a group of Soul Suckers was doing up on this hill. You do realize that's a Black Angels camp down there, don't you?"

"That's why we came up this way. Tiny mentioned seeing the lights, and since we owed him a favor, we figured we'd take a ride up here and make sure there was nothing to worry about. There's nothing to worry about, right, Sam?"

The older man nodded, not looking at me. Sporting one heck of a red mark on his cheek that would likely become a bruise in a few hours. "Nothing to worry about at all."

The bullshit was thick with these guys. "Good, then. No sense in bothering this man anymore if there's not a problem."

Goose stared my way, locking eyes with me and not letting go. I could stare down the best, though. Had learned in the military to keep my cool and control the situation with very little action.

It worked, too. Goose broke first. "I'll tell Tiny you're keeping an eye on things."

Tiny again—the enforcer of the Vegas Black Angels crew. What he was doing dealing with the Soul Suckers, I wasn't sure, but they were making sure I knew where their orders had come from. Which was fine. I could play the name-drop game, too.

"You do that. I'll mention it to him, too. He's been a little on edge lately—your friend Coyote must have done some serious shit to stir up the hornet's nest in Justice."

Goose's smile faltered, his stare hardening. "Don't know much about that. Heard there was a fire. Maybe even a dead girl, though I don't know what such a tragic accident would have to do with Coyote."

As if I didn't already know it was some Soul Sucker named Coyote who'd killed a woman named Leah in Justice. As if Alder Kennard hadn't already told me about the other fire the Soul Suckers had set, the one that had burned his fiancée's trailer. I knew, all right, and I wasn't about to let them off the hook. "Really? I heard different."

One of the other bikers chuckled. "Tell the asshole not to tag his work next time."

His work. Like killing a woman was just a normal day at the office. Which, for guys like these, it might have been. A thought that made my blood run cold—they'd kill Mercy without a second thought. Especially if it worked in their favor.

"Well," said Goose, shoving the older gentleman backward. "I believe our work here is done anyway. Right, Sam?"

The guy nodded, looking beaten-down and defeated. "Absolutely. All done."

Goose laughed before heading my way, passing by far too

close on his way to his bike. Purposefully looking at the name on my coat before smiling my way.

"Hope to see you again, Parris."

I nodded, keeping my eyes on all of them. Not relaxing my stance until every last one had driven up the driveway and turned onto the road leading down the mountain.

Leaving me alone with Sam.

"You okay, old man?"

Sam huffed. "Why would you care?"

I wouldn't, except for one reason. "I'm a friend of Mercy's. She called me to step in." But that really wasn't it, and watching that man—likely twenty years my senior—pull himself together to glare my way struck me with a truth hammer I couldn't avoid. "Besides, I'm not like them."

Sam looked me up and down, wiping blood from the corner of his mouth and not giving me an inch. "Could have fooled me."

Because I looked like them. Because I'd been them, just not as bad. Maybe. Fuck, I wasn't even sure anymore. I'd done bad things thinking I was right because there were reasons backing me up. Reasons that made me feel less like a murderer and more like an avenging angel.

And it was all such bullshit.

I reached inside my jacket, pulling out the same pen and notepad I'd used last night. The one I'd written the same numbers down on for Mercy. Hoping Sam would eventually trust me enough to use them just as she had. "Look, you run into those guys again, let me know."

He took the paper, though I had a feeling it would likely end up in the trash. "We don't need more bikers around here."

They definitely didn't. They needed me, though. "I'm not just a biker."

But I was. At least on the outside. And by the distrust in Sam's eyes and the way he turned and headed for his house without waiting for me to leave was just the way the people of Justice should have been treating me. It was what I deserved.

It was what I'd earned.

Chapter Six

MERCY

It took me hours to calm down from what happened at Sam's house, but I did. I had to. There was a little boy who had a birthday party, and no way was I disappointing him. Even though he was running around the apartment in his superhero cape, his Iron Man underwear...and nothing else.

"You'd better get dressed, young man. You can't go to dinner in your undies."

He swooped past me, giggling as he asked, "Why not? It's *my* birthday."

That smart mouth had definitely come from me. I loved his confidence but knew that sass would eventually bite me in the butt. He was going to be a handful as he got older for sure. But for now, I could still grab him and snuggle him and force him to follow the rules. Most of the time.

"Why not?" I captured him in the hallway outside the bathroom, tugging him into my embrace from behind and kissing his neck loudly. "Because it's against the law. So, unless you want Mister Alder to drag your cute little booty to jail tonight, you'd better get dressed."

He laughed, the sound something I would never get enough of. "There's no jail in Justice."

He was right—no jail, no police, no first responders. Just the Kennard family...and Parris. A thought that wouldn't let me go even as Beckett raced away from me.

The image of that big, hulking man infiltrated my thoughts for the millionth time that day. I owed him a big one for helping me that morning. He'd texted just as I'd gotten to the school to pick up Beckett, a simple *Problem handled. Sam is fine.* I sure hoped it was the truth because I certainly wasn't okay. My hands wouldn't stop shaking, and my heart jumped with every noise from outside. I'd even called Sam after that text to check in on him, but he hadn't wanted to talk. He'd only said thanks for sending Parris up the hill and that he'd talk to me later. Didn't really sound fine in any way, but there was nothing I could do. No way to make the man talk without being pushy, and I wasn't really prepared for that.

Nor was I prepared to have a naked Beckett—sans cape, even —go screaming down the hallway.

That kid.

"Beckett Cole Bell, I told you to get dressed, not run around this house butt naked."

"But it's my birthday, and I'm wearing my birthday suit."

God help me, but I laughed. Really, really hard. He wasn't wrong.

———

"I'll get the cake ready." Katie patted my arm and stood from the table where we'd been sitting, taking her empty teacup with her. The birthday dinner had definitely been a success—friends of my parents sat at a table in the back, chatting with Vol and his wife, whom I'd known practically since birth. Shye and Alder had been sitting with Gage at another table, but the big, burly mechanic followed Katie into the back. Not that I could blame him. After the Soul Suckers had attacked her in this very restaurant and nearly kidnapped her, he'd finally stopped following her around like a puppy and had basically claimed her as his girl. He rarely left her side anymore.

The lucky bitch.

I kept my eyes on Beckett, trying hard not to think about the disappointment he must feel. Not that he seemed disappointed— his friend from school had come to the dinner, and the two were playing with cars along the bottom of the bar across the room. He seemed happy as a clam and silly as always.

I was not feeling silly because the one person I'd invited who hadn't shown up was the one who'd promised both Beckett and me that he'd be there. Parris had missed the entire dinner, something that would likely bother me for days.

Weeks, maybe.

Hell, months.

I always had been one to hold a grudge.

"You did well, honey. That boy is a good egg for sure," old Vol said as he took the seat Katie had left empty, setting his cup of coffee down in front of him. The man had been great friends with my parents before they'd up and left for Florida. He was as much family as anyone else.

"Thanks, Uncle Vol."

He sat back, watching Beckett with a smile on his face before looking my way again. "So, Beckett mentioned a man named Parris was missing. Want to fill me in on who that is?"

I shrugged, feeling more like an idiot with every passing minute. Knowing everyone in town would be gossiping about my business if Vol's wife got her teeth into this particular story. "I don't really know much about him. He's in town because of the Kennards."

"Well, if he's with the Kennards, he must be good people."

Sure, he was. "If he were that good, he wouldn't have told Beckett he'd be here and then not shown up."

Vol nodded, a frown forming on his face. "Maybe something came up."

Something came up, my ass. "Maybe."

I gave Vol a quick side hug then headed into the kitchen to help Katie, needing a minute to clear my head from thoughts of errant bikers and disappointing men.

"Oh, good," Katie said from where she stood before a two-tier, red, white, and blue cake with superhero figures all over it. "I grabbed a candle in the shape of a six because I was worried Beckett wouldn't be able to actually blow out six candles. What do you think?"

I passed Gage, who stood in the corner like some sort of sentinel, and came around the counter into the cooking area of the kitchen. The cake was even better up close—bright and shiny and colorful. Exactly what Beckett would want.

"I say go with the six. He's got a lot of hot air in him so I'm sure he could blow the individual ones out, but he might spit on the cake doing it."

Katie nodded. "Fair point."

With that, she set a blue six candle into the top tier, moved Iron Man off to the side, so he wouldn't melt, most likely, and then grinned.

"Time to light it up."

Gage appeared at her side, lighter in hand, pulling her away from the counter as if she might ignite. "I've got this."

Katie's bottom lipped popped out, a firm pout on her pretty face. "I can light a candle."

"I know you can." He kissed her hand, the one with the burn scars along the palm from her run-in with the Soul Suckers. "I just want to help."

God, they made me jealous. And slightly sick. There was no doubting they were in love. Meanwhile, I was on the outside looking in. Alone. Katie had Gage all over her ass on a daily basis, and I couldn't even get Parris to show up to a party he'd promised to attend. Not that we were dating or anything, the way Katie and Gage were. Not that it should have mattered so much to me that he hadn't showed. Beckett might have been disappointed, but there was no reason for me to be.

And yet, I was.

Super big idiot.

Gage led the way into the dining room, holding open the door for Katie to carry the cake and cutting the lights as she and I strolled toward the table where Beckett sat with his friend. I focused on his smile, his glowing grin, as we all began singing happy birthday to him. One voice powered over the rest, making my skin go cold.

Parris stood directly behind Beckett, one hand on my son's shoulder. Smiling as he belted out the words. As if he'd always been there. He hadn't, though, and as grateful as I was for him showing up, I had to remember that he was a couple hours late.

"Happy birthday, buddy," I said as Katie set the cake down in front of Beckett. "Make a big wish."

Beckett grinned up at me, that holey smile embedding itself into my mind like a snapshot, before closing his eyes and blowing out his lone candle. Birthday done—wish made—cake about to be served.

"Who wants ice cream?" I asked, cataloging those who said yes or nodded as I glanced around the room, trying really hard not to focus on Parris for too long. He looked good. Tired, though. Exhausted, really. I couldn't help but wonder what he'd been up to all day to make him look that way. Not that it was any of my business.

Katie and I served cake and ice cream to the crowd, both of us working in concert to accomplish the task in minimal time. I even smiled at Parris as I handed him his plate, nodding at his whispered thank you. I might have thought evil things about him, but I held myself together. That was about the best I could do.

I was standing near the bar watching my friends and family chat and celebrate with my son when Parris finally made his way over to me. My entire body went stiff, my muscles locking down as if ready for an attack. Which wasn't at all what I got.

"Sorry I'm late." His voice cracked, that weariness evident in the tone.

I almost felt bad for him. Almost...but not quite. "You should apologize to him, not me."

"I did. But I'm apologizing to you too.

"I don't know why."

"Because I'm an asshole."

I snorted, unable not to laugh. "I figured that out already."

Parris grabbed my hand, tugging me around until I faced him. "But I'm not a big enough asshole to break a promise to a kid. Not without one heck of a reason."

God, his eyes always froze time when they locked on me. "So, what's the reason?"

"For being late?" He sighed when I nodded. "Bullshit stuff with the clubs."

"That answer is weak."

"It is, but it's the best I can do right now. I don't want that life affecting yours. Or Beckett's."

And that right there might have been the only thing he could have said to make me melt even a little for him. "You could have called to tell me you'd be late."

He cocked his head, looking decidedly arrogant. "Check your phone, woman. I called and texted."

I tugged my phone from my back pocket, nearly smacking my head when I saw I'd left it on do not disturb. Four texts all from Parris and two missed calls, plus a voice mail. Yeah, he'd tried, all right.

"Oh." A simple response. Not enough, but the most I could do.

Parris accepted my nonanswer without hesitation. "He looks like he's had a good time, though."

"He has." I took a deep breath, reaching for his hand, squeezing those rough fingers. "Thank you for showing up."

His eyes burned into mine, the lust there obvious. The interest clear. And God help me, but I knew my own looked the same way. There was something between us, some sort of connection that refused to be ignored. Chemistry, people called it. Attraction.

Whatever the word, the feeling was likely going to get me in far too much trouble.

"You're welcome," Parris said finally, weaving his fingers with mine and holding on. Sending shivers racing up and down my spine. His hands were as rough as I'd expected, something that I'd definitely remember in my dreams tonight.

"Time for presents," Beckett yelled, breaking the moment. I

pulled away from Parris, looking up at him as I moved toward the gift table. Giving him a smile. He grinned back, his eyes holding mine the entire time. Have mercy, the man had a way of looking at me that was better than foreplay.

Beckett managed to behave with manners through most of the gift opening, though he did toss the clothes I'd bought him over his shoulder with a whiny "Mmmooommm" when he opened them. I made up for that with a set of Legos I knew he'd been wanting and some premade slime. I hated the stuff, but he loved it. For his birthday, I would deal with the gross substance.

His last present wasn't a present at all but a card. Beckett didn't read much, but he could make out sight words and chop and blend simple ones, so it wasn't a real surprise when his eyes grew big after he'd been staring at the opened card for a few seconds and he began to practically vibrate in his seat.

"Are you serious, Mister Parris?"

Parris nodded, shooting me a wink as he said, "Sure am."

"What is it?" I asked, moving to read the card over Beckett's shoulder.

"He's going to take me to get a bike."

Another promise. Another chance for disappointment. I stared right at Parris, cocking my head. He nodded as if he knew where my thoughts had gone, catching my little boy who'd basically flung himself across a table into the big man's arms. Everything inside of me melted at the sight, the backbone of steel I'd developed as a single mom turning to mush in three-point-two seconds. And still, I worried.

Don't be like his dad.

"When can we go?" Beckett asked, bouncing in Parris' big arms. "I'm ready now."

Parris laughed as if that level of enthusiasm hadn't been expected. "The bike shop is closed right now, but how about

Sunday? That gives you all day tomorrow to look at the website and pick the bike you want."

And plenty of time for him to back out.

But Beckett wasn't as negative as I could be, couldn't remember how his dad had up and left us with nothing. He still held on to hope. A luxury I didn't have.

"Mom, can I go on that site and look? Please."

I gritted my teeth, pulling a smile for my baby from deep within me. "Of course you can."

Beckett jumped down and raced toward his friend, the two boys talking excitedly about all the places they could go once they both had bikes. I only had eyes for the man of the hour—the one who'd just promised my boy something big.

The one who had better not disappoint my son.

I kept my voice low as I cornered Parris along the bar. "You know he'll expect you to follow through on that."

"I do."

"Don't flake on him."

He nodded once, watching Beckett play with his friend. "I made him a promise, and I'll make good on it. I swear."

Somehow, against my better judgment, I believed him. Either I was losing my edge, I was a bigger idiot than I'd thought, or Parris was just that darn good.

I really hoped it was the latter.

I sighed, wishing this uncertainty would go away. Wanting things that made me nervous. "You didn't need to buy him a present, you know."

Parris twisted his face into an expression of pure insult. As if that hadn't even crossed his mind. As if my even stating the obvious fact was somehow a shot to his character. "What sort of man comes to the birthday party of his girl's son and doesn't bring a present?"

His girl. As if he'd laid claim to me, like how Gage had laid claim to Katie. Like Alder and Shye, who I could see cuddling out of the corner of my eye. His girl? I hadn't even gone on a date with the man. Hadn't even gotten to know him.

I hadn't been anyone's girl in a long damn time, and that wasn't changing tonight. "I'm not your girl."

He pinned me with a steely gaze, stealing my breath as he said, "Not yet."

Alder appeared at Parris' elbow, giving me a break from the look that had just set my panties on fire. This was bad. So bad. The man seemed to want to give me everything I could have asked for, and yet he didn't seem like the type I should want to be with. What was that saying? The heart wants what the heart wants. My heart suddenly wanted Parris. As did the rest of my body.

"Mercy," Shye said, totally stealing my attention. "I was hoping to talk to you about a business opportunity."

Business. Lady business. Lady parts. Good lord, was Parris still watching me? I needed a fan. "What sort of business opportunity?"

The little blonde smiled shyly, living up to her name as always. "You know Alder and I are getting married in a couple of weeks, right?"

The invitation hung on my refrigerator, so I nodded.

"Well, there's so much going on, and all the planning is really tricky. I was hoping I could hire you to help me."

I...hadn't expected that. "You want me to plan your wedding?"

"Yes. I'm afraid I'll forget some detail that might be important, and Alder says you're really organized."

I was, always had been, but I'd never worked as an event

planner. "You know I don't do that for a living, right? I never have."

"I know, but Alder's sure you'll do great, and I trust him."

Trust. I shot a look at Parris, the word rebounding in my head. Such a fragile thing. Such a foreign concept. The very idea of being able to trust a man so thoroughly nearly unnerved me.

Shye was a very lucky lady.

And I could always use a little extra money.

"Okay. I'll do it."

I shook hands with Shye as if we'd made some sort of business arrangement—which I guess we had—and listened as she began laying out what she wanted and whom she'd already contacted or hired for various parts of the event. Meanwhile, I kept feeling watched. Couldn't stop from sensing someone staring at me. When I looked up, that someone was Parris, and the look said so much more than words could.

I want you.

I need you.

You're mine.

I was in so much trouble.

Chapter Seven

PARRIS

As I looked across the restaurant at the good people of Justice celebrating the sixth birthday of one of their own, there was only one thought in my head. *I shouldn't be here.*

"You shouldn't be around that kid," Alder said, appearing beside me out of nowhere and confirming my thoughts.

Not that I would let him know my own doubts about the entire situation. "Why not?"

He looked past me to where Mercy stood with Shye, the two women deep in conversation. "You sticking around once this whole Soul Suckers thing is over?"

Damn. When that man went in, he headed straight for the jugular. "I might."

Gage sidled up to us, the big man appearing more deadly calm than usual. He looked across the crowd to where Beckett and his little friend sat on the floor with a pile of metal cars between them. "You think he's safe with you? If your biker friends see you with him, are they going to target him?"

Fuck. "I'm not putting him at risk."

But I was, and they both knew it. As did I.

"You got two options, the way I see it," Gage said, those dark eyes locked on mine. "Either you hustle the fuck up on this whole wooing thing so you can keep an eye on them twenty-four seven, or you walk away. Your call. But Mercy's stubborn—she won't leave that hardware store. She wouldn't even move in to one of Alder's properties when I took Katie home with me. She and Beckett are alone on Main Street after dark."

Alder huffed. "So damn stubborn."

Stubborn...or fiercely independent. I had a feeling it was the latter. "I get that."

"So you'd better decide how you're going to play this," Alder said. "Because we're already spread thin, and adding even more security to Main Street because she won't move and you've brought attention to her is a problem."

"I'll take care of it." How, I had no idea. But I would. I'd follow through on my promise to get Beckett a bike, then I could begin to figure out how to get out from under Cartel's thumb and maybe—just maybe—convince Mercy to give me a shot.

Fuck, I never would have thought it possible, but dealing with Cartel might have been the easier of the two non-bike-related tasks.

"You planning on telling us where you and Deacon snuck off to?" Gage asked, piquing my interest and pulling my attention from the shit situation I was likely about to find myself in to whatever Alder had been dealing with.

"We were in Vegas." Alder shrugged, ever the good liar, but a liar nonetheless. I saw right through that bullshit line.

"Not that one," I said, knowing that had been the excuse he'd used when he'd headed out to save Jinx from the Soul Suckers. Not that she had been his mission—her presence had been more of a surprise than anything. Still, that was how I saw the situation and why I felt I owed him as much as I did. He'd picked up the pieces when I'd failed. I wouldn't forget that. I also wouldn't forget that he'd disappeared with Deacon for a whole damn day. "You and Deacon went running off again. Anything I need to know?"

"We were out hunting."

No way was that the truth. "Get anything good?"

The smile that crept across his face was one filled with pride. "Sure did. Got exactly what we needed to."

Gage furrowed his heavy brow. "I have no idea what we're talking about."

"You watch the news?" Alder asked, looking from Gage to me and back again.

I could only shrug. "Not often."

"You might want to. And hey, my brother Bishop's in town with his girl Anabeth, in case you didn't know. You should meet him." With that, he strolled away as if he hadn't just lied his way through our conversation then dropped a bit of a bomb on me. Another brother? How many Kennards were there?

Gage seemed just as unhappy about what had just happened as I did. "I don't like this."

Me neither. "Feeling left out of all the fun?"

"A little bit." His head whipped around as his girl Katie laughed, his eyes zeroing in on her as his lips twitched once. As if wanting to smile but holding it back. So whipped.

"Enjoy it, man," I said, unable not to take a good long stare at Mercy as she walked away from Beckett. "You've got a good woman to take care of. Focus on that."

"I am," Gage said, still watching Katie. "Believe me, I am."

I patted him on the shoulder then followed after Mercy, who'd headed for the kitchen. Alone. Time to take the first step, which included walking through those swinging doors into the back of Katie's restaurant. Mercy didn't hear me enter, too focused on whatever she was doing to pay attention. I took a moment to look her up and down—to really take in how her jeans hugged her ass, how her shoulders and back tapered to a narrow waist before flaring again at her hips. The woman was pure sex appeal, all feminine and soft, with curves for days and legs that didn't quit. She also had a backbone of damn steel. I was attracted to both sides of her. And I never had been a patient man.

"Beckett sure does have a lot of friends in Justice."

Mercy jumped, spinning with a pile of dirty plates in her arms, her light eyes and full lips opening wide. "Jesus, Parris. You scared me."

Yeah, I obviously had. I closed the distance between us, taking the plates from her arms and setting them on the counter before pinning her against it. Blocking her escape from me just for a minute. Needing a moment with her full attention on me.

"That wasn't my intention."

"No?" she asked, all breathy and wild. Definitely liking my closeness. "What was your intention, then?"

"Just to spend a little time with you. Alone."

"Oh."

That was all I got—one syllable. But it was more than I needed because her body was having a full-on conversation with mine. Breaths coming fast, cheeks pinked, and a slight arch to her back, pushing her closer to me. Yeah, that hot little body of hers was talking all right, and I definitely liked what it was saying.

I reached out and tucked a lock of her hair behind her ear, palming her neck. Feeling her pulse under my thumb and the same damn rhythm through my cock. "The things I want to do to you, beauty..."

She licked her bottom lip, her eyes locked on my mouth, her expression so damn needy. I broke. I'd wanted to kiss that mouth—to taste the sweetness of her—since the first moment I'd met her. Wanted to know how those plush, pink lips felt against mine since I'd seen them through the glass at the hardware store. I refused to hold back another second.

So I did exactly what I wanted to—I kissed her. Grabbed her around the waist and yanked her into my arms as I practically bent her backward. Pressed my lips to hers and ran my tongue along her bottom one, making her open for me before plunging my way inside. Overpowering her and running the kiss like a military operation—with speed and power and decisiveness. And good goddamn, she tasted as sweet as I'd imagined. So hot and soft and delicious. I couldn't stop myself; I had to have more. Needed it. I picked her up and set her ass on the counter before pulling her closer to me. Bringing us together from shoulder to hip. Trapping my hard cock between us and rocking into her as I gripped her hips and held her in place. Moving against her like a man possessed because that's what I was—overtaken by her. Completely out of control.

And I loved it.

At least, until she yanked herself away from me and shoved me backward. "Stop."

Ice water straight to my balls would have been more comfortable than the sound of her voice in that moment. I took a step away, licking the taste of her from my lips. Fighting to catch my breath.

"Okay," I said, holding my hands up and taking another deliberate step back. Giving her room to escape if that's what she wanted, even though I definitely didn't. "I stopped."

"You can't just go around kissing random women." She slid off the counter, flushed and shaky and obviously affected but also mad as hell. Stubborn didn't begin to describe her—Mercy Bell was goddamned pigheaded.

But I could be just as dogged and determined as her. "Trust me, beauty. There was nothing random about that kiss."

Her cheeks darkened, and she refused to look in my eyes. "I don't like people taking from me without asking."

That statement dropped a lead ball right into my gut. I nearly growled, ready to burn the fucking world down. "Did someone hurt you?"

"What?" She cocked her head, her eyes going wide when she understood where my rage was coming from. "Oh no, nothing like that. I just—"

"Because I will kill the fucker for you."

"Stop. You will not."

I would, but she obviously didn't need me to do so. "Then what do you mean by take? Because where I'm from, sweetheart, the definition isn't one that instills a sense of calm."

At least, not in relation to her. The women Edge and Ravel used—the ones they drugged and fucked and left behind when they grew bored—floated through my mind. Guilt. So much fucking guilt weighing on me for not doing more. For accepting the bullshit as standard practice. For participating. But I could do better. Mercy made me want to *be* better. When it came to her, I'd do anything to make sure she never got taken advantage of. Not even by me.

Mercy, meanwhile, seemed to be calming down. She even shrugged a single shoulder in response to me. "I just meant, if I wanted you to kiss me, I'd ask you to."

Well, that sounded...appealing. "Okay. So, ask."

Those eyes flashed, that ornery trait of hers showing itself once more. "Maybe I don't want you to kiss me."

I stalked closer, caging her in against the counter again but not touching her. Not taking from her in any way. Playing the game by her rules this time. "Oh, you want me to, Beauty. I can tell."

"Bullshit."

"That naughty mouth. But fine. I'll wait for you to ask next time." I ran a finger along her bottom lip, then took a step back. Releasing her once more. "Want help with these dishes?"

She crossed her arms, raising that chin up in an act of defiance. "I won't be asking."

"For help with the dishes?" I grinned, leaning against the counter at my back. Casual as fuck but with intention. "No need to. I'm offering my services to you."

"I meant for a kiss. I won't be asking for a kiss. From you."

That slip, that almost stutter of her words—she'd be asking all right. And soon.

I shook my head and edged past her toward the sink, making sure to brush along her arm and sending her a cocky grin when I saw her shiver. "Yeah, you will. It won't take you too long either."

Not soon enough, though. She didn't ask right then, instead falling in beside me to load the dishes into the industrial cleaner after I rinsed them. We worked well together, quiet but not needing more conversation. Soon enough, all the dishes were loaded and the kitchen set back to rights, which was both a blessing and a curse. The party was over. Time to go back to my reality, while she and Beckett returned to theirs. Without me.

"Come on," I said as I held open the kitchen doors for her. "Say goodbye to your guests, and I'll walk you and Beckett home."

"We don't need you to guard us."

So damn stubborn. "You may not need it, but I'll worry if I don't see you safely home. Besides, my momma raised me to be a gentleman." I leaned into her, moving nice and close so I could whisper in her ear. "She also raised me to take care of what was mine. That means I'll be walking you home, beauty."

She pulled away but didn't leave. Didn't argue with me. Instead, she nodded once before turning for where Beckett sat with Gage at the bar. Not without one last shot, though. "I'm never going to be yours, Parris."

My grin kicked up as Gage caught my eye, obviously having heard that. Yeah, she was stubborn. But so was I.

"We're all cleaned up," I said. "Once everyone's gone, I'll walk these two home."

Gage glanced down at Beckett then over to Mercy, who didn't say anything to dispute my offer. I considered that a win.

"Sounds good."

Ten minutes and a handful of goodbyes later, Gage held the back door open for us as we left for the evening. Mercy walked a step in front of me, that head held high and her eyes focused anywhere but on me. Beckett...well, he was a softer touch.

"So, Sunday, Mister Parris?" the little boy said, practically bouncing down the alley. "That's when we'll go get my new bike?"

"Sunday. I have your mom's number, so I'll let her know when I'll be here for our trip."

"And we'll go to a real bike store? One that sells lots of bikes?"

"Yep. It's over in Crystal Falls." I glanced at Mercy, shrugging. "It's supposed to be one of the best in the area for mountain bikes."

She nodded, looking thoughtful. And still totally avoiding my gaze. "Sounds good. We'll need to get you a helmet, buddy."

"Aw, Mom. Why?"

"I wear a helmet," I said. "Smart dudes wear helmets—you only get one brain."

Beckett gave me a thoughtful look, then shrugged. "So long as it's a cool helmet. Maybe they have an Iron Man one."

And with that, the crisis of protective headgear had been averted. Score one for Team Parris.

When we reached the rear entrance to their building, Beckett grabbed my hand and tugged. "Want to come upstairs? Mom has a computer—we can look at the bikes on the website."

But as much as I definitely wanted to, I had a feeling Mercy needed a break from me. She'd been quiet since our kiss, and I didn't want to push her. Not yet.

Luckily or not, just as I opened my mouth to answer, my phone rang. Loud and jangly, the sound shattered the stillness of the night and brought Mercy's eyes to mine. And she did not look happy.

"You should get that."

I reached into my pocket and silenced the device, holding her gaze. Not even glancing at the screen so I could make a point to her—she was my priority in that moment. "I'll call them back once I get you two inside—I'm sure it's work." I threw her a quick grin then dropped down to come face-to-face with her son. "Thanks for the invite, Beckett, but I should pass tonight. I'll be here on Sunday though, okay?"

I held out my fist for a bump, but the kid didn't offer his in return. Instead, he dove for me, practically throwing himself into my arms and almost knocking me off-balance.

"Okay," he said before squeezing and hugging me with everything he had. "Thanks for the coolest birthday ever."

My heart shattered and reassembled itself, the boy taking up a huge portion of it as I hugged him back. "You're welcome, little man. Be good for your mom."

"I'm always good." He dropped to his feet, heading inside the door his mom held open for him.

Mercy watched him race up the stairs before turning my way once more. "Thanks for coming."

I rose to my feet, craving a closeness with her she wasn't ready to give. Wanting so badly for her to ask me for a goodbye kiss even as I knew there was no way that was happening. I'd never been a patient man, but this woman was going to force me to learn. And I planned on being an eager student.

So I didn't push, instead giving her space. And time. And every ounce of my attention once more. "I gave the boy a promise that I'd be there."

"Yeah, well—not everyone follows through."

I had a feeling those words weren't really directed at me. Maybe they were more for Beckett's real dad, whom I knew nothing about. Was he still in the picture? He definitely didn't live with them or I'd have noticed something, so I didn't have that sort of shit to worry about. But he'd apparently left a few scars that needed healing. Something I knew all too much about.

"I'm not everyone."

She smiled all slow and warm, sweet. Her eyes locked on mine, her body relaxed and soft finally. Receptive. "No, you're not."

Ask me, I thought, watching those lips for any sign of movement. For any indication that she wanted me to kiss them as badly as I wanted to do the kissing. Taking a chance, I inched closer. Leaning into her body. Not enough to touch but enough to feel her warmth, to hear the way her breath stuttered. To smell that floral aroma that seemed to float around her. I wanted to touch her so badly, to grab her and pull her into my arms. She seemed to want the same, opening herself to me. Standing still instead of retreating. Accepting my closeness. Her mouth opened, the tip of her tongue appearing to wet the flesh before hiding once more as she—

My phone rang again, totally interrupting the moment and making me want to throw the thing at the wall. The heat dissipated, the cool air of the night replacing it. And Mercy? Well, she took a step away from me, and I knew we were done for the night.

Fucking phone.

"Work again?" Mercy asked, looking doubtful. Something I simply wouldn't put up with.

"Definitely. No one but my crew and the Kennards have this number."

She looked up at me again, cocking her head to the side. "And me."

I leaned closer, wishing once more that she would just ask me to kiss her. Wanting her taste on my lips one last time before she walked away for the night and left me to myself. "And you, beauty."

That smile grew, but the evening was over and we both knew it. She whispered a soft goodnight and headed inside. Kiss denied. Door closed between us once more. That was fine. I'd wait her out. She'd ask me eventually.

And still, I stood in the alley in front of that door. Watching as lights turned on above me. Knowing the two Bells were back where they belonged, safe and secure and performing whatever nightly rituals they'd developed over the years. Washing up and getting ready for bed—something so simple, and yet something I desperately wanted to be a part of. I was tired all the way to my bones, and curling up in a soft bed with that woman by my side seemed almost heavenly compared to what I'd likely end up doing tonight. Something I wanted but couldn't have. Yet.

When my phone rang for the third time, I finally tugged it from my pocket. Two missed calls from Edge and one incoming. Fuck.

"What?" I said as soon as I swiped to answer, turning away from the door I wanted to break through so as not to foul that space with the nonsense I knew was coming.

"I want you at camp. Now."

"What's wrong?" I hurried down the alley toward where I'd parked my bike, listening closely for any clues as to what was wrong. The only thing I heard was the sound of a party going on.

Edge laughed, growing louder over the line. "We've got pussy all over the place, Parris, my friend. Get here. I need someone to help contain the madness."

Fuck my life. As I reached my bike, I looked up at the buildings lining Main Street. Only one had any sign of life in it—the hardware store. A warm, golden light glowed from the upstairs. From Mercy and Beckett's home. I'd have given anything to be there with them, enjoying a quiet evening after the birthday party. But that simply wasn't in the cards for me. Instead, I got the mess back at camp. The one I had grown far too weary to want to clean up anymore.

One more kill, I thought. Wolf—once he was done and my debt to my sister's memory had been paid, I was through. I'd find a way out. Until then...

I took one more glance at the glow over the hardware store before turning my back on it.

Stay safe, beauty.

"I'm on my way."

Chapter Eight

MERCY

S aturday morning, I snuck downstairs—coffee in hand—to look over emails received overnight. A totally normal thing I did weekly, but for some reason, I couldn't get my head into work. Fine, not just *some reason*—I knew where my focus had gone, where my attention seemed to be pointing, and it wasn't to customers and sales. It was to the man who'd infiltrated my life and taken me completely by surprise. The one who'd kissed me like a man claiming ownership of a woman would, before backing off completely after just one word from me. I had no idea how to handle a man like Parris, but he sure seemed to know how to handle me.

"Not going to pay the bills in kisses." I shook my head, sipped my coffee, and refocused on the screen. Work, work, work—that was my priority. That was what I needed to devote my time to. Build the business, take care of Beckett, and make sure there was some money left over for me to enjoy life just a little bit. That didn't seem like too much to ask.

I was deep in my email inbox, noodling over the idea of how to handle custom works for customers, when a loud knock coming from the alley door sounded through the store. Fear raced through me, making me grab my phone and rush for the front of the building instead of the back. Beckett was still sleeping upstairs, and whether that was a good thing or not I wasn't sure. All I knew was I needed to figure out who was outside and how much help I was going to need to make them leave.

Knowing no one in the Kennard family could make it to me as quickly as I would likely need them to, I grabbed the shotgun from under the counter before heading toward the alley door. One shot. I just needed one good shot—not to kill, but to maim. To hurt. So long as there weren't a whole lot of men back there, I could handle this.

Still, the door seemed way too close to me, and my heart beat louder with every step toward it. Another knock sounded, this one harsher. More forceful. I gripped the gun with sweaty palms and took a deep breath as I finally closed the distance between myself and the door. The metal felt cold against my hand, but I leaned closer, taking advantage of the security features my dad had installed many, many years ago. Long before anyone had even heard of the Soul Suckers.

But when I looked through the peephole, it wasn't a biker standing outside. Well, it was, and technically the one I feared the most but for so many crazy reasons having nothing to do with death.

"What are you doing here?" I said as soon as I opened the door.

Parris—looking more tired than even the day before—held up a bag from The Baker's Cottage and shrugged. "Hi."

I blinked. Again. Still trying to make the vision before me turn into something I might have expected to see. "Hi. You make a wrong turn or something?"

His brow furrowed, the exhaustion battling with what I could only describe as dejection. "I didn't mean to bother you." He glanced at the gun in my hands, darting his eyes to mine. "And I really didn't mean to scare you."

Something in his tone, in the tiredness there, warmed my heart a little bit. The mother in me worried about him, and the woman I'd been brought up to be couldn't help but want to take care of him. I tugged my robe tighter around me and stepped back, giving him room to pass me. "Come on inside."

"I don't have to."

"No, please. I didn't mean to snap—it's still early, and I haven't had much coffee yet."

And yet, he paused.

"I wasn't sure if you drank it, or I would have grabbed some for you." He looked down the alley, frowning. "Want me to go get some from Katie's? I'm sure they—"

"Parris, get inside and come upstairs with me. There's coffee brewing already."

That arrogant smile lit his face for about half a second. "Yes, ma'am."

He passed me then waited as I hauled the shotgun back to the front of the store. When I pushed through the doors separating the selling space from the back room, he hadn't moved, but his eyes...they saw. They noticed everything.

"Was that even loaded?"

I nodded. "Always. Just in case."

He frowned, those eyes that held so much exhaustion sharpening slightly. "And Beckett?"

As in, did Beckett know about the gun. "He knows it's there, what it does, and why he should never touch it. When he gets a little older, I'll teach him to shoot the same way my dad taught me."

"Did you always keep a gun behind the counter?"

"No. Not until the bikers showed up."

Why I'd chosen bikers instead of Soul Suckers, I wasn't sure, but the word definitely affected him. He sagged a bit, that frown deepening. I couldn't take it back, though. The word sat between us, heavy and dark. Creating distance. Creating friction.

"I'm sorry you feel the need to be armed," Parris said before yawning widely. "Sorry. It's been a long night."

"Want some coffee?"

He nodded. "That sounds amazing."

"Come on, then." I locked the alley door before tugging Parris down the hall. The man followed close behind me as we trudged up the stairs to the apartment, not saying anything. When we reached the apartment door, I held it open and let Parris lead the way inside. The rooms sat quiet, which told me Beckett was still asleep. But the sun was lighting up the spaces, and that little monster rarely slept in. He'd be up and rolling any minute now.

"No Beckett?" Parris asked, as if reading my mind.

"Still sleeping. Why? You disappointed to only be able to spend time with me?"

And though I'd meant the question as a joke, the tension those words created nearly overwhelmed me. Parris darted his eyes to mine, locking me in that predator gaze again. Making me tremble in ways that had nothing to do with fear.

"I will never be disappointed in time with you, beauty." He

huffed a laugh, setting the bag on the counter. "You need to quit looking at me like that."

"Like what?" I asked, completely breathy and out of sorts.

Parris practically jumped in front of me, forcing me back until my hips hit the kitchen table. "Like you want me to kiss those sweet lips of yours again but are too afraid to ask for it."

This man. "I...I don't..."

He hummed as he tucked a lock of hair behind my ear. The action familiar and sweet, something I noticed he did often enough to have become almost expected. "You're not ready to ask yet. I get that. But you will be."

He tapped my nose then gave me my space, heading back to the counter to unpack the bag. Giving me a few seconds to collect my thoughts and calm my breathing. The man was dangerous, and I liked it. Too much.

"I figured everybody liked breakfast stuff," he said, catching my eye and giving me an almost shy sort of smile. "I grabbed a bunch of pastries and sandwiches that Katie had for the mill guys."

For the men who worked at Alder's lumber company. I'd grown accustomed to hearing their trucks running up and down Main Street, though why they'd be working on a Saturday, I had no idea.

As if reading my mind again, Parris said, "Apparently the weather's going to stay warm for a bit, so Alder's got them working hard during this heat wave. Something about beetle wood."

"Beetle kill pine," I said. "It's what he harvests."

"That's it. I couldn't think of the words." He shook his head and yawned once more. "Come eat something. I want to feed you."

Oh, my heart. "You didn't have to do this."

"Of course I didn't, but I wanted to say thank you for letting me crash your party last night."

I grabbed a few plates and set them on the counter before walking toward the opposite end. "I'm sure it was boring to a man like you—a kid's sixth birthday party."

He shook his head, dead serious as he said, "It was the most fun I've had in a long time."

This man was going to break through my defenses in no time. Of that, I suddenly had no doubt. Instead of falling for him, though, I reached into the cabinet and grabbed a mug. Holding it between us as if it were some sort of talisman. A sort of shield, not that I had any doubts that Parris could be warded off with anything other than some seriously strong magic.

I didn't know any magic, but I could brew an amazing potion. One I had a feeling he'd appreciate. "So...want some coffee?"

Parris practically groaned. "God yes."

With a smile trying hard to force its way onto my face, I poured him a cup, repeating the process for my own seeing as how I'd left my cup downstairs. But once the dark liquid was swirling, I froze. And frowned. "I don't have cream, but I've got milk of both the cow and the almond variety."

Parris simply shook his head. "Not needed. Black is perfect. Thank you."

I handed him the cup of black coffee, grabbing a spoonful of sugar for my own. "So, you just decided—"

"Mister Parris!" Beckett's screech made Parris jump back, and my little six-year-old ball of energy jumped at him before even looking my way. "Are we going to get my bike today?"

Parris laughed, hugging Beckett—and thankfully not spilling hot coffee on him—before setting him on his feet. "Not today—

today, you pick your ride while I go buy a truck. Tomorrow, we take my new truck to buy your new bike."

"Aw, man." Beckett's pout pulled heavy and thick, but the smile that broke out as he saw one of Katie's homemade donuts cleared that right up. My boy knew better than to take, though. "Mom, can I have a donut, please?"

"Sure. Go ahead."

Beckett practically leaped at the counter, earning a chuckle from both Parris and me. As soon as Beckett was settled at the table with his donut and a glass of milk, I moved behind the counter again. Needing something firm and solid between me and the man taking up so much space in my home. And my life.

"You're buying a new truck?"

Parris huffed, taking a sip of coffee before setting his mug down. "It's getting colder, and I'm too old to deal with motorcycles in the snow."

That caught my attention. I'd noticed the slight graying of his hair and the wrinkles around his eyes. Subtle—not excessive—but there. And my curiosity was definitely piqued by them. "How old are you?"

Those eyebrows rose high on his forehead. "You getting personal with me, Miss Bell?"

"Sorry. I just—"

"I'm forty-two," Parris said, totally interrupting my apology. Smiling when I turned back around. "I'll be forty-three soon enough, though. What about you?"

I gripped my coffee mug a little tighter, thinking about the age difference. Ten years wasn't that bad, was it? "A lady never tells her age."

Parris shrugged and raised his own mug to his lips. "Fair enough."

But my son, bless him, knew no boundaries. "My mom's thirty-two. And I'm six."

Parris grinned. "That I knew, little man."

"So...a new truck." I nodded, practically rolling my eyes at Parris' grin. Yeah, I was changing the subject, and he knew it. "It's supposed to be warm for a bit. Why do you need one today?"

He took another sip of coffee, keeping his eyes on mine as he swallowed then lowered the mug. "I can't fit a bike on the back of my Harley."

"No, you can't. You could just use my SUV, though."

"Thanks, but I need to grow up and deal with driving a cage eventually. Might as well be now."

"A cage?"

"Car. Truck. Ride. Vehicle not on two wheels and open to the ground beneath my feet." He shot a glance at Beckett before locking those light eyes on mine again. "Sometimes, life hands you things that need more protection from the elements."

God, he was so hot. And there. And he actually seemed to enjoy spending time with Beckett. I should not be having the sort of thoughts about him that I was. Naked thoughts. The kind that had woken me up again last night and left me a needy mess.

"Hey, Mister Parris!" Beckett jumped to his feet as soon as he finished his donut. "Want to play *Minecraft* with me?"

"Sure thing, little man." Parris leaned closer and dropped the volume of his voice. "What the fuck is *Minecraft*?"

I laughed. "Like Legos but a video game. He likes to build houses in it."

"Huh." He took a step back, looking me up and down. Making me feel much more naked than I actually was. "You planning on working today?"

"Yeah. Beckett and I usually head down to the store around ten."

"Okay. I'll hang with the little man until you're ready, then I'll run and deal with this truck while you get your business on."

"You know you don't have to stay."

He shrugged. "I want to."

As if things were that easy. As if coming into a little boy's life was something simple and quick. As if Beckett wouldn't be devastated when Parris left again.

As if I wouldn't as well.

"Don't..." I stopped, trying hard not to get choked up. "Don't make him promises you can't keep. He's gotten enough of that from the men in his life."

Parris' brow tightened, his lips turning down. "Anyone still in the picture? His dad, maybe?"

That question almost made me laugh. "Not in the least. He left us a long time ago."

"Not to sound like a dick, but good."

"Good?"

"Yeah. His stupidity is a gift to me." He squeezed my elbow as he leaned past me to put his empty cup in the sink. "I've only got to get through your defenses now."

"And if you can't?"

He locked his eyes on mine. "I never stop fighting for what I want, beauty. Not ever."

Breathless. I had gone completely breathless.

"Good to know," I whispered, unable to find the strength for more words.

"Go. I've got him." Parris ran a finger down my wrist then turned away, heading toward the living room. "All right, little man. Tell me all about this Mineshaft thing."

Beckett giggled, looking way too excited to have Parris involved in our morning routine. "It's Mine*craft*."

Parris grinned my way. "*Minecraft*. Got it. Teach me how to play it."

I watched Parris disappear into the other room, standing in my kitchen long enough to finish my coffee and catch my breath. My god, the man did things to me. Bad things. Things that made my heart race and the blood inside of me warm. Nothing good could come from an attraction that strong. Nothing but hot sex and broken dreams. I might have been down for the hot sex if Beckett weren't the one who'd suffer right along with me at the whole broken dreams thing.

Still, I liked him. More than I cared to admit. And when I snuck to the doorway and peeked into the living room, I liked him even more. My son and Parris sat side by side on the couch, the older one dwarfing the younger. Parris was a big man with a big personality and a lot of arrogance, but as he sat there with Beckett, I could also see the carefulness about him. The way he gingerly touched the screen on Beckett's iPad, how he listened to the child beside him. Good lord, a man being kind to my kid was the hottest thing ever. Instant aphrodisiac. I needed to step away before I jumped him.

"I'm going to get dressed," I said, swallowing hard when two sets of light eyes met mine. "Behave, okay?"

My heart jumped a little when both of them said *Yes, ma'am* at the same time.

"Trouble, trouble, trouble. That's what he is," I whispered to myself, hurrying down the hall toward my bedroom. Once safely locked inside, I stripped off my robe and headed for the bathroom. A quick shower was all I needed. Just a couple of minutes under the hot water to recenter myself and bring my brain back online.

Still, a little makeup likely wouldn't hurt anything.

Ten minutes, three outfit changes, and more mascara than I'd worn in a year later, I walked across the dining area to the living room. Parris and Beckett were still on the couch, but *Minecraft* had obviously been abandoned as the iPad lay beside my son. He leaned against Parris instead, the two of them watching cartoons on the television mounted to the wall across the way. Parris had his arm around Beckett and was playing with the boy's hair, and Beckett...he looked completely and utterly at ease. Comfortable. Safe.

I was pretty sure the huge shift within my body was from my ovaries exploding.

"Ready for work, buddy?"

Parris looked up, giving me that sexy once-over before locking his eyes on mine. "He sure is."

Beckett turned off the television and jumped to his feet, grinning. "I'm going to be a super good helper today."

That was new. "You are?"

"Yeah. Because Mister Parris said—"

"Mr. Parris said that was a conversation between men." He gave Beckett a wink. "Go get your stuff so I can talk to your momma."

"Okay. See you later, Mister Parris."

"Bye, little man." Parris followed Beckett—who'd gone running to his room, likely to get dressed for the day—and stopped right in front of me. Almost touching but not quite. Bringing all that heat with him and practically bathing me in it.

He was far too sexy for his own good.

But I still wasn't asking him for a kiss. "A conversation between men?"

"Yup," he replied, looking quite pleased with himself. "Nothing bad, I promise."

"Were you cussing?"

He frowned. "I might have once or twice."

"Do I need to know what this manly conversation was about?"

"It was about taking care of your woman, and for Beckett, that means you." He leaned even closer, making me drunk off his scent, his lips brushing my cheek as he whispered, "For me, too."

"I'm not yours." But my argument sounded so damn weak. And he knew it.

Parris grinned and inched back. "You will be. Someday."

"Not happening."

"Happening."

"Are you always this stubborn?"

"Are you?"

"Yes."

"Then we're a matched set." He dove in and kissed my cheek, chuckling when I gasped. "Had to."

"I didn't ask."

"No, you didn't. But if your body were any more primed for my kiss, you'd be underneath me." He laughed even harder as I rolled my eyes. Not that he was all that wrong.

"Go buy your truck. I have stuff to do."

"Busy day planned?"

"I need to get in touch with Shye. She wants my help planning the wedding. And then I have some orders to fill."

He grabbed his coat from where he'd hung it on the back of a chair, looking out the window that overlooked the front of the store. "You don't get many walk-in customers, do you?"

"In Justice? No. Very few."

"Good."

"Why is that good?"

"The fewer people shopping, the less chance the wrong person will walk in."

My stomach dropped, and every thought went to the little

boy likely picking out mismatched clothes in the other room. "Do I need to be worried about that?"

Parris paused, the beat between me speaking and him answering far more noticeable than I wanted it to be. "No."

That didn't sound all that reassuring. "No, or not really? Or not right now?"

"All of the above." He grabbed my elbow again, tugging me closer in that way he tended to do. Bringing me against him as if needing to feel me close. "I have to deal with this truck this morning. You be careful out there."

Out there. As if the danger were all around us. Which I guess it was. "You, too."

"Aw, see? You do care." He headed for the door, laughing when I flipped him off. "That's my girl."

"Still not yours."

"Yet."

"Never."

"So damn stubborn."

"My dad would say tenacious."

"When I finally meet him, I'll tell him he's right about that." Parris paused, looking toward the hallway and raising his voice as he hollered, "Bye, Beckett. I'll see you later, little man."

"Bye, Parris. I'll take care of my mom for you." Beckett raced out—missing a shirt—and bumped fists with Parris. The two working through some sort of combination of hits and movements I had no idea how to follow.

"Good man, young one," Parris said when they were through. "Stay strong for her."

"You too."

Parris grinned, raising his eyebrows as he caught me looking. "See? It's just a matter of time, beauty."

But I wasn't ready to admit defeat just yet. "Don't hold your breath."

Still, as Parris headed out the door and Beckett returned to his room to finish getting dressed, I gave myself a single moment to admit that the man was right. If he managed to keep up this attention, I'd fall for him. Hook, line, and sinker. Two days, and I was toast.

It was just a matter of time until I got burned.

Chapter Nine

PARRIS

I'd left Mercy's place with a smile on my face. Every minute I spent with her, I saw the wall she'd built around herself crumble just a little bit more. She might not have been ready to ask me for another kiss just yet, but I was close. So damn close.

"Crystal Falls Bike and Hobby. Milt speaking. How can I help you?"

I tapped the button for speaker and set the phone on the table in the motel room I'd been staying at. The place wasn't much, but it was behind The Jury Room and owned by Deacon, someone I needed to track down eventually. Once I got done with Milt.

"Hey, Milt. This is Parris. We spoke yesterday about a bike for a six-year-old boy."

"Yes, of course. We have you on the books for a private appointment tomorrow, is that correct?"

"Yeah. I just wanted to make sure you would have everything

we need. His mom mentioned something about a helmet last night."

I'd ridden a bike all through elementary school without a helmet and had never had a problem, but Beckett needed to be safe. Kids these days wore helmets, which meant I needed to make sure Beckett had one. A good one.

"Of course," Milt said. "We have all sorts of helmets in many sizes. I'm sure we'll have something he needs."

Just *something* would never be good enough. "And they're good ones, right? His mom will castrate me if I buy him a helmet that cracks the first time he takes a tumble."

"All good ones. There are regulations for bike helmets, and we only buy from reputable manufacturers."

"Perfect." I yawned, fighting hard against the exhaustion tugging me down. Needing sleep more than just about anything...except to make sure Beckett got what he needed. "I just wanted to make sure we could buy the bike and he could ride it around once we got home."

Home. The word struck me, shooting a picture of the little apartment over the hardware store straight into my head. I hadn't thought much about what home meant in years, having never really had one. My dad had been moved from base to base, so I'd gotten used to leaving things behind and living in new places at a young age. I'd been alone for most of them...until Dad remarried. A woman to call mom—though I never did—entered the picture, and I was no longer alone on those moves. Then Ashley had come along, but I'd already been halfway out the door, so I hadn't really gotten to know her well. Not until much later— post military years. After my dad had died and left me alone in the world, when I'd joined the same club as her husband. When I'd decided to try out the whole family thing.

Not what I needed to be thinking about.

Basically, between being an Army brat, my own military years, plus my time in the clubs and in prison, home was a foreign concept. But I was beginning to think I'd found something to hang that moniker on. I just needed to figure out how to earn my access to it.

"I'm sure we'll have exactly what you need," Milt said, yanking me from my memories and bringing me back to the here and now. To the cheap motel room I rented in a town I was new to and the danger lurking around every corner. But I could buy Beckett a bike and keep him safe from any falls that might happen, keep him from busting his skull on the trail. At least it was something. I just hoped it was enough.

Nothing had been enough for Ashley.

"Great." I rose to my feet and began to pace, needing a little blood flow to stay awake and keep my focus. To move past those failures and work on something new. Something good. Something I might be able to do right. "I'll see you tomorrow, then."

"Excellent, sir. We'll be here."

I ended the call with a tap and then scrolled through my text messages, looking for the one about the truck. A guy named Jackson who worked with Gage and Alder at the mill. He had a ten-year-old pickup for sale with low miles and a strong engine. Exactly what I was looking for. I found the message and verified I had the time and place noted so I could check out the truck and make sure it was what I needed. If so, I'd be buying it. That meant I needed to head into Rock Falls to the bank and pull out some cash. Which likely meant running into some Black Angels and dealing with their bullshit. Not what I wanted, but something I could prepare for. I glanced at the clock—time to go.

Three hours later, I made the final turn toward Justice, my inner jacket pocket heavy with an envelope of cash and my phone dead silent. I didn't want to hear any more shit from the Black Angels—not today. I'd run into two on my trip, and that had been more than enough. I had a list of things to get done, and dealing with their drama was not on it.

Still, I'd made a few calls while I'd waited for the tellers to verify I had the cash at my bank and count out the money. I was still looking for this Coyote from the Soul Suckers. I'd even called in a few minor favors to collect information on him, something I rarely did. Favors were the name of the game in my world. It was why I was working so hard to help Alder and Deacon keep Justice safe—I owed Alder for saving Jinx's ass. Plus, Deacon still owed me for supplying him and Alder with info on the Soul Suckers in the first place. Having another favor owed—from a Kennard, no less—would be a boon for sure. I just had to find the man who'd ghosted the world as soon as he'd killed the chick in Justice and give his info to Finn. Tricky, but not impossible. And something worth working toward.

I rolled into the lot at The Jury Room but didn't head for the motel. Two cars sat outside the bar, not exactly what I'd been expecting since Deacon had closed the business just a couple of nights ago. He hadn't wanted to deal with the bikers coming in and making trouble for his patrons, and I didn't blame him. The Black Angels were bad, but the Soul Suckers wouldn't be concerned about any collateral damage that got in their way. Neither crew was exactly what you'd call loyal customers.

The first car I recognized—Deacon's. Totally normal for the thing to be parked in the lot, even with the bar closed. The second car worried me. I didn't recognize it, hadn't seen it around town, which meant a stranger was holed up inside. I grabbed my gun from the saddlebag on my bike and tucked it into my jacket pocket, wishing I had my shoulder holster. I hadn't wanted to wear it around Beckett that morning and had forgotten to put it on once I'd returned to the motel. Stupid mistake on my part and one I wouldn't be making again. No matter what TV shows and movies portrayed, no one with gun experience would tuck their firearm into the waistband of their pants. Misfires and accidents happened, and no man wanted to shoot his dick off. Which was why my loose gun was in my jacket pocket instead.

Shoulder holster...always.

I stepped inside the bar with my head up and my eyes sweeping the room, my hand in my pocket and holding the gun. Just in case. Deacon looked up when the door opened, giving me a chin nod and a smile.

"The man of the hour. Get over here, Parris. There's someone I want to introduce you to."

No holster needed, apparently. I let go of the gun and strolled to the bar, eyeing the man sitting at it. Cop. Definitely a cop. No way was he anything but, even though there was no badge or sign of any law enforcement affiliation. I could practically smell the job on him, though.

"Parris, this is Zane Grogan. He works for the county sheriff's office. Zane, this is Parris of the Black Angels."

I shook the man's hand, waiting for him to lay out how the conversation would be going.

Zane didn't take long. He tipped his beer bottle—no, wait, root beer—my way and came out swinging. "So, I hear you're planning on taking out the Soul Suckers camped outside of town."

That wasn't what I'd been expecting. "Deacon—"

"He's good, Parris." Deacon gave me a look, one filled with confidence. "He works for the sheriff's office but is on our side."

I plopped into a seat, the exhaustion of the last few days of minimal sleep catching up with me. "Somehow I doubt that."

"The Soul Suckers killed our sheriff," Zane said, looking pissed as hell and ready to fight. "I want payback."

I shook my head, the last five years of chasing that same demon without success weighing on my mind. "Vengeance won't fix things."

"No, but it'll make me feel better."

"I doubt that." I caught Deacon's stare. "You got any coffee by chance? I'm beat."

"You look it. Rough night?" He turned to the back of the bar, reaching for one of them pod thingies to brew a single cup of coffee. Not my usual choice, but beggars couldn't be choosers.

"Rough couple of days."

Zane huffed. "Tell me about it."

I caught Deacon's smirk before his face went flat again, some sort of phony concerned look appearing. "Zane's boss' body was found yesterday."

The sheriff Gage had killed when the guy had threatened Katie. I had a feeling Deacon's *good friend* Zane didn't know that part of the story. "Oh yeah? Where at?"

Deacon handed me the cup of coffee, almost seeming to wait until I had taken a pull of the hot beverage before saying, "Rock Falls. At the Soul Suckers' clubhouse."

I choked. No way around it. Coffee burned up my nose and down my throat at the same time, and I coughed for about a whole minute before I finally caught my breath. "The fuck?"

"Yeah," Zane said, handing me a couple of napkins. "The Soul Suckers tried to hide it, but they did a crap job. My forensics crews were all over that scene."

I glanced at Deacon, knowing there was no way the Soul Suckers had just *left* a sheriff's body at their house. The man looked cool as a cucumber, though. Almost arrogantly cool. Damn, did I like him.

"They know how he died?" I asked, even though I already knew the answer.

"Gunshot wound to the chest." Zane picked at the label on his bottle of soda, staring at the dark glass as if it held all the answers he needed in life. "Likely a rifle but it'll take a few days for the autopsy. Ballistics could take months."

"Sounds like a slow case."

"Right. Which is why I'm in for this hit on the Soul Suckers. They don't deserve to keep breathing on my dime."

In prison. In other words… "So, you want them all dead."

Zane took a strong pull of his root beer before slamming the bottle down. "Yep."

That simple. "All of them. An entire clubhouse of riders."

"Why? You can't handle that."

Never let it be said I wasn't a confident SOB. "I can handle anything. Can you?"

"Definitely."

I shrugged, taking another drink of my coffee—not choking this time—before nodding toward Deacon. "Then you've got the right crew to help you."

"Deacon said you guys already had a plan."

A shit one—Deacon in the air on sniper duty, Finn as backup, and me going in all guns blazing to take out as many of the Soul Suckers as I could. Adding another man to the team, especially one who might know his way around a firearm, changed things. As did still having my own crew in town.

"We do, but we'll need to rework it if you're involved."

Zane grinned, the smile growing all slow across his face. Man, that was a lot of teeth. "There's more than just me."

That caught my attention. "What do you mean?"

It was Deacon who answered. "Zane has his own crew of

sorts. Think of them like the white knights of the Rocky Mountain Front.”

“White knights…like saving people and shit?”

“Something like that.” Zane turned my way. “I’ve got nine guys to help, plus me. All well trained in various things that we could use. Surveillance, sharpshooters, snipers like Deacon, demolitions experts—”

“Whoa, whoa, whoa. How the fuck do you know these people?”

“You two aren’t the only ones who were in the military.”

I hadn’t pegged him as a brother-in-arms. Definitely not a Marine like me. He didn’t have the sociopathic air to him of the SEALs I’d met, and he definitely didn’t fit the Special Forces mold. There was only one thing that came to mind.

“You an airman?”

“Yup. Fifteen years wearing the uniform.”

Huh. Okay, I could see that one. “Where were you based?”

“Tampa, mostly.”

Tampa, where the Air Force intelligence offices were located. I had a smarty on my hands. “You see any action?”

His face went blank, the look of a man trying real fucking hard not to remember. “Yeah. Quite a bit.”

Well, okay then. “So, ten guys?”

“Right.” He took another pull from his root beer before setting it down. “I can get you a list of their qualifications for the planning, though we might be better off if I just join you and Deacon on that. I know my team.”

My day had just picked way up. “Let’s talk tomorrow. I’ve got things to do in the morning but can make myself available later.”

“Nah, tomorrow’s Sunday. I don’t plan or commit murders on the Sabbath.” The guy stood up, looking dead serious. Meanwhile, I could only stare. No murders on the Sabbath…was he some sort of religious zealot? A holy roller with a gun? Had he just become the most dangerous man in the room? Had I somehow walked into an episode of the *Twilight Zone*?

I glanced at Deacon. The sniper was practically grinning, looking way too pleased with this turn of events. So maybe Zane wasn't a zealot, just a really religious person who took that whole eye-for-an-eye thing seriously.

Twilight Zone for sure. "So...Monday, then?"

Zane nodded. "I'll call you on Monday, and we can work something out. I don't want to wait too long, though."

"Sure. Of course. Just not on Sundays."

"Right." The guy smirked. "No murders on Sundays for me or my team."

"All righty, then."

"Thanks for your help today, Zane." Deacon reached across the bar and shook the lawman's hand. "You'll hear from us."

"Good. Let me know if there's anything else you need."

I stared at Deacon as Zane walked out, waiting for the door to close behind him before I shook my head.

"What the fuck just happened?"

"What just happened is we found ten experienced soldiers to back us up on taking out the Soul Suckers. You ready?"

"Yeah." Always. Except I had a little boy I'd made a promise to. "Just not tomorrow."

"What? You don't kill on the Sabbath either?"

Fuck me, I'd almost let that comment go. I couldn't now, though. "That guy religious?"

"Very." Deacon frowned, glancing toward the door Zane— Mr. No Killing on the Sabbath—had walked through. "Zane is deadly as fuck but searching for grace at the same time."

"I find that..." I didn't even have a word for it. Deacon did, though.

"Contradictory? So do I, but the man has skills and knows how to keep his mouth shut. We can use him and his team."

True facts, though I'd learned a long time ago that if something seemed too good to be true, it likely was "You're sure we can trust him?"

"I'm sure."

"You willing to bet your life on that?"

Deacon never even faltered. "Absolutely."

That was enough for me. "Then I'm in."

"Excellent. Let's toast to that."

I yawned, unable not to. "I'd rather have another coffee."

The barkeep frowned. "You okay?"

"Yeah, just tired. The fucking Black Angels are running me ragged."

"Too many missions?"

"Too much partying." I shook my head at his glare. "Not me, them. I've somehow become their designated babysitter."

"Sounds like fun." He handed me back my mug, having refilled it. "Mercy know about that?"

Her name on his lips pulled me up short. "Any reason she should?"

Deacon raised his hands, trying hard to look innocent under all that attitude. "I'm not trying to slow your roll, but that girl is Justice royalty. You mess with her, you'll have the whole town coming down on you."

I stared into my cup, my stomach churning. Mercy's big blue eyes danced through my thoughts, and the memory of her lips on mine gave me just the shot of energy I needed to speak my truth strong and sure. "I'm not messing with her."

"So, you're sticking around, then? After we kill the Soul Suckers."

"Which we won't be doing on Sunday." I raised my mug in a toast, knowing there wasn't much I could do to lighten the mood considering the topic at hand. "I'll stay. If she'll have me, I'll stay."

"You've decided."

I caught his eye, staring hard. "She's mine."

He didn't back down, though. "And Beckett? Because he's part of the package."

"I'm aware."

"Good." He wiped down the bar, not looking at me. "People in town are going to talk. Everyone here knows how bikers tend to treat women."

Like property. Like whores. Like sperm receptacles.

Not at all like how I wanted anyone—especially not me—to see my beauty.

"I'll treat her like a princess. Like a goddamned queen. If she's willing to let me in, I'll never do anything but right by her. And Beckett."

Deacon nodded, moving to straighten some of the bottles on the back shelf. Still decidedly *not* looking at me. "That's all we can ask. For you to be good to them."

"I plan on it."

He stopped, finally turning my way, and gave me a sad look. One I didn't understand at all. "You need to be good to her for sure, but be better to him."

To Beckett. "That's a done deal."

"Then you'll be fine."

And for the first time, I thought just maybe I would be.

So I settled in, and I wrapped my hands around the mug of coffee. And I gave the man a shrug when he shot me a curious sort of frown. "I'm taking him to buy a bike tomorrow. And a helmet. My little man needs a helmet."

Deacon smiled. "He definitely does. You taking Mercy's rig to buy it?"

Because I couldn't exactly toss Beckett and a bike on my motorcycle. "No, I'm buying a cage. In fact, I need to go meet up with this Jackson guy."

"You looking at his truck?"

"Yeah. How'd you know?"

He shrugged. "It's Justice. I know everything."

Well, shit. "You know anything about this truck?"

"I do." He grabbed his jacket and turned off the lights behind the bar. "Come on. I'll take you up to Jackson's place. Make sure this deal is fair for both of you."

"I'm in. But I don't want to take too long."

"You got plans tonight?"

Remembering the glow from the window over the hardware store, I nodded. "Yeah. At least, I hope to. If I can get this deal finished in time."

"These plans include Mercy?"

I grunted as I climbed into his truck. "And Beckett."

He turned the key, bringing the big engine to life with a half smirk on his face. "We'll have this deal finished, then."

Chapter Ten

PARRIS

Hours later—after spending far more time laughing with Deacon than negotiating anything—I had a new-to-me truck, a plan for dinner, and a second wind that I hoped would get me through the night. But even my good attitude hadn't prepared me to come face-to-face with a positively giddy Katie when I walked into The Baker's Cottage.

"So, I hear you want to take dinner to my neighbors."

Yeah, so Deacon may have known everything that happened in this town, but it was because he was the biggest gossip I'd ever met.

"Deacon called you."

She shrugged, practically bouncing in place. "I never like to reveal a source. But you should be grateful because I was able to start right away. As soon as Beckett's mac and cheese is done, I'll wrap everything up for you so it stays warm." She nodded toward the back, rushing through the restaurant. "Will you need a bottle of wine? No, Mercy probably wouldn't like that with Beckett awake. Everything will be packaged in a way that you won't need plates, but what about the rest? Do you want me to send along plasticware to eat with?"

I followed her into the kitchen, my head spinning from so many words. Goodness, the woman could talk. "Uh, I mean...I assume Mercy has some."

Katie didn't even pause, simply headed to the cabinet where all the carryout containers were stacked and grabbed three packages of utensils. "Sure, but then there will be dishes, which Mercy will want to do right away. That takes time away from you while you're there. If I give you plasticware, you can just toss them in the garbage and be done with them, therefore being able to spend more time with Mercy and Beckett." She gave me a grin and a wink. "But especially Mercy."

Smart woman. "Good call."

"I'm a planning sort of girl." She grinned when Gage came in through the back, totally missing—or ignoring—the glare he sent me. "Hey, babe. I'll be ready to shut down in a few."

"Cool. Everything okay in here?"

In other words, was I harassing his woman? "I'm just picking up dinner for Mercy and Beckett."

Gage bent down to give Katie a quick kiss. "They know you're coming over?"

"Not yet."

He nodded and then grinned, an almost disturbing sight. "Good luck with that."

Katie smacked him on the chest as she passed, heading straight for the short oven in the wall. "Ignore him. He's just cranky."

I looked from one to the other, suddenly thinking maybe I'd

missed an update. Not likely, seeing as how I'd been with gossipmonger Deacon all day. "Something wrong in town?"

Katie shook her head as she finished whatever she was doing. "Nope. He's just always cranky."

Ah. "Sounds like a personal problem."

Gage glowered at my grin. "One all these fucking bikers in town are responsible for."

Okay. I could give him that. I didn't answer, instead watching Katie as she sorted and plated and...did things to food I wasn't sure how to explain. But when she was finished, the kitchen smelled amazing and she had a huge grin on her face. Both things I took as good signs for a successful dinner.

"All set." She handed me a bag filled to the brim with containers. "Go feed the family."

The family. As in *my* family. They weren't mine, though. Not yet, at least. "Thanks. You've got my credit card on file?"

She waved me off. "Of course. Go. Before Gage gets even crankier and makes you mop the floors or something."

I nodded, giving Gage a chin nod. "Thanks. I appreciate you staying open for this."

"No problem," Katie said, even as Gage gave me a look that said it definitely *was* a problem in his mind. Not that I could blame him. If Mercy were truly mine, I'd be just as protective of her and selfish of her time. If not worse. Okay, definitely worse, but mostly because *her* included Beckett. I'd be twice as cranky as Gage.

Lord help the town of Justice if that happened.

I walked out of the restaurant, bag of food in hand, and headed down the street. The cold had held off most of the day but was descending quickly over town. I'd be thankful for the truck I'd bought once the temperatures dropped. Heat would be much appreciated.

I hadn't even made it to the corner when the rumble of Harley engines stopped me in my tracks. Out on the highway, a group of bikes passed by. Soul Suckers by the looks of them, which only made me more aware of how vulnerable I was. My bike sat parked in a garage around the block that I'd rented from Alder, most of my weapons in the saddlebags. I had a knife in the pocket of my Black Angels jacket, but that was it. One blade and a bag of food. Not exactly ready for war.

Thankfully, the Soul Suckers rode on past. Likely just a group trying to scare the people of Justice. A pain in the ass but not an immediate threat. That didn't completely calm me, though. That group could have turned. They could have come straight down Main Street and stopped at the hardware store. They could have been inside Mercy's apartment before I'd even gotten a chance to call for backup. And if I hadn't been close enough to know those bikers were around? No one would have been able to help the Bells.

Mercy and Beckett being down here alone was asking for trouble. I'd need to figure out a way to convince her to listen to me, to persuade her to move out of town to someplace more defensible. To let me hole up her and the little man somewhere and keep them safe.

Which I already knew would never, ever happen. Stubborn women didn't bend.

I sent a quick text to Gage, knowing there was no way Mercy would leave that business. Already accepting her stubborn streak as something impassible. The text was simple—*let's chat tomorrow about how to keep Main Street safe after hours*. He sent back a thumbs-up emoji. That would have to be good enough for tonight because I wasn't canceling this impromptu dinner.

When I reached the front of the store, the fixtures under the awning bathed the sidewalk in light and the open sign hung in the door. Mercy and Beckett were inside, laughing and talking about something. I stood just outside the light for a solid minute, watching the scene. Memorizing it. The smiles, the joy, the comfort. I wanted to remember every detail. To be able to play that scene back when things got rough, because they would. Because plans had started to form in my head, ones that would yank me from one life and drop me into another. Ones that could cost me everything. Ones I had the full intention of exploring... after tonight.

I walked inside and joined the two Bells, hopeful for the first time in a number of years. "Anyone hungry? I brought dinner."

"Mister Parris." Beckett came running, hugging my hips before skipping back toward his mom. "Mister Parris is here."

Mercy smiled, looking confused. "I see that. And you brought food?"

I shrugged, thankful. The woman seemed happy to see me, and I would never not be grateful for the chance to put that look on her face. "I figured you might be hungry."

"I'm starving." Beckett raced into the back, yelling, "I'll go wash my hands."

Mercy passed me, heading to the door to lock up and flip the sign before coming to a stop right in front of me. Looking so fucking beautiful, it made my heart lurch to life in my chest.

"You brought dinner."

I held up the bag as if in offering. "I did."

"Sort of presumptuous, don't you think?" Her snarky words were softened by the smile on her face and the way she grabbed the bag from me, how she led me through the back room, flicking off lights along the way to the rear stairs that would take us to the second level. How she never asked me to leave.

Mission accomplished, in my opinion. "Maybe, but I figured you wouldn't mind."

"Oh, really? And why's that?"

Time to roll the dice again. "Because you'll be asking me to kiss you later."

She laughed, which wasn't quite the reaction I was going for. But at least she didn't punch me in the face. "Never gonna happen."

"We'll see." I held open the door for her, letting her slip past me once again as we walked into her little apartment. I set the bag on the counter and started pulling things out. "Katie said all of this is packaged to eat in the containers. She even sent plasticware."

"No dishes to wash? Excellent. That woman is a saint."

Score one for Katie.

Dinner ended up a raucous affair with Beckett running the show, constantly regaling me about his day and all the things he'd done and the bikes he'd looked up. The kid must have spent hours online researching options. Mercy and I couldn't fit a word into the conversation, but neither of us seemed to mind. My beauty sat there watching her son with a soft smile on her face, and I was just happy to be included at all. Such a difference from the quiet of the motel room or the chaos of dealing with my crew.

"And I really wanted the red one, but the wheels on the blue are better for trails, and I think I want to ride the trails. Right, Mom?"

"Right." Mercy tapped a finger on the table. "How about less talking and more eating, buddy?"

"My belly's already full." He pushed aside his plate. "May I be excused?"

Mercy frowned at the barely touched macaroni dish but simply said, "Sure."

Beckett might have been done with dinner, but he wasn't

with me. He glanced my way then at his mom. "Can we watch a movie tonight?"

We. As in all three of us.

Mercy caught my eye, an expression of hesitancy on her pretty face. "Of course, though I'm not sure if—"

"Got any good ones?" I asked, focusing on Beckett instead. "Maybe something funny."

The little man gave the movie choice some serious thought, screwing up his face and looking to the ceiling before a grin broke out. "I've got *Zootopia*. It's my favorite and funny. We should watch that one."

"Done. Let's watch it."

Beckett jumped up from his seat and took off running across the room. "I'll go get everything ready."

And then he was off, and I was left alone with Mercy. Just where I wanted to be.

"That kid has two speeds," I said, shaking my head. "Sitting and full speed ahead. There is no in-between."

"Sounds about right." Her smile dipped, her brow furrowing and that pretty, pink tongue flashing for just a second to wet her bottom lip. "You don't have to stay, you know. If you have things to do or something."

As if anything could be more important to me in that moment. "I want to stay. If you don't mind."

Those light eyes stabbed into me. "You're asking permission now?"

"I figured I'd invaded your life enough for one day, so I could go if you demanded it." I grabbed her hand where it sat on the table and leaned closer, dropping my voice a bit just in case little ears were nearby. "But I'd really like it if you didn't demand it because I missed you today, beauty. You and Beckett."

Her cheeks flushed, and she smiled so prettily that I nearly fell out of my chair. "I'd like it if you stayed."

"Then I will."

I helped her clean up our mess, seriously thanking Katie in my head for being so thoughtful about the whole no-dishes thing, and then followed Mercy into the living room. Beckett had blankets out and the movie all cued up and ready to go on the television. He sat dead center on the couch as if he simply had to be between me and his mom. Which was fine. I could play by his rules.

"You ready, Mister Parris?"

I took the seat on the left, letting my arms fall across the back of the couch. Allowing my fingertips to brush along Mercy's shoulder as she sat way on the other side of the piece of furniture.

"Ready. Hit play, little man."

Not even half an hour into the movie, Beckett fell asleep. His garbled snore gave it away.

"He sounds like a man," I said, fighting to hold back a laugh at the grunts coming from the kid.

"I know. It's only when he sleeps in a funny position, though." Mercy rose to her feet, reaching as if to pick up the boy. I nudged her out of the way and did it myself, knowing his weight wouldn't bother me much but would be something she might struggle with. She let me pick up Beckett, blinking twice once I had him in my arms. Not moving.

"Which way?" I finally asked, and Mercy—looking startled at my question—jumped into motion.

She led me down the hall to a small room with beige walls and bright-colored posters all over. She tugged down the bedding for me, giving me room to lay the sleeping Beckett in the middle of the mattress. Then I moved out of her way, knowing this was a mother-son moment.

Mercy pulled the covers over Beckett then tucked a little bear under his arm. She leaned down to kiss his forehead, whispering a quiet "love you" against his hair. So sweet, this woman, and such a good mom. Something I'd never taken the time to appreciate in anyone before but that was such a fucking turn-on with her. Her dedication to her son was obvious, her love overflowing. I wanted to bask in the warmth these two people exuded. To stay right there in the middle of their happy bubble.

But I also wanted time with just Mercy, which was obviously what I was about to get. Mercy rose to her feet and gave me a look. One that spoke volumes. That twisted something in my gut and made tingles shoot off in my spine. Hard. One glance, and I was hard as stone for her.

The little temptress grabbed my hand and tugged me from the room, swinging those hips more than usual. Not letting go of me until we reached the living room once more.

"You don't have to watch this," she said, waving toward the television screen where the movie sat frozen, having been paused before we'd taken Beckett to bed.

"I liked it." I shrugged when her smile showed up all crooked and cute. "Besides, now I need to know what's been happening to the predators."

She laughed, reclaiming her seat and curling into the blanket there. But this time, we didn't have a six-year-old between us. I took full advantage, plopping much nearer to the middle of the sofa and tugging her closer. Wrapping an arm around her and breathing her in as she pressed play.

"Comfortable?"

She sighed and nodded, snuggling into me. Giving me more affection in a matter of seconds than I'd had in years. A blessing, this girl. A total motherfucking blessing. One I wasn't about to let go of or take advantage of. One I was planning to appreciate.

We watched the rest of the movie in silence, her fiddling with my fingers and me completely focused on her every breath. Her every sigh. The woman was my true north, the biggest sign I'd ever been given in this life of mine. Everything I could have wanted and needed plus more. I'd take watching G-rated movies with her any day of the week because being in her presence was better than anything else out there.

But it was as the credits began to roll that things took a turn for the better. Mercy finally made a move, twisting to face me, rising up to her knees so she could look me in the eye.

"Parris?"

Fuck, but that one word on her lips made my balls tight. "Yeah?"

"You brought us dinner."

I nodded, completely focused on her mouth. Unable to tear my gaze from it. "I did."

"That's sort of like a date."

"Only sort of?"

She hummed and leaned closer, not pulling away when my hand happened to land on her ass. Not backing off for a second as I squeezed that luscious flesh.

"Was this a date?" she asked, sounding like sex and need and all sorts of good things.

I shrugged, lying back against the arm of the couch as I pulled her down to lie on top of me. Gripping her ass with both hands because it sure seemed like I could. "Do you want it to be a date?"

"I don't know." She bit her lip, suddenly so damn nervous. "I haven't been on a date in a long time."

"I'm pretty sure you don't forget how to date. Besides, how long could it have been?"

It took her a while to answer me. Many seconds spent simply staring down at my face as her expression shifted from worried to embarrassed to something close to sad. "Not since Beckett, really."

Six years alone. Not nearly as long as me, but still too long. This woman deserved to be worshiped, not stuck up in some apartment and forgotten about. Not relegated solely to the job of mom.

"I promise to be gentle with you," I said, grinning and holding her in place when she nearly jumped backward. "On our dates, I mean."

"You think there'll be more?"

Oh, my beauty. "I fucking promise it."

She relaxed in my arms, dropping down to rest more of her weight on me. Adjusting her legs to tease the fuck out of my aching dick without even touching the poor bastard.

"Parris?"

She was going to make me come in my pants like a teenager if she kept saying my damn name like that. "Yeah, beauty?"

Her voice dropped and softened, her words barely audible. "It's been that long for more than just dating."

I shouldn't have been happy about that. Not at all. Shouldn't have wanted to beat my chest and call her mine at the thought that she hadn't been touched in years. I was an asshole, a selfish, hypocritical jerk who was way too happy to know that the pussy I was after hadn't been claimed in so long.

I was also a man with the most beautiful woman in the world lying across him. Caveman tendencies came along for the ride.

"I figured as much when you said you hadn't dated since Beckett." I brought her closer, brushing my lips against her chin. Lightly. Softly. Trying my hardest not to break my promise to her. Not to take. But damn, did I want to taste her once more. "Ask me, Mercy Bell. I made you a promise, and I'll stick to it. So I need you to ask me if you want this to go any further tonight."

I ran my hands down to her knees and up to her shoulders, pressing her against me. Shifting my hips so she could feel how hard she made me. How much the feel of her fed the beast within me. She shivered, her entire body seeming to respond to my touch before she lowered her head and pressed her lips to mine in the briefest of touches. I was about to groan, about to cling to her and beg her to say the words, when she reached for the remote to mute the television. The light from the screen lit up her eyes, and the silence that fell only made me so much more aware of how hard my heart was pumping. How heavy my breaths were. And my beauty took advantage of the quiet to whisper the five sweetest words known to man.

"Will you kiss me, Parris?"

And just like that, the leash she'd placed around me snapped. I kissed her, all right—hard and fast, plunging my tongue to tangle with hers as I fisted a hand in her hair and yanked her body into a position that gave me more access to her. Her thigh dropped to wedge itself against my straining cock, and I made sure to press one leg between hers, weaving us together. Giving her pressure where she needed it and letting our bodies begin to learn one another. I never gave her a break from the kiss either. Never took it easy on her. Instead, I pushed her hard and fast and demanding. Giving her everything I had and taking from her without pausing. Without allowing her a moment to catch her breath. And she liked it, groaning into my mouth as she bent her legs to straddle my hips. To move into a position as if to ride me. Just the thought of seeing her naked and bouncing on my cock had me groaning loud and fierce in the quiet of her little apartment.

Something that made her pull away from me.

"We shouldn't do this out here, but we can't go to my room," she said, signaling to me that we were about to be so much more than just kissing.

"No?" I pulled her closer again and bit my way down her neck, tasting every inch I could reach. Spreading my fingers wide so I could touch as much of her as possible. "Why not?"

She moaned, sighing softly as I slipped a hand under her shirt and let my thumb drop to caress her breast. "We might wake up Beckett."

Jackpot. "Don't worry, beauty. I'll hold my hand over your mouth when I make you scream."

She jerked back, giving me that fiery glare I'd practically fallen in love with already. "You're so arrogant. As if you could make a woman scream. That only happens in the movies."

Challenge fucking accepted. I flipped us over, tugging her to the edge of the couch while I dropped to my knees before her. Spreading her long legs around my shoulders.

"Oh, my beauty. You should know better than to challenge a man like me. I *am* going to make you scream now."

"You can't."

Stubborn. My girl was so damn stubborn.

But so was I. "I can and I will."

Those light eyes locked on mine, steely resolve behind them. "Prove it."

Aw, hell yeah. "Done."

Chapter Eleven

MERCY

Prove it.

Two words that rebounded in my head the second I said them, that ramped up the ache brewing deep within me. The man made me want, made me crave something I knew I shouldn't have. Made me say things like *prove it* when confronted with his attitude. I had no idea where those particular words had come from or why I'd pushed Parris the way I had, but I couldn't take them back. Couldn't stop the train I'd set into motion. And to be honest, I didn't want to.

"Done." Parris yanked my legs apart and pulled me lower on the sofa, running his hands up my thighs. Tugging on the jeans I wore just enough to tease me of his intentions. When I arched and tried to scooch back, he held me in place. Pinning me with his eyes and his hands as he rubbed his thumb over me, hitting just the right spot with a touch that was both too little and too much at the same time.

"I'm going to strip these dick-tease jeans right off that curvy ass of yours, beauty. Are you okay with that?"

That voice—that deep rumble. It did things to me. I nodded, unable to speak. Unwilling to break the moment of heat and sensation growing between us. Parris didn't seem to mind, though. He did exactly as he'd said—he unfastened my jeans then pulled them down and off, tossing the denim to the floor before spreading my legs wider. Before baring me to him even more.

The entire situation felt so out of control. From the fact that Beckett lay sleeping only a small distance down the hall, to the scratchiness of the couch fabric. From the darkness of the room —lit only by the television as it silently looped the trailer for the movie we'd been watching—to the stillness around us. Parris was the only thing that moved in the apartment, the only creature to make a noise. Breathing hard and heavy in the silence of the night as I shivered under his heavy gaze. Half naked but fully exposed.

"Parris," I whispered as I tried to bring my knees together. The man didn't let me move, though. Didn't allow me an extra inch of space away from him.

"You really are my beauty," he whispered, inching closer to run his nose up the length of my thigh. Sending shivers shooting all along my skin. "You sure you want to do this here? You might never look at your couch the same way again."

That attitude—such a turn-on and yet so annoying at the same time. "You act as if you're some sort of gift to women everywhere. I'm not a virgin, Parris. I've had sex before."

He slipped his thumbs under the edges of my panties, teasing me. A cocky smile spreading when he made me gasp with a particularly well-placed flick. "You've never had sex with me, which is all that matters. And I'm not a gift to women everywhere. Just you." He kissed my thigh, taking his time to suck gently on the flesh before retreating once more. "I'll do anything to be a gift to you and this slick pussy."

Those filthy words coming from that sexy mouth had me trembling. I couldn't speak, couldn't answer him. Could only watch as he wrapped his hand around my panties, brushing his knuckles against me.

"Tell me your secret, beauty. How wet does this pussy get for whatever toys you have hidden away?"

Oh no. I hadn't been prepared. Hadn't been ready for him. Not like this. Not with that sort of question.

"What makes you think I have toys?"

He cocked an eyebrow up and shot me that trademark smirk. "You're a woman with needs that haven't been being met. I know what that means—I bet you've got a cock-shaped something tucked away in that bedroom of yours. Should we go get it? Let me try it out on you?"

That thought had me dripping. Not that I would tell him that. "Why? You think you'll need the help?"

One second, I was sprawled on the couch, still mostly dressed, with Parris' big, bulky frame between my spread thighs as I taunted him. The next? He'd ripped my panties right off. One tug. One yank, and that last bit of protection between him and my pussy was gone. Vanished. I'd gone from mostly dressed to almost completely naked, and he looked so damn proud of himself.

"I liked those."

"I'll buy you more." He brought my knees up and over his shoulders, his rough hands pulling me lower on the couch. Spreading me wider. I was on display just for him. His face was *right there*, his breath warming my skin. The skin with a light layer of hair over it as I'd stopped my waxing appointments years ago but refused to sport seventies-style bush.

I really should have shaved that morning. "Maybe we should—"

"Fuck, beauty. I'm going to eat you all up."

I groaned. Couldn't help it—not with his breath teasing me. It was a loud groan, too. Far louder than I would have liked for it to be considering he hadn't even really touched me yet. I was a desperate, needy mess, and I was going to die of embarrassment because of that. It had been a long time since I'd had a man between my thighs, since anyone had taken an interest in me as someone other than Beckett's mom. This was all too much, too fast. Too enticing and dangerous. Too...thrilling.

I was a mom, for fuck's sake. Thrilling had long since said goodbye in my world.

Which was why I needed to end this, to stop him. "Parris, I—"

He ran his nose along my flesh, bumping my clit and knocking all thoughts of stopping him right out of my head. One touch, and he had me ready to do whatever the hell he wanted. Ready to ride his face or his hand, maybe even his thick erection. Didn't matter so long as he kept touching me.

"I changed my mind—I won't buy you any panties because it's a shame to cover up such a pretty pussy. And to think, this has just been here waiting for me to come take care of it." He blew over my damp flesh, chilling me to the bone even as he set every part of me on fire.

I arched into him, flexing my fingers as if to grab hold. "Parris, please."

"My poor, lonely pussy. Let me give her a kiss, beauty. She needs some attention." He licked his lips, pausing with his thumbs rubbing deep into my thighs. Holding me open until I met his gaze, those light eyes freezing me in place. "Give me permission to kiss you, Mercy."

The way the man said my *name*. Pure foreplay. And completely irresistible. "Please."

"I'll take that." The first swipe of his tongue took me by surprise. It shouldn't have—his face had basically been in between my legs for minutes at that point, not to mention he'd flat out told me what he wanted to do. I'd given him permission—practically begged him—with that please. Still, I hadn't expected the explosion of heat and wet to come down so quickly. Hadn't been ready for my body to react the way it did, with shivers and trembles and sparks of sensation firing from my toes to my fingertips. I hadn't been ready for Parris at all. But damn was I glad he was there.

"More," I moaned as he worked his lips and tongue against me. As he teased me toward a peak I knew I wanted to fall from. I ran my fingers over his cropped hair, needing something to hang on to. Finding nothing and growing more frantic the longer he left me hanging there. On the fourth pass with still no way to secure him to me, I huffed. "You need to let your hair grow."

Parris froze, looking up at me. Questioning. And then, without warning, he knocked all the breath right out of me with one simple move. He wiped the back of his hand against his mouth. As if I'd somehow soaked his chin.

Oh my god, I'd soaked his chin.

"What's that?"

My mind didn't want to focus on anything but the man's lips and chin. The shine there. Wet. I was wetter than I'd ever been before, and he had the proof of that. I couldn't tear my eyes from his chin, from the moisture left behind even after he'd done his best to remove the traces of my arousal. I tried to retreat—wanting to close my legs, push him away, and cover myself—but Parris refused to budge. Holding me open and keeping his thumb moving over my clit in a cruel and yet sensual little dance that had the finest hairs on my body standing on end.

"Beauty." Parris gave my thigh a squeeze and pressed a little harder against my clit, making me gasp. "Why do I need to let my hair grow?"

If my face and neck had been any hotter, they might literally have gone up in flames. "Parris—"

"Tell me." He pinched me. Not my thigh—oh no, that wouldn't be like him at all to go easy on me. No, the man pinched the flesh right at the curve of my ass. His knuckles brushing against my opening. His eyebrow arching up as if to make a point. And it did.

I licked my lips and turned away, unable to look at him a moment more. Not wanting to see his reaction as I made my admission. "I want you to grow your hair so I have something to hold on to."

Silence. Deep, heavy silence greeted me. Nothing to listen to but the sounds of the two of us breathing. For seconds, I hung out on a ledge of shame, wishing I hadn't opened my mouth. Hoping he didn't take that as some sort of commitment and run away. Wanting so badly to—

"Mercy Bell." He grabbed my attention with my full name, forcing my eyes to his. That slow smile crept across his face, so arrogant and smirky. So sexy. "Quit hiding from me, woman."

"I'm not hiding."

Lies, and he knew that. "Just so you know, I've worn my hair in the Marine high and tight for decades not because I like it, but because I never had a reason to change it." He leaned in to give my pussy a soft, luscious kiss. "Until now. You've given me a reason to do something different."

"No. I didn't mean—"

"You want something to hang on to while I lavish this sweet

pussy with my attention." He began massaging my thighs again, spreading me just a little more with each push and pull. "I'll give you that. I'll also give you a reason to need to. You ready?"

"For what?"

"For me to eat you until you scream my name."

I'd like to say I rolled my eyes and said something quippy back, but that would be a lie. Parris never gave me the chance to respond. He dove in, basically face-planting into my pussy. Lips and tongue and fingers—oh my, his fingers—driving me straight up that hill of desire without a single pause or delay. The sounds I made—the grunts and moans and squeaks as he worked me over—should have embarrassed me. Instead, I loved them. Loved knowing that he pulled that from me, that his touch was releasing something I'd kept locked up inside of me for far too long. This man did that—he pushed me to let go. Forced me to drop the tough-girl act of a single mom and simply let me be me. The me who needed to be touched and kissed, who needed to come.

My god, did I need to come.

"Parris, I can't." I bent my legs, placing my feet on his shoulders and pushing up, up, up. Blatantly providing him with the room to do something more. Anything more. To just...get me there. "Please, I want to come. I need it."

Parris never missed a beat. He groaned against me, slipping two fingers inside and thrusting deep. Giving me the *more* I'd been craving. Filling me with a third finger once he'd gotten me good and ready for it. So full and yet not enough. Never enough.

The sounds of his invasion—the slick, wet sucking noises as he fucked me with his hand—were so much. So loud. So embarrassing. But I couldn't care. I rocked my hips against his hand and face, chasing that release. Needing to come so badly and knowing he was going to get me there. Him—a man. A real man.

Not plastic or silicone or battery-operated anything. Parris was staking a claim on my pussy, and I was all in to let him.

"Come on, beauty," he said, driving his fingers inside of me faster, keeping his thumb on my clit as he pushed me further and further up the hill. "I want to see you come. I need to hear you scream my name. I promised I'd make you, and I'm a man of my word."

I chuckled, trying hard to argue, but really, it was exactly that on the tip of my tongue. His name. The word I wanted to chant as he controlled my body, as he tore away everything between us and brought us together for this moment. His scent covered me, his heat warmed me, and his body made me feel so fucking good —of course I wanted to taste his name on my lips as I crashed.

And I did.

With a flick of his thumb, Parris broke me. Sent me flying as quivers rocked my body. My legs clamped closed around his head, holding him to me, and I grabbed hold and held on to him as best I could. I didn't scream, though. There were little ears in the house that might have heard me. And no matter how good the man had made me feel, that was a thought that never left my mind. Something I couldn't forget.

"I'm disappointed," Parris said as soon as I began to calm down, as soon as I released him from my grip, even as he kept teasing me with slow, shallow thrusts of his fingers. "You didn't even have to bite your arm to keep from screaming."

I huffed a laugh, already wanting more. Already needing to feel him on me. Inside of me. Pinning me down and taking what he needed from me. Yeah, that had to happen. "Maybe next time. Speaking of which..."

I tugged him up the length of my body, pulling his hand free from between my legs and forcing him to rise to his knees. Kissing him deeply so I could get a taste of myself on his lips. So I could experience us together. Only breaking away to whisper, "I really hope you have a condom on you."

Parris froze, the stark look falling over his face telling me his answer before he could.

I couldn't believe it. "Seriously?"

He shook his head. "I don't carry them around with me."

"Why not?"

"I'm not a manwhore, beauty. I don't just fuck anything with a pussy that comes toward me."

That totally didn't fit my image of the man. "Are you telling me you're selective in who you decide to fornicate with?"

He laughed out loud at that one. "Good goddamn, you're fun." He ran his hands up my thighs again, this time grabbing my ass. Massaging me. "I still need to make you scream."

"I don't have any condoms, though, and I'm not on anything."

He shook his head, breathing over my breast. The moist heat of his mouth seeping through the thin cotton of the shirt I still wore. "We don't need anything."

I jerked back, pressing my hand to his forehead and holding him in place. "Parris, we can't—"

"I'm not a boy," he said, a growl in his voice. "I wouldn't fuck you without protection and risk you getting pregnant like that. You think I don't know the position that would put you in?" He leaned in as soon as my arm relaxed, kissing me on the lips once more. "I'm going to make you scream tonight, beauty. And I'm going to do it without coming inside of you."

Parris always seemed to be taking me by surprise, but this— his understanding of my hesitancy to have unprotected sex—took the cake. "You're serious?"

He kissed me again, moaning slightly when I bit his bottom

lip. "Sure. I mean, I have no problem fucking that ass so long as you're down with it."

Parris laughed and held me still as I bucked against him, trying my hardest to get away.

"That's not an option, mister."

"No?" He slipped a hand deeper under me, teasing my crack with his fingers. "You might like it."

"I might punch you in the face."

"Kinky." He moved back, taking me with him. Rising to his feet and carrying me as if I weighed nothing. "Come on, beauty. I can't fuck your ass on this couch."

"Parris, I swear on everything I own, if you even try—"

He dropped me. Not on the floor but on the bed, letting me fall to the soft surface and bounce as he crawled over me. Pushing me up the mattress so he could cover me with his heat and weight. Stopping my words and leaving me breathless when he stared down at me with those blue eyes I'd come to like so much.

"Beauty," he said, his voice calm and deep. Sure. "I won't do anything you don't want to do. But I will make you scream. I made you a promise for that, and I fully intend to keep it. Besides, I've been wanting to come because of you for days. And not just by my own hand." He licked a trail up my neck, stopping to bite my earlobe before he whispered, "Though that hasn't been too bad either. Jacking off to thoughts of you has been pretty fucking hot. Thanks for wearing those jeans—they make your ass look downright bitable."

I groaned as he began to rock against me, dragging his thick cock over my wet flesh. Teasing me. I had no idea what he intended to do, but I was in. Didn't matter. I wanted to feel that deep release again and see him get his. I had a feeling the man had an incredible O-face.

"You were right about one thing," I said, arching harder.

"What's that?"

"I do have toys. And you're not the only one needing a little release because of seeing something you like in a good pair of jeans."

He groaned, rocking harder. Gripping my hips with a hold just over the edge of painful. I didn't stop him, though. Instead, I pulled my knees up, adjusting the angle so he could hit the best parts just right. Shaking as he nudged my clit with the head of his dick. Squeaking out a cut-off moan when he rubbed over my clit and made sparkles appear behind my eyes.

"That good?" He drove a little harder, his actions deliberate and careful. Pumping his hips faster when I nodded, when I reached out to hang on to his shoulders. Not sliding too far down but definitely putting us into the realm of some sort of sexual act without penetration. I adjusted my grip, squeezing him closer, bringing our bodies together from shoulders to hips and tightening my legs around him.

"I wish you were inside me right now."

He lurched forward, a growl in his voice as he said, "Fuck, beauty, me too. I want to come so bad. You're just so wet and soft and... Fuck, I gotta come."

"So, come. I want you to."

He shook his head, grunting as I met his thrusts. "Have to make you scream first."

He jerked back and down my body, burying his face in my pussy once more with a groan that I felt in my spine. But this time, there was nothing gentle or building about his attack. He came at me full force—three fingers inside, his mouth pressed against my clit and sucking hard, and his thumb...held tight against my asshole.

"Parris, I don't... I can't..."

I couldn't speak, and he didn't let up enough to answer me.

Every nerve ending in my body fired, every ounce of desire and need and craving swirling together to feed this tsunami of sensation about to crash over me. It took no time, this attack by him. None at all until I was a tumbling, pulsing mass of girl riding his hand and face as I came all over him.

And pressed the pillow against my face to deaden the sound of me screaming his name.

"Fuck." Parris jumped to his knees, his heavy cock in his hand. Stroking quickly and with a grip much tighter than I would have though comfortable. "Gotta come. Need to come."

But he'd just given me the best orgasm of my life. I couldn't make him come alone. So I sat up, and I added my hand to his. Following his rhythm and pressure. Leaning in to take the tip into my mouth as he grabbed my head and slowed. As he gently, carefully, fucked my face.

"Lean back. There you go." He sped up a little, not pushing too deep but letting me lead as I sucked. As I tightened my lips around him and hummed. My hand kept a similar pace at the base of him, twisting and sliding to bring him closer to his own release. Holding on to the thick, hot flesh as I adjusted my position to give him everything I could.

It was when his legs started to shake that the dam broke. That the words tumbled straight out of that filthy mouth of his. "Fuck, beauty. Those dick-sucking lips look so good wrapped around my cock. I want to get you on your hands and knees to really fuck that mouth of yours. Want to wake up in the middle of the night buried inside your throat. Damn, your suck is good. So good. A little more. Suck me deeper."

He growled and shifted us again, his knees on either side of mine as he fucked into my mouth. Deeper and harder as I held on to his hips and dug my fingers into the flesh of his ass. As I took everything he had to give me and moaned for more.

He must have liked that—the moaning—because he cursed under his breath and grabbed my hair. Tightening his hold and moving my head how he needed to. Cupping my face with his other hand and rubbing a thumb over my cheek. Hard and soft, brutal and gentle. That was my Parris—a dichotomy in human form. And I found that way too fucking hot to resist.

"Gonna come," Parris grunted suddenly, losing his rhythm and speeding up his breaths. "Gonna come, gonna come, gonna —fuck."

He pulled out of my mouth, his hand dropping to stroke his cock a few more times. Coming all over my shirt. The one I hadn't taken off. The one still covering me as if I'd been too shy to strip fully for him. Somewhere deep inside of me, I really wished I had removed it. That I could catch a glimpse of his come on my breasts. That I could have that debauched image to remember.

Next time.

"Damn, beauty." Parris collapsed beside me, breathing hard and reaching for my hips. Tugging me closer. "That mouth should be labeled as some sort of weapon."

As if mine were the only one. "Ditto, sir."

He chuckled and wrapped himself around me, enveloping me in a warmth I hadn't expected. "You kept your shirt on."

"Yeah."

"It was hot."

"Really?"

"Made me think you were trying to hide a little of yourself from me. Like you were shy or some shit." He bit me, making me jump at that shot of pleasure-pain. "Like I gotta work up to seeing you fully naked."

This man was going to have me ready to go again in seconds

if he didn't quit, not that I wanted him to. "And that's hot? Making you work for it?"

"I like goals." He sighed, slipping his hands up under the shirt to palm my back. "First, I made you scream. Next, I'll get you to take this off so you can show me your tits."

"You're quite the charmer." But I couldn't stop laughing. This man was rough around the edges, but there was a soft side there too. One no one else got to see. One that made me feel special and cared for. Even if I didn't know anything about him.

I mean, he was a snuggler. How bad could he really be?

"Parris?"

"Yeah, beauty."

"Thanks for making me scream."

He laughed and kissed the top of my head. "Thanks for letting me fuck your face. Next time, I'll bring condoms."

"I'm looking forward to it."

"Me too."

Chapter Twelve

PARRIS

I woke up hard as stone with a soft, warm ass pressed against my cock. Mercy slept soundly, cuddled in tight to my body. The feel of her, knowing she was right there next to me, wasn't enough, though. I still wanted to make her mine. Wanted to fuck her hard and deep, to come inside her. Feel her quivering all around me as I pushed her over the edge. I wanted her eyes on mine in the morning and her kiss to be the last thing I felt before sleep took me. I wanted snuggling and eating her pussy and her lips around my cock and her laugh as I stripped her down. I wanted a life with her. All of it.

I wanted *her.*

Unable to stop, the desires coursing through me driving my actions, I rolled my beauty underneath me, rubbing my body over hers as I bent to take a thick nipple into my mouth. I sucked her hard, using my teeth to give her a little friction as she moaned. Popping off when I heard a gasp that told me she was awake.

"Can you be quiet?" I asked, still rocking my hips into hers. Slipping my cock through the wetness of her pussy but not entering her. Not crossing that line. Not yet. Someday, I'd ride her bare. Someday, we'd be wanting whatever our union could bring us. Today was not that day, so I held back.

Mercy nodded her answer and grabbed me by the shoulders, pulling me up her body to press her sweet lips to mine in a kiss that seared me to my soul. This moment—in the dark with this woman in my arms—was it for me. No, not just it—everything. Mercy Bell had exploded into my life and become the meaning behind it, the reason to keep going. My true north. Even without actual sex, with only what we could do to each other with hands and mouths, this had been the greatest sexual experience of my life, and there would never be enough. I would never stop wanting more from her, craving her. Needing to grab that ass and hold her against me. Wishing for more contact, more touch, more feel of her.

Mine. She was mine. And knowing I was hers as well might have been the hottest and most terrifying thing ever.

Mercy pulled her knees up, bracketing my chest as I kept rolling into the cradle of her hips. As I teased her with pressure and lift, with my cock against her. On one thrust, she adjusted a little too far, and I slipped inside. Just the tip, but we both froze, both gripping the other and moaning as if that small connection, that breach, was the greatest sensation in the history of sex. And it was. To me, and hopefully to her. I wanted more, but I couldn't. We couldn't.

Not yet.

"I won't do that to you," I whispered as I pulled back out and wedged a hand between us to realign my cock in a safer spot. "I won't give you another baby until I know you're ready for one."

Mercy kept those light eyes on mine, looking so sweet and vulnerable and perfect as she murmured my name.

"Parris—"

"A boy does that," I said, kissing her again. Closing my eyes as tingles burned their way up my spine. This woman was so hot all over, she practically melted me. There was nothing like her heat. "I'm a man. I would never hurt you that way. I would never abandon the family I made. I promise you, Mercy."

"Oh fuck," she said as she circled her hips into mine, arching her back and thrusting to meet my movements. Losing control of herself and doing what she could to ride me. "Someday. When you're really mine."

That word on her lips—priceless.

"I am yours. I will always be yours." I rocked into her again, slower this time. Not trusting myself after feeling the slick heat of her around the tip. After being that much closer to burying myself inside her. Fuck, I wanted to. Wanted to so badly, I almost broke. Almost pressed myself deep inside her. I resisted, though it took me backing away to do it. Took me holding my breath, needing a few minutes of calm before I could ease into the motion we both needed.

Mercy kept holding me through all of it, kept that hot little body pressed against mine and her hands gripping me tight. And when I began to move again, when I leashed the beast of my control and let myself tease her once more, she groaned and moved with me. Pulling me down to rest more weight on her, burying her face in my neck as I increased my pace. As I pumped with more force, more speed—with everything I had so I could watch this girl get off. I loved to see her come.

"This right here," I said, groaning under my breath as her pussy positively soaked me. "This is mine. All of you, all of this. I want the pussy—you know how much I want the pussy—but I want you too. I'll do right by you, beauty. I'll spoil you rotten and treat you like a queen, then bring you to bed at night and fuck you like you need me to. Nice and hard and deep. Filthy. I'll make this pussy weep for me every night once you're mine for real."

I grabbed her hips and tugged her against me as I thrust forward, grinning when she bit her arm. Knowing she wanted to chant something—oh or god or my name. Whatever. Words wanted to form, and she couldn't let that happen because of little ears right down the hallway. That was fine, though when she dropped that arm, I swear I heard her say she was mine. My gut plummeted, my entire body going cold on me. Mine. She'd said she was *mine*. Quietly, softly...as if she didn't want me to actually hear the words. As if it were an admission she wasn't truly ready to make. I'd take it, though. Bank those words and honor them. I'd live up to what it meant to be hers in every way I knew how, starting with making sure she got to come before I did. Giving before taking.

I slipped a hand between us again and pressed a finger against her clit, rubbing hard as I rocked my hips into hers. As I laid my cock along the length of her opening and gave her the pressure she needed. And fuck, she felt so good. Hot and wet and ready for me. Too ready. The urge to slip in again—to bury my cock inside of her tight heat—dug its claws into my mind, so I pulled away. Giving her my hand instead. Thrusting two fingers deep and curling them, searching for a spot that would make her want to scream some more. Keeping my thumb against her clit and rubbing as I humped the fucking mattress and hoped to last even just a few seconds longer than she did because I was close. Hard and leaking and so damn ready to explode.

The sounds of my fingers invading her body, of the wetness sucking me in, filled the quiet of the night. A top note to the background of our heavy breaths and whispered curses. She was close. Her legs had begun to shake, and she couldn't keep her eyes open, both signs I'd already picked up on. A few more thrusts, a little more pressure, and I'd have her. She'd break for sure. I just needed—

"Fuck, Parris," she said, far louder than she probably should have. She tossed her arm over her face and covered her mouth, making me chuckle even as her pussy locked down on my fingers. As her slick walls clenched and released around me. As she came all over my hand.

Hottest thing ever.

I jumped up her body, lining myself up to slide between those soft pussy lips again. Coating myself in her wetness as she twitched and moaned and got hers. As I teased her clit just a little more, rubbed the head of my cock on it and forced every shudder from her body. It didn't take me long to follow her, just a couple of thrusts before I dove forward, holding my weight on my arms as I fought back the urge to roar like a fucking beast. Making sure to come on her stomach instead of near her pussy just in case. Honoring my promise to her—I'd give her a baby when she was ready. I'd give her ten of them if she wanted me to. But not yet. Not until I knew she was good and truly mine and I was hers. Not until I could give her more of a commitment than some words whispered in the heat of passion. She deserved better than that.

"Seriously," she said as I dropped all of my weight onto her, needing a moment to catch my breath. "We need an all-night convenience store in Justice."

I laughed, licking up her neck to get a taste of her. "I'd say the hardware store could fill that purpose, but then we'd have to staff it."

"I have no interest in staying up all night," she said, reaching for a tissue from the stand next to the bed to clean up the mess between us. Grabbing another and handing it to me with shaky fingers and a shy sort of smile. My beauty.

Unable to resist those lips, I gave her a slow, deep kiss, rubbing the tissue over her stomach and mine. Taking care of my girl before pulling back enough to whisper, "I'll stay up all night if it means being inside you."

"You have a one-track mind," she said, giggling softly.

"I'm in a bed alone with you, and we're both naked. Yes, my mind is stuck in one gear right now." I tossed the tissue to the floor, grabbed her around the waist, and rolled with her so she could lie across my chest. Wanting this feeling of contentment to last me forever. Every day. Every second. This was motherfucking blissful, and I'd never get enough of it.

But my girl needed her rest. So I ran my hands up her naked back, massaging her as I whispered, "Get some sleep, beauty."

She sighed, scratching her fingers along my chest. "I would, but someone keeps waking me up."

"You complaining?"

"Not really, but I have a feeling I'm going to put my coffeepot through a workout in the morning." She yawned, snuggling closer as I kissed the top of her head and held her a little tighter.

"Worth it," I whispered, knowing she'd agree.

Mercy wasn't any sort of insomniac. She fell asleep within minutes, her breath evening out and the thump of her heart slowing. Me? I stayed awake, all the promises and opportunities of being with a woman like my beauty slamming into me and making my brain refuse to quiet.

I wasn't good enough for her.

But I could be.

I'd been a fucked-up man for a long time, working undercover for the Black Angels, spying on the men I was supposed to see as my brothers, sabotaging their missions when necessary so they didn't upset the balance the national president demanded. Doing Cartel's dirty work for him. All so I could keep searching for Wolf, the man who'd murdered my sister. All because of some fucked-up revenge fantasy. I needed to end that shit. I'd been sliding downhill since I'd earned my nomad patch. When I'd come for one of the guys who had killed my sister, the one who had also been trying to take out the big prez so his crew could gain power over the Black Angels. Cartel may have been running my show, but the president owed me big-time. That debt was about to come due. It was time to return to my nomad status for good.

Nomads were bound by no house, no crew. I'd let Cartel stick me in Vegas for far too long, let him tell me what to do like I was some sort of prospect. It was time to take back what I'd earned. My freedom.

I'd given of myself for too long—it was time to start taking what I needed. And what I needed was the little woman sleeping soundly on my chest to be mine and the boy in the other room, too. I needed them to be safe and cared for, and I needed to be the man doing that job. I needed it like I needed air.

Closing myself off from my past and starting new couldn't come soon enough, but there were things that needed to be handled. People who needed to be cut out of my life. Assignments that needed to be finished. The only way to do that was to go in full force. Twenty-four seven. No stopping, no time off, straight mission.

Which meant I needed to leave Justice for a few days.

I crawled out from under Mercy, tugging on my jeans in case Beckett woke up, and grabbing my phone before heading out into the living room. The thoughts of how I could accomplish my extraction from club life rolled through my head, not allowing me to think of anything else. I paced the small living room, typing notes into my phone. Working out a plan that could end with my escape or me dead in the ground. Either way, I wasn't riding with that Vegas crew again.

I figured there were five things that had to happen before I could close the current chapter in my life and come back to my little family. A task list.

Tell the national prez all about Edge and Ravel, and how they were about to blow the club apart with Cartel's approval.

Take out Edge and Ravel so that explosion wouldn't happen.

Tell Jinx what really happened to her mom.

Tell Cartel I was out of the spy game for good and was reclaiming my nomad status.

And when all that was done, there was only one more thing I'd need to accomplish.

Convince Mercy and Beckett to forgive me for walking away in the first place.

Chapter Thirteen

MERCY

The morning sun brought a glow to the room that matched the one in my chest. A night with Parris in bed, even without actual sex, had been just as wonderful as I'd dreamed. More so. The sweetness of his hands on me, the roughness of his voice in my ear. The body-blistering heat between us. Nothing had ever felt so good. My entire body buzzed with the strain of muscles that hadn't been used in far too long.

Smiling, already calculating when I could slip away from Beckett to buy condoms so Parris and I could move from almost sex to real sex, I rolled over. I reached for the burly biker who'd slipped so easily into my life. And I found an empty bed. Empty and cold.

Even as I jumped to a sitting position—as I tried to calm my heart—my stomach dropped. *Maybe he's in the bathroom.* The thought didn't make me feel better, though. Mostly because the apartment sat far too quiet and still, too much like it usually did on a Sunday morning before Beckett awoke. I knew Parris wasn't there—just knew it. Still, I crawled out of bed and pulled on my robe, hoping against hope that I was wrong. That Parris was awake and sitting in another room silently for some reason. Maybe he couldn't sleep with another person beside him. Maybe I snored.

I had better not be a snorer.

Padding through the apartment, the fear that Parris had left only grew. Every room sat empty; every seat unoccupied. Gone. Just as I'd feared.

It was when I made it to the kitchen that I found the note, and the tears began to form. A simple white slip of paper next to the coffeepot was the scariest thing I could have seen. I knew what it was—a Dear John letter. Or Dear Mercy letter. Dear beauty, maybe. The name didn't matter—it was a kiss-off. I didn't want to read Parris' words, didn't even want to look at whatever he'd left behind, but I couldn't ignore it. So I crept to the counter, and I picked up the stiff paper with a hesitant hand, and in my head, I cursed the man under my breath. Leaving a note and slipping out in the middle of the night was child's play —cowardice—something I hadn't expected from a grown man. Something I hadn't been ready for. My fault, that one. I should have known Parris wasn't exactly the forever type. Not that I was already thinking of forever. A morning after wasn't too much to ask for, though. Was it?

The guy was such an asshole for doing this to me.

I unfolded the paper with shaking hands, needing to take a deep breath before I could really focus on the harsh lines of his writing. Before I could read the words he'd left behind.

Beauty -

I need to end a few things in my life before I can take a place in yours. You're still mine—I'll be back for you.

Parris

PS: I'm yours as well

PPS: Tell Beckett I'm sorry—we'll deal with that bike as soon as I get back.

All the hurt inside of me, the ache of loss and the pain of such a swift departure, turned to white-hot anger at the line about Beckett. Parris had promised my son something, and he wasn't even going to follow through on that. Couldn't even spend a couple of hours to give my son the experience he'd been so excited about. What sort of person let down a child that way? Walk away from me, fine. But don't make the leaving harder on me by screwing over my kid. That was just...being an asshole.

The petty side of me also couldn't help but notice he'd left the note right next to my coffeepot. One of my favorite parts of the day was drinking that first cup of coffee in the quiet before Beckett woke up. What sort of man ruined my first cup of coffee by leaving an *It's not you, it's me* brush-off note by the coffeepot? What sort of man not only abandoned you and your son with only a few bullshit words and also took away the joy of *coffee*?

"An asshole."

"Who's an asshole?"

I jumped and spun, my heart doing the same inside my chest as Parris came walking through the door with a bag from The Baker's Cottage in his hand. I had to stop for a second, to center myself on the note still in my hand as I stared at the man who'd written it. Who was not supposed to be here anymore.

If my heart pounded any harder, he'd hear it from across the room. "I thought you left."

"I did, and I am, but I'm nothing if not a man of my word. That means there are a couple of things that needed doing before I go." He grabbed me with desperate hands, yanking me close with a hunger I felt down to my toes. Kissing me without reserve, with passion and need and desire as he cupped my ass and held on. As I looped my arms around his neck and hugged him closer yet. This was so perfect and yet utterly wrong. Soothing and yet painful at the same moment. I couldn't resist him, though. Not for a single moment. I wanted him so badly, was so happy to see him, that I was willing to take whatever I could get from him. The hurt, though...it burned. And it was only going to get worse.

I finally had to break the kiss and place my forehead against his chest, still clinging to him. Still wishing he would change his mind. Still hurting so much because of that stupid slip of paper.

"You're leaving."

He tightened his hold on me and kissed the top of my head, squeezing me in his thick arms as if trying to deny my words. "I know you're going to be pissed as fuck about this, but I *have* to go. I need to settle a few things before I can be here a hundred percent."

That didn't ease any of the worries inside my head. In fact, it gave me more. "Are you married?"

He stepped back, looking me square in the eyes. "No."

"Have a girlfriend?"

"Yeah... She's right here."

"I'm not your girlfriend."

"You are, you just don't know it yet." His lips kicked up into that sexy smile I liked so much. "You're going to fall in love with me."

I was already halfway there, but he was leaving. That fact

changed everything inside my head even though my heart needed a few hours to catch up. "Not happening,"

He hummed, leaning closer so he could murmur against my lips. "You're mine, beauty. That's a done deal."

Pretty words could never replace hurt. "Yet you're leaving."

"I am, and I might not be back for a few days."

"Parris—"

"The guys from the bike store in Crystal Falls are going to be here at three."

That redirected my thoughts for sure. "Wait...here?"

"Yeah. They're loading up the bikes that should work for Beckett's size and coming here."

"You said—"

"I know what I said, but last night changes things. You giving me a shot changes things." He tucked my hair behind my ear—a habit for him, it seemed—before cupping my face as if I were something precious and dropping down to look me in the eye. "I know this doesn't make sense, and I wish I could tell you everything, but that would put you and Beckett in danger. I won't do that—I refuse to do *that*. I know I need to be a better man for the two of you, which means shutting a few doors in my life. That takes time. The quick way is to get out of town, deal with my shit twenty-four seven, so I can lock those doors up tight to keep all that stuff away from you two." He ran a thumb over my cheek, sighing. Looking so intense and serious. "I won't disappoint the little man, though. He wanted a bike today, and I promised to get him one. A real man comes through and stands by his word—the bike store will be here."

Oh, my heart. My poor, weak heart would never stop wanting him. Especially not when he said the right things. When he showed how much he cared about my son. But who would be caring about him?

Likely just me. "Will you be in danger?"

He paused, still staring into my eyes. Looking like a man weighing the pros and cons between lying and telling the truth. Thankfully, he seemed to choose truth.

"Yeah, I will. But trust me—I'm coming home to you."

Another promise, one I wasn't sure I should believe in this time. This was all just so...*much*. Dangerous and cutting and a reminder of all I'd already been through. I stepped out of his hold, pulling away and crossing my arms over my chest. Needing a barrier between us. Unable to comprehend what had happened overnight and then this morning. The vast change that had occurred.

"This is crazy." I shook my head when Parris tried to reach for me, pinning him in place with a glare. "I know nothing about you—not your age, your hometown, if your parents are still alive, what you do for the club—"

"I'm forty-two, but we've had that conversation before." He waited, that smile reviving itself, until I nodded. We *had* talked about that. "And I grew up as an Army brat, so I don't have a hometown. My parents are both dead. What I do for the club falls into dangerous territory—ask me something else, and I'll tell you."

"Just not that."

He shook his head slowly, keeping his eyes on mine. "Just not that."

I took a deep breath, still glaring. Letting my mind wrap around what I wanted to know, which was everything. "Do you have any siblings?"

His smile disappeared, a tic forming in his jaw. "My dad remarried when I was in high school and had a daughter with the woman. They named her Ashley."

"Where is she now?"

"Dead." One word, rough and clipped. Obviously, Ashley was a sore subject for him.

"I'm sorry. I had no idea."

"Of course you didn't." He inched closer, carefully caging me against the counter as if I were some sort of rabid dog. Slipping his hands to my waist as he tugged me closer. All his movements slow and careful. Calculated. "Anything you want to know, I'll tell you. Maybe not now, but later. I promise."

I didn't have a lot of faith in that vow. "Fine. Where do you live now? Do you have a home? What do you do to make money? Why do you wear a nomad patch when most bikers I've seen have one that specifies a town? What's your real name, and why do they call you Parris?" I swallowed once, refusing to give up the upper hand in this conversation and going in for the kill question. "How long do you intend to stay in Justice once the Soul Suckers are eliminated?"

The pounding of little feet pulled Parris up short before he could respond, and we both turned to watch as Beckett came running around the corner into the kitchen and dove at the man. Skinny arms wrapped around a thick neck, my baby giving away his affection so freely. So willingly.

Beckett didn't even wait to let go of Parris before he asked, "Are we going to get my bike now?"

Ice picks to the heart would have hurt less than to know what was coming and not be able to protect Beckett from the pain. I kept my mouth shut, letting Parris deal with his broken promise. Letting him be the one to tell Beckett he wouldn't be sticking around.

Parris set my son back on his feet, crouching so they were face-to-face and looking the boy square in the eye. "I'm really sorry, little man, but I have to go out of town for work."

Beckett's face fell, his lip quivering, and my rage at the man intensified. "But why?"

Parris didn't falter under that sad, whiny voice. He placed one hand on Beckett's shoulder and kept looking him in the eye. "You're still getting a bike today. I made you a promise, and a man is only as good as his word."

My son's voice was too soft, too weak when he asked, "How, if you're not taking me?"

"The bike store is bringing you their bikes so you can shop from here."

It took a few seconds for those words to sink in, but when they did, the change was instant. Beckett grinned, glancing at me with excitement clear on his expressive little face before refocusing on Parris. "Really?"

"Really. You pick out whatever one you want. They'll have helmets too." Parris turned to catch my eye. "I told them to bring me the best because I had a precious little boy who needed all the protection in the world."

Ice picks. Seriously.

Beckett wasn't one to let someone off easy, though. "I wanted you to come with me, Mister Parris."

"I know, bud. But I have to do a few things to be able to stick around. Gotta put in the time now so I can enjoy your company later."

"So you're coming back?"

Again, Parris shot a look at me. Again, hanging on to my son as if physical touch would cement the vow he was making. "Absolutely. Give me a few days, and I'll be back. And then we'll go riding that bike of yours."

"It's cold outside," Beckett said. "Mom said it might be too cold to ride."

"It is cold, but we've got coats. And hey, I'll be riding my bike this week. It goes way faster because of the motor, and I'll be okay."

Beckett took a moment to watch Parris closely, then nodded. "Then I'll do the same. I don't know how to ride, though."

"I'll teach you," I said, wanting so much to fix the world for him. Knowing I was a poor substitute for the father he'd never had.

"Mom," Beckett whined, which was exactly what I'd expected from him. "This is a boy thing."

Parris nodded once, a firm look on his handsome face. "Totally a guy thing."

As if learning to ride a bike was somehow gendered. I must have frowned or huffed or showed my irritation, because Parris chuckled quietly.

"I promise," he said, still holding on to Beckett's shoulder. "When I get back—if your mom hasn't already taught you everything you need to know about bike riding—I'll teach you."

"Deal." Beckett dove in for a hug, hanging on to Parris with a grip that defied his little body. My throat tightened as I watched the two men embrace, as I let the reality of what was happening settle over me. Parris was leaving us. He could claim all he wanted that he'd be back, but he'd inserted himself into our life only a few days before and was already walking away.

Just like Beckett's dad had done.

Parris was promising he'd come back.

Just like Beckett's dad had done.

One more man failing my son, and this one was all my fault because I'd known from day one that being with a biker was a bad idea.

Parris rose to his full height, a red-faced Beckett on his hip and those light eyes locked on mine. "I have to go now, but I'm coming back. And I'll have answers to all your questions when I do."

"Sure," I said, eyeing Beckett. Not able to say what I really wanted to because I didn't need to take away the boy's hope so soon. "Be safe."

"Take care of each other, okay?" Parris kissed Beckett on the forehead before setting him down, his voice rough as he said, "You should reach out to the Kennards if you need anything."

Because he wouldn't be available to me. "I know."

He gave Beckett one last fist bump. "You take care of your momma."

Beckett—my baby, my heart in human form—nodded. "I will."

Parris stepped in front of me, trapping me against the counter with his big body. Looking down at me with an expression that totally gutted me. "Three o'clock. Don't forget."

For the bikes. "We'll be here."

He leaned closer, pressing his lips to mine. Kissing me slow and deep and in a way that screamed I was his before pulling away once more. "I'm coming back."

I could barely hear my own voice as I whispered, "You'd better."

But I knew right then he might not. Probably wouldn't. Men left. Even good men, and Parris wasn't what I would have ever considered a good man. He'd tried—put in the time and really given Beckett and me a taste of what we'd been missing. But he wasn't going to stay. And no matter what words fell from his lips, I had a feeling he wouldn't be coming back to us.

"The bike guys have my card," Parris said as he moved toward the door. "Beckett can get whatever he wants."

I nodded, trying hard not to watch as he opened the door. As he stepped outside. As he shut the slab of wood and formed that barrier between us. As he—

"Oh, and Mercy?"

I looked. Couldn't help myself. "Yeah?"

His eyes burned into mine as he said, "When I get back, I'll have everything we need to finish what we started here last night, so be ready."

With a thud as he closed the door, he left, and my heart shattered right there in my kitchen.

But I had Beckett to worry about, the little boy with the brave face but the teary eyes. The one who had jumped at the chance to welcome Parris into his life, had shared his heart with the man, and might have to learn that his acceptance hadn't been enough.

We hadn't been enough.

"Mister Parris brought donuts."

I turned my back on my son, unable to hold in the tears a moment longer. Not wanting him to see me break. "Yeah, buddy. He did."

Beckett had always been a smart, sweet boy, though. He came up behind me and wrapped his arms around my waist, hugging me. "I like Mister Parris, Mommy."

I sighed and patted his back, wishing for things that likely could never be. Wanting so much to have the right words to say to explain what was happening and how much it sucked. But I couldn't find them. All I could think about was the man who'd just walked out the door on us. About his flaws.

Unstable.

Demanding.

Likely a criminal.

And heartbreakingly mine.

"I like him too."

Chapter Fourteen

PARRIS

I left my heart in that little apartment over the hardware store and headed toward the county line, needing to pick up Deacon before we could enact part one of my withdrawal from the life I'd been living. Before I could kick off the plan I'd been working on all night as my beauty had slept. I was ready, I had a solid strategy, and I was willing to do just about anything to escape my past and head for a future in Justice. It was just going to take a murder or two.

Deacon was standing outside when I got to his place, ready for me. But looking rough.

"You look like shit," I said as soon as I turned off the engine on my bike.

Deacon could only shrug a single shoulder. "I haven't been sleeping much. Everything good? I'm not used to my team being late."

That was a dig, but one I deserved. I *was* late. Just a few minutes, but he was telling the truth—most military men weren't late. My only excuse was a little boy with a big heart and eyes that could see straight down to my soul. "I had to make sure my birthday present to Beckett would make it."

"What did you get him?"

"A new bike."

Deacon's lips kicked up in a sort of half smile. "The biker bought the kid a bike. Fitting."

"Yeah, but I was supposed to take him to the store to pick it out. This mission threw that option out the window, so I had to make arrangements."

"Mercy taking him instead?"

Mercy. My girl. The woman who might never forgive me for walking away, even though I was doing it for all the right reasons. The one who had looked at me with so much relief when I'd walked back into that apartment. Relief that had quickly turned to disappointment. Hopefully, she'd realize soon enough that everything was for her. Every action, every minute away, everything.

"No, I didn't want to add anything more to Mercy's plate. I'm having the store brought to him this afternoon."

Deacon's smile shifted to a full-out laugh. "You're whipped already."

Completely and totally. I'd do anything for those two, and I really didn't give a fuck who knew it. "There's no shame in my game, Gramps. That's one hell of a woman and her son is important to her, so he's important to me."

He nodded, seeming almost proud. "That's the best way to look at it."

It was, but work wouldn't wait because we wanted to gossip about our love lives. We had a meeting to get to. One that had been my idea and still filled me with a sense of unease. "All right, enough jawing. Let's go deal with this shit."

I started my engine and walked the bike backward, managing a three-point turn in Deacon's sad excuse for a driveway before rolling up the hill. He followed me in his truck, both of us heading toward Sterling as we'd planned. It was time to deal with Cartel.

Sterling sat just past the city of Crystal Falls—home of the bike store I was supposed to take Beckett to. As much as it killed me to break my plans with the little man, I knew he was safer in Justice. If any of my crew or the Black Angels leadership in Crystal Falls had spotted us, rumors would have exploded through the club. I'd be putting Beckett and Mercy in danger, and that wasn't fucking happening. I'd left them behind to make sure danger wouldn't come their way, to cut off the head of one of the monsters at their gate.

I could only hope no other beasts came for them while I was dealing with this one. I'd burn the entire town of Justice to the ground if they didn't keep my little family safe while I was protecting their asses and getting mine out of the situation I'd ridden into. Just a couple of days—that was all I needed. At least, I hoped it was.

We pulled up outside the same diner where I'd met Cartel before, but we didn't go inside right away. Instead, I hopped into the passenger seat of Deacon's truck.

"What's the plan?" he asked, looking straight ahead, his jaw hard. The soldier ready to go to war.

Thank fuck for that. "From what I can tell, the Black Angels aren't working well with the Soul Suckers. I think Cartel wants to demand they pull out but can't or won't for some reason."

"So, we need to push him."

"Yup."

"Anything else I need to know?"

Fuck. "The man's responsible for the death of my sister, helped get me my nomad patch so I could hunt down the men who killed her, and holds the fact that there's still one murderer out there I haven't found yet over my head."

Deacon nodded, looking deep in thought. "So basically, the man's a boil on the ass crack of humanity."

"One with a lot of power in the club."

"Will he be missed?"

If we killed him. A definite option depending on how things went. "Yes, but not enough to bring in the law."

"Just more bikers." Deacon let out a deep breath and opened his door. "Let's get this done, then."

Calm, smooth, and ready to fight. Damn, I loved that man. We walked into the diner together, neither of us talking. Not needing to. This wasn't a social visit; it was a mission. One I was determined to be successful at.

"Parris," Cartel said when he saw me, that oily smile of his sliding up his face as he noticed I wasn't alone. "And you brought a friend."

Cartel didn't stand up, so I took a seat in his booth, Deacon slipping in beside me. The two of us stared down the man across the table, serious and solid. Cartel didn't look a damn bit worried, but he should have been. He had no clue what he was up against.

"The team in Justice knows the Black Angels are working with the Soul Suckers," I said, starting off the conversation.

Cartel shrugged. "We knew that would happen. It's not as if we'd ride around in their colors."

"True. But Justice isn't going to sit back and take the invasion like most places. There are already plans in the works to start picking off bikers as they roll past town."

Cartel's smile fell. "No Black Angel dies because of the Soul Suckers. Period."

"Then you've got a problem. You've also got a club president out of control."

"Edge again?"

I nodded, knowing the exact button that would set him off. Aiming right for it. "He's bringing attention to the club because of his...predilection."

"What predilection is that?" Cartel asked, as if he didn't already know.

"Women and making them bleed. He drugs them, carves into their skin, then kills them when he gets bored. He's back at it. Here."

Cartel didn't look convinced, which was why I nudged Deacon's boot with mine.

"This ain't Vegas, son," Deacon said, picking up right where I'd left off. "Girls go missing around here, you'll have more law on your ass than ticks on a dog. I've got the acting sheriff asking a whole lot of questions already."

Cartel pursed his lips, looking from Deacon to me. "You got one out. Why can't you handle the rest?"

Jinx. He was talking about Jinx and how I managed to keep her safe from Edge...for a while, at least. "I knew Jinx because of my connection to her mother. She trusted me, which is how I pulled her from Edge's circle. She's not out, though. He's still looking for her."

Cartel sat back, tapping his finger against the table and watching the two of us. Silent for a long moment before he said, "Bring her to me. I want to talk to her about what happened with Edge."

He wanted to see Jinx. My reply shot out of my mouth as Deacon stiffened beside me. "Not happening."

The warlord didn't like being told no. "Are you disobeying a direct order?"

"The girl isn't involved," Deacon said, taking over the conversation and laying down one hell of a hard line. "We've been tracking Edge with other women—ones who are likely to turn up addicted to something or dead. He doesn't keep them around long, and this place doesn't offer the anonymity of Vegas. His connection to the girls will get out."

"Which is why I need the girl—Jinx. I want to hear her story directly."

No, he didn't. He wanted to find a bargaining chip to use with Edge. Something to offer him to make him calm the fuck down. I wasn't letting Jinx be gambled away again. "Her presence isn't an option."

The warlord looked ready to kill, and he turned that evil gaze on me. "You failed your sister, you tried to protect this girl's mother and lost her, now you're doing the same for the daughter. Do you really think I'm just going to let you hide her away from me?"

I didn't get a chance to answer—not that I would have had one other than a simple and direct *fuck you*—before Deacon took over again.

"The girl is under Justice watch now," Deacon said, his voice harder than usual. His line in the sand growing stronger and deeper. "You come for her in any way, and you'll die. Period."

Cartel turned the full force of his snakelike stare on Deacon. "Is that a threat?"

"Of course not." The bar owner sat back, spreading his arms over the back of the booth and...chewing on a toothpick, of all things. "I'm just letting you know how that'll work out if you try it. Jinx is nonnegotiable."

The warlord looked ready to flip the fucking table. "Who are you, anyway?"

The grin Deacon shot the man looked about as wide and big as one could get. "I'm Sniper."

The man had just given himself a road name. That wasn't done in this world—road names were assigned by the club—but he looked calm and cool and sure as hell about breaking that protocol. Cartel would have no reason to even question the lie, and I sure as hell wasn't outing him.

"Sniper," Cartel said, accepting the name as true, leaning forward and pointing at the man beside me. "The girl belonged to the Black Angels until her ownership was transferred to the Soul Suckers, from what I understand. I don't remember seeing anything about Justice in her file."

"Possession is nine-tenths of the law, and that girl is in Justice." Deacon moved the toothpick from one side of his mouth to the other, looking thoughtful. Cagey as fuck, but thoughtful. "I'm not an unreasonable man, though. I want her off the books, and I'm willing to earn that freedom for her. How do we make it to where she doesn't belong to the Black Angels or the Soul Suckers?"

Cartel inched back, interest making his eyes that much brighter. "Are you really a sniper?"

Deacon didn't miss a beat. "Yup."

"I've got a proposition for you, then."

"Let's hear it."

I waited, keeping my face neutral as Deacon went down a road we hadn't planned on. Cartel sat a little deeper, eyeing the sniper like a spider about to trap a fly in a web. I couldn't imagine Deacon being the type to fall into a trap.

Cartel would likely try, though. "Beyond our own internal

issues, we've run into a few problems with a couple of Soul Suckers that are in town."

"What sort of problems?" Deacon asked.

"Let's just say their trafficking efforts didn't stop at the norm."

The norm...as in normal. That wording struck me. He wouldn't care too much about women being trafficked. He didn't participate in such ventures, but just like with Jinx, some members were allowed to take liberties so long as things were kept quiet and didn't bring attention to the club. If he wanted these men dead—

"Kids," Deacon said, picking up the same thoughts I had and sounding more disgusted than I'd ever heard him. "They sold kids."

My entire body lurched, my muscles locking down as the world went red. I could only think of one thing, one kid—Beckett. And if anyone had even thought about taking that little boy from his momma, I'd have torn the world apart to get him back.

Jesus, these fuckers deserved what was coming to them.

Cartel kept his snake stare on the sniper, his face hard. "Three children that I know of. One was the great-niece of a brother of ours, which brought attention to our club. Still, the brother reached out to the big prez looking for retribution, and we've agreed to provide that."

Translation—the Soul Suckers had stepped onto Black Angels turf and taken a big shit, causing issues with law enforcement and fucking with one of our own. Either incident could really mark a man for death, but seeing as how the victim here was a child, I had a feeling that was the reason the warlord was out for blood. No wonder he hadn't wanted to pull the crews out—he'd been working his own revenge this entire time. Had been keeping his enemies close so he could find the perfect time to strike.

Perfect time and perfect weapon. Cartel had definitely found the perfect weapon in a former Special Forces sniper.

Deacon may not have known club rules, but he was smart. He'd been picking up what Cartel was hinting at. "So we take care of these problem Soul Suckers. What do we get?"

Cartel spun that web a little bigger. "The girl."

I had to jump in there. "Black Angels don't own her—Soul Suckers do."

Cartel glanced my way. "You take care of these couple of men, and I'll personally pay that debt."

Jinx. Free and clear of the club. I owed her that. Big-time. This hadn't been what we'd come for, but it would take a huge stress from my shoulders and give Jinx options. Fuck me, Deacon had just worked some major magic on his tangent, and there was no way we could turn down that offer. So long as Cartel played it honorably.

"And you make sure Edge knows she's off-limits?" I asked, leaning forward. Seeing a way to make amends for at least one of my biggest regrets. "Because we're not making a single move if that chain isn't broken. No Soul Suckers coming for her and no Black Angels either. The girl has to be completely free."

"I'll lay down the law with the club—no one will get a pass if they go near her. That includes Edge and the Vegas boys."

Deacon looked my way, likely weighing the options but leaving the final decision up to me. I knew Cartel better, knew his tricks. The responsibility of keeping us safe and deciding if the warlord could be trusted would fall on my shoulders.

I had to take the shot. "If Sniper's in, we're good."

Deacon shrugged as if we were talking about trading a used

car instead of a human being. "Sure. I've got nothing better to do. I'll even take care of it today if you can get me the details."

Cartel's eyebrow jumped, the only tell of his surprise. "You work fast."

"I want these fuckers out of my town," Deacon said, his voice gritty and dark. "If cutting down a couple of them helps move that along? So be it."

The warlord nodded. "Fine, but Parris brings me the proof."

Which meant there would be other jobs to deal with once this was done. More club business to do before I could cut myself free.

"Agreed," I said, knowing I'd likely regret that decision along the way. "But any Black Angel comes for Jinx, and they're dead. Period."

Cartel practically growled. "I don't like threats, Parris."

"And I don't like men who can't keep their word. You say she'll be Justice's free and clear, then she'd better be Justice's."

Cartel sat back again, looking from me to Deacon. Likely still trying to spin the web that could trap us. "Done. You deal with this problem, and I'll put my own word up that the girl is yours and safe from our crew."

"From all Black Angels," I said, spotting a trap in his offer. "I don't want some fucker from Oregon showing up because you decided to play a battle of words."

Cartel put his hands up, that oily smile back. "No games, Parris. She's off-limits to all Black Angels, not just the Vegas crew."

I nodded once to Cartel, catching Deacon's eye and letting him know this was on. Two dead bikers for one girl. Not what we'd planned, but I couldn't pass up this opportunity. I owed Jinx, and this was the first step in paying that debt.

Deacon held a hand across the table, shaking Cartel's when

he extended it. "Send everything you've got on the marks to Parris. I'll put a plan together."

The warlord looked impressed. "You really are in quite the hurry."

"Jinx's freedom is worth the rush."

"Understood." Cartel sat back, watching as we slid out of the booth. Not that he was quite ready to let us out of his web just yet. "Before you go...I heard a dead sheriff was found at the Rock Falls Soul Suckers clubhouse. You wouldn't happen to know anything about that, would you?"

Deacon shrugged, completely nonchalant. "Only what I saw on the news."

The warlord's nod screamed his disbelief. "Could have sworn I heard different."

But Deacon was a cagey motherfucker when he wanted to be. He was also sarcastic as hell. "Maybe your ears need cleaning."

Cartel laughed, shaking his head as if truly entertained by the barkeep. "You are a good one, Sniper. Come see me when you're done with this project. I may have more opportunities for you."

"The only opportunities I want to hear about are ones that take the Soul Suckers out of Justice. Black Angels, too." He grinned, showing far too many teeth. "Unless you want missing bikers in your ranks."

We didn't give Cartel the chance to reply, walking out of the restaurant instead. My phone pinged before I reached my bike, a dossier on the two Soul Suckers including locations, pictures, and every bit of pertinent info showing up in my email. Cartel was not fucking around.

"You sure you're up to this?" I asked as soon as we made it to Deacon's truck. Needing to know this was what we were doing. We, as in me and him—a mission without his usual partner of Alder Kennard.

Deacon didn't even falter. "Do I have you as backup?"

"Yeah."

"Then I've got this."

"And that sheriff he was talking about?"

"Don't know nothing about that." Deacon grinned a wolfish sort of smile. One that made his lie that much weaker.

"You're a good liar, barkeep."

"I'm a better sniper." He paused, fiddling with his keys before frowning. "What's this about Jinx's mom?"

Fuck. "I put in a call that Edge and his buddy Ravel were coming in hot on Jinx's mom—I wanted to get her out of the club and away from them."

"But they got to her first."

"Ravel did. He used her addiction against her." He also took out a hell of a lot of anger on her, something I wasn't supposed to know about. It's amazing what witnesses will say when you've got their head in a vise. "She didn't make it out."

"Jinx know?"

"No, but she has her suspicions."

"She's a smart girl."

"Yeah. She is." And a free one...soon. Real fucking soon. My payment to her for my failing her mom.

Deacon wasn't done yet, though. "So when we're done with these two child-sellers, do we take out Cartel?"

That one pulled a laugh from me for sure. Simple, easy— murder the warlord and call it a day. "Damn, son. You're not as clean as I thought."

"I have no idea what made you think I was." The sniper hopped into his truck, leaving the door open to finish the conversation. Looking so much like the soldier he was. Ready to go to war, calm about it. Knowing he had the skills to come out alive. The man was a wall of warrior, a strategist laying the groundwork to pull off whatever mission came his way. If anyone could take out Cartel, I had a feeling it was Deacon Manns. Unfortunately, dropping the warlord could cause more problems than not.

"Another time, old man," I said, bumping my knuckles against his before heading for my bike. "Let's focus on one murder at a time."

"Suit yourself," he said with a shrug. "Lead the way, Marine. We've got some planning to do."

Chapter Fifteen

PARRIS

Deacon Manns planned a mission like no one else I'd ever met. Fast but specific, incredibly detailed, and yet with room to make adjustments should things go sideways. The man was a major asset for me. He was also a giant pain in my ass.

"If I were baseball commissioner, the first thing I'd change is that damn designated hitter rule. It's ridiculous." Deacon couldn't be seen—he was stationed too high up in a tree at the back of the property where the two Soul Sucker marks were staying—but I couldn't possibly lose track of him because he kept talking. Endlessly. "Then I'd start looking at ways to bring down the price of tickets. It shouldn't cost a mortgage payment to take your boy to a game, right?"

My boy. Just the thought of the kid made my heart lurch a little bit. Beckett might like to see a game. Maybe I could take him and Mercy to Denver for a long weekend, get Beckett his own hotel room—one of those ones with a door connecting to ours. That way, I could spend my day showing that little boy how much fun baseball games could be and spoiling him rotten with sweets and souvenirs. And at night, I could spoil his mommy with my hands and tongue and cock. Make her quiver all over until she begged me to stop. Yeah, I'd be planning that out for sure. Once I got this shit out of the way and could go back to being a nomad.

Deacon, meanwhile, was still stuck on his dream of somehow becoming the commissioner of Major League Baseball. "Yeah, costs are too high. I think the player contracts could also use a little adjusting. Free agency—"

"For fuck's sake," I said, unable to listen to another rant. "Are you like this when you work with Alder?"

"Not really, no. I tend to talk a lot more with him."

I suddenly had a newfound respect for the elder Kennard. I was about to say so, but a car turned onto the road leading to the cabin we were staking out. Time to get down to business.

"Incoming," I said, lowering my voice now that we had company.

Deacon also grew quieter, his words clipped and his voice hard. "Roger that. Red sedan rolling up."

I looked through my binoculars, watching as the car came to a stop and two men stepped out. They each wore a Soul Suckers jacket, the club emblem plain as day on the back. What I couldn't see were the names on the front.

"Visual confirmation on Soul Suckers members, but no names yet."

"Roger that," Deacon replied. "No visual here."

Fuck. We had to be sure these were the right guys—the ones Cartel had fingered for trafficking kids. The ones we would kill in payment for Jinx's freedom. If they were the wrong men, we'd just be murdering Soul Suckers without reason.

I had to be sure. "I'm moving in."

"Veer slightly east. The cover is better than in the other direction."

"Got it. Try not to shoot me."

"I make no promises."

I chuckled softly, creeping through the woods at a fast pace. Heading for the cabin.

"I got one inside the house," Deacon said, huffing into the microphone. "Bastard ran in like he was about to shit his pants."

"Let's hope he comes back out. Otherwise, this is going to get messy." Because house cleanup hadn't been on our agenda. I wanted this done in a particular way—outside, no waiting, no staking out as these two fuckers jacked off in the house or whatever they had plans for. Get in, get out, leave no trace. That was our plan. And it would work if we could just get sight of the name tags on the jackets and the shitter would come back out of the house.

"Yo, Bama," one guy yelled, and I grinned. Sometimes fate handed you a gift.

"Confirmed target—Bama." I slowed my pace, moving under the boughs of a heavy pine tree as I brought my binoculars up. "Light-haired mark standing at the rear of the car yelled the name."

"I heard it. Bama is coming back out. We need confirmation of blondie over there."

Yeah, we did. And I had a feeling the only way we were going to get it was for me to out myself.

"Cover me. I'm rushing the targets."

"Try not to get shot."

"Always the goal." I raised my weapon—a nice, semiautomatic tactical rifle—and raced forward, aiming straight at the blond guy by the trunk.

"Back up," I yelled, taking him by surprise and not giving him a second to even think. "Back the fuck up, and drop to your knees."

Blondie turned, and I finally got to see that handy-dandy name badge. Grudge. Exactly the person I was looking for.

"Targets confirmed," I said, knowing Deacon could still hear every word through his receiver. "Fire when ready."

"What the hell is this?" Grudge said, his hands up and his eyes wild. "Bama."

But Bama was already on the ground, blood spreading from what looked like a single gunshot wound to the head. Even I was surprised by that—Deacon was fast and accurate, but also sneaky as fuck. He'd likely shot the man while I'd been running up on Grudge, taking advantage of our distraction and my noise to hide the guy's fall, though he also had to have a suppressor on his weapon. No way could me yelling cover the sound of a gun firing.

My admiration for the Special Forces sniper grew more every minute.

I walked up on Grudge, knowing he'd be dead already if Deacon had wanted to take that shot. Feeling as if I should bear some of the weight of this mission along with him.

"You know why we're here?"

Grudge shook his head, still staring at his fallen buddy. I tapped his chin with the end of my rifle until he tore his eyes from the body and met my gaze. Pale, shaky, terrified—exactly how I wanted him.

So I crouched down, keeping my gun on him as I put on what my former teammates had called my killer face. "You fucked with the wrong town. The wrong kids."

Grudge's eyes went wide, as if he was only just realizing what he could have possibly done that was bad enough to deserve death. As if he'd had to dig through tons of offenses to come up with one that crossed the line. The thought made me sick to my stomach, not that I would ever let on to that.

The Soul Sucker began to tremble all over. "I didn't set the mark."

I bumped his chin with my rifle. Harder this time. "Who did?"

Not that it mattered, but having something like another name to hunt down might entice Cartel. Might give me more negotiating room.

Grudge licked his lips and swallowed hard before saying the one name I hadn't expected. "The Wolf."

Wolf. The same man I'd been hunting for years. The one who'd killed my sister. My own ghost on the wind.

This mission had just turned into an opportunity. "Where is Wolf now?"

"Last I heard, he was in Texas."

"That's all you know? Texas is a big state, motherfucker."

"San Antonio," he yelped. "He's got a house there."

Which was all the information I needed. "Thanks for the tip."

And then I shot him.

I had Grudge dragged halfway to where Bama's body lay when Deacon finally joined me. He surveyed the scene with a frown on his face and a tight grip on his rifle.

"Everything okay there, Deacon?"

He lifted a shoulder in a lazy sort of shrug, his lip curling a bit. "I never wanted to be a soldier for hire."

Not many people did, but sometimes you took the opportunities that were available. "You've killed before and gotten paid for it."

"Not like this."

I dumped the second body on the first, rising to my full

height to look over at the sniper. "The military paid you money to kill people. You and Alder have killed since then, too."

"One was for our country's safety and the other for personal protection."

"Killing in exchange for safety is the same as killing for money—different prize. Besides, this isn't for money. It's for Jinx's safety."

"True." He took a deep breath and blew it out. "And the kids."

My gut clenched, and the world swam with red again. *The kids.* The ones these fuckers had taken from their families. This kill was definitely about the kids—if these two would have gotten anywhere near Beckett, if they would have set their sights on him while I wasn't there to keep him safe, if they'd have taken him...

I wanted to kill them all over again just for the possibility that they were such a threat to that boy.

Deacon tugged my thoughts from the brink of rage with the logistics of disposal, though. "We should load these guys into their own trunk and drive them out of here."

Destroy the evidence, hide the bodies, move on with life. Those words were practically a mantra.

"Yeah. That sounds good." I lifted Grudge's feet while Deacon handled his shoulders. It took us a few minutes and some serious Tetris skills to get both bodies shoved into the trunk of the sedan, but eventually, we did. The lid shut and everything.

"I'll drive this one," I said, knowing the risk would be on me should the cops pull us over. "You lead the way."

"Sounds like a—"

But he didn't get to finish his statement because right then, the rumble of a bike engine coming up the hill broke the silence around us. Deacon moved to the front of the car where his long-range rifle sat, pulling a handgun out along the way but holding it low. Armed but not obvious. I had no qualms about making sure whoever was coming our way knew I was packing. I hopped onto the trunk, lazily pointed my gun down the driveway with one hand, and waited.

As soon as the biker turned into the drive, I knew things were about to go sideways. I recognized the man—Tiny, the enforcer for the Vegas chapter of the Black Angels. Though why he'd be coming to see a couple of child-stealing Soul Suckers, I had no idea.

The big man rolled to a stop, planting his feet on the ground as he killed the engine, but not dismounting his ride. He removed his helmet slowly, looking over Deacon and me with a slight smirk on his face. As if he knew shit we didn't. Which I sincerely doubted considering there were two dead bodies under my ass.

"What's doing, Parris?"

I shrugged, keeping my gun pointed his way and not even attempting to hide it. "Nothing. What's brought you up this way?"

"Just checking on some friends of mine. Maybe you've seen them—two Soul Suckers named Grudge and Bama."

I shook my head, keeping my eyes firmly locked on his. "Can't say that I have."

"This is where they've been staying."

"Wouldn't know anything about that. My friend and I came up here to do some hiking and haven't seen anyone else."

Tiny's smirk grew. "Hiking."

"Yup. Hiking." With guns. No way did he buy that bullshit line, but that didn't mean I wasn't going to try to sell it. "Good for the soul and all that."

Tiny nodded slowly and deliberately, as if actually thinking over my words even as his eyes strayed to where Deacon stood beside the sedan. "You're the barkeep."

"Sure am." Deacon strode forward, stopping when he reached my side. Rifle in hand. "Though the bar's closed for now. I'm remodeling."

Tiny didn't seem surprised. "Too bad. I was hoping to find a place to throw a party."

As if anyone would just let him come strolling into Justice like that. "Maybe you should stick to Rock Falls."

"Or maybe I should throw my party right on Justice's Main Street instead. Heard there's a good restaurant there."

I locked down every muscle, hoping like hell Deacon had the same skill. That he wasn't giving away any sort of fear with his expression or some sort of tic.

Tiny wasn't done with us, though. "I also hear good things about the hardware store there. Sounds like they've got lots of supplies for a man like me."

Translation—sadistic, brutal, and into causing pain just like Edge and Ravel. Yeah, Mercy's store would definitely have supplies he'd like, but he wasn't stepping foot in there unless it was over my dead body. I didn't reply, though, didn't give him a weapon against me, but Deacon wasn't exactly one to hold his tongue.

"You might want to think twice about going anywhere near Main Street, son."

Tiny chuckled, locking eyes with me. "Speaking of sons, I bet Wolf could catch a pretty penny for that little boy you've been seen with."

That leash I'd been tethered with, the one to make sure no one noticed how much Mercy and Beckett meant to me, the one that held me back from making quick decisions in regard to them so as to keep them safe—it snapped.

I was on Tiny in a heartbeat, knocking him off his bike and beating him in the face before I could even take a breath. He fought back, rolling me underneath him and getting a few good shots in. I wasn't about to just take it, though. That wasn't my fucking way. I pushed off from the ground and rolled again, straddling the big enforcer and bringing my fist down with a snap to pound into his throat. Hitting bone like an eye socket or jaw would break a man's hand—hitting something soft and delicate like a throat could do more damage to the opponent and save a few fractures. I'd always hated casts.

Tiny wasn't unaccustomed to fighting. I had just shrugged off Deacon's hold on my arm—the man seeming to want to break the two of us apart—when Tiny punched out and up. It wasn't a fist that connected with my side, though. By the deep burn that set in, my only guess was that he'd stabbed me.

"Break it up," Deacon said, finally grabbing hold of me and yanking me off Tiny. The big man stayed on the ground, coughing and choking as I struggled to my feet. Yup, definitely stabbed, though not deeply. He must not have had a good hold on his blade, which sat on the ground beside his hand. I kicked the thing away and fell back against the sedan, trying to catch my breath.

"You fucking stabbed me."

Tiny gagged and rolled over, crawling to his knees and spitting before he could reply. "You punched me in the throat."

"Aren't you two supposed to be on the same crew?" Deacon asked, holding both his gun and mine, which I must have dropped in my rush at Tiny. Good thing. Otherwise, the man might be dead.

"Yeah." I pressed my hand against my wound, double-checking how badly I was bleeding. Which really wasn't that bad. "But same crew or not, you don't fuck with kids."

Tiny laughed, the sound mumbled and wet. "Your play is so obvious." The man pushed off the ground and rose to his feet, still breathing heavy. "Edge wants the girl. Bring her to him, or you and I will be dancing. And I'm not afraid of collateral damage."

This motherfucker. "You come anywhere near that boy or his mom, and there'll be nothing left of you but some entrails for the scavengers to make a meal out of."

"You two are over-fucking-dramatic." Deacon laughed in that sarcastic way he seemed to have perfected before pinning Tiny with a look that would have had most men shaking in their boots. "Besides, won't matter in the end. Tiny here goes for Jinx, and the Kennards will have his head before he gets a finger on her. And he dares to come for the boy? We won't even need the Kennards."

"You think you can snipe me, old man?" Tiny asked, eyeing the long-range rifle Deacon held.

But the sniper had mad skills at a lot of things, including knowing when to go serious as fuck. "Nah. Shooting from so far away distances me from the kill and makes the death of the mark quick and painless. You come anywhere near a child of Justice, it won't be a bullet coming for you." He stepped closer, smiling brightly, looking far too happy as he said, "I'll cut your fucking dick off and leave you to bleed out in the woods instead. See what kinds of critters the smell attracts."

Tiny huffed a laugh, but Deacon never broke his stare, never backed down a single inch, which definitely seemed to throw the enforcer off his game. The big man finally took a step back, nodding to the older, smaller barkeep.

"We're done for now."

"No shit," Deacon said. "Don't take my warning lightly. I'm nothing if not a man of my word."

Tiny glared my way, but I just raised my eyebrows and stared right back, letting Deacon take the moment. Knowing Tiny would think twice before stepping foot in Justice if he had a functioning brain cell in that head of his. Still, even as the enforcer mounted up and started his engine, even as he flipped us off before making a 180-degree turn and gunning the engine, my gut churned. The man knew about Mercy and Beckett. If Tiny knew, others did as well. That fact put them in more danger than I'd planned for. *Fuck*.

Still, we had a plan—me and Deacon. We also had the Kennard crew if we needed them, and I had a feeling we were about to need them.

I waited until the rumble of Tiny's engine had faded completely before I finally turned to Deacon, not quite ready to get to the heavy stuff just yet. "You threatened to cut off the man's dick but called me dramatic?"

Deacon shrugged. "You said entrails. That word seemed more dramatic."

"Than cutting off a man's dick?"

"Yeah."

"Okay then." I cracked my neck and sighed, trying hard to line up details in my head that simply shouldn't go together. "We need to deal with these bodies, then get to Main Street, maybe track down Gage and work out a protection plan for him to keep an eye on Mercy."

Which would never be enough. He would always place Katie as his priority, a fact that I couldn't argue because Mercy and Beckett were mine.

"I can deal with the bodies alone. You need to go see that warlord and prove to him that you killed these two fuckers and then maybe get that stab wound looked at."

"I'm fine." But I didn't sound fine. Not in the least.

Deacon must have heard the strain in my voice. "In the

history of the world, no one who has ever said they're fine in that tone has actually been fine."

I couldn't really argue that. "He mentioned the hardware store. They know about Mercy and Beckett. I have to get down there."

"I can send Zane and his crew to Main Street."

An intriguing idea but one that didn't sit well with me. One—I hated cops. Two—I didn't know that crew well enough to be certain they'd keep my family safe. Because yeah, Mercy and Beckett were mine, and the thought of them being in danger made me want to fly down this mountain just to make sure they were protected.

Without answers or plans or even options, the only thing I could do was grit out a tired and breathy, "Fuck."

Deacon grabbed my arm, forcing me to meet his gaze. "I trust Zane, and I'll make sure he knows how important these two are... to all of us."

Which was about as good as I could get considering all that needed to be done. "You'd better. It might take me a day or two to get back there."

"I'll make sure she's covered."

Fuck, I hated this. But there was more to think about than Mercy. More to consider. "And Jinx?"

"Jinx is with Finn. He won't let anything happen to her. And once you confirm the mission was completed, she should be a whole lot safer."

True facts. I still didn't like this, though.

"Fine, but Zane's crew had better not fuck this up." I popped the trunk and took out my phone, snapping a couple pictures of faces, gunshots, and name badges so Cartel couldn't question my completing his mission, then slammed the lid once more. "And Deacon?"

"Yeah?"

My heart lurched, my body rebelling at heading in the wrong direction. At riding away from Justice instead of toward it. A couple more days. Hopefully, just a couple more days. "Make sure my boy is taken care of."

The barkeep's face fell, his eyes sharp but haunted. "As if he were my own."

I took the man at his word. As much as I hated it, I needed to block out my thoughts and worries about Mercy and Beckett, needed to get my head in the spy game. Because I had a meeting with a warlord to arrange, and it was one I wasn't sure I'd walk away from. Night would be falling soon enough. It was time to get back to work.

Chapter Sixteen

PARRIS

Cartel was still at the diner when I rolled into the lot. Or maybe he'd somehow gotten word I was coming and had returned. Either way, the man spent way too much time lording over his booth in the back, and I had smiled at the waitress more than I should have needed to.

"Well, look who the cat dragged in." A woman at the table closest to the door stood up, looking really fucking pissed off. At me. I paused, staring at her, trying to place her face. To pinpoint how I knew her because I did know her. She looked familiar, and that voice—I'd definitely heard it before.

My brain refused to put a name with that face, though. "Do I know you?"

Rage lit up her eyes. This chick looked ready to kill. "You really are an arrogant prick, aren't you?"

The *arrogant prick* slipped the pieces into place. This was— well, hell, I still didn't know her name. Whatever it was, she'd been at one of Edge's parties. She'd taken me home with her and gotten pissed when I'd had to leave to meet Cartel. That had happened pre-Mercy but seemed so long ago. Had that really been just last week?

"You don't remember my name, do you?" Mystery Hookup said, crossing her arms and glaring hard. "You fuck that many women? Hard to keep them all straight or something?"

No, but she hadn't been memorable. Or wanted. And she was nothing more than a roadblock at this point. "I'm just here to meet with someone."

"Another chick? Which one? Let me tell that bitch how you're going to walk out and leave her with nothing."

I caught Cartel's eye from across the room, and the interest in his expression grated my nerves. He'd be using this interaction against me for sure, which meant it needed to end. Immediately.

And obviously, I was the only one who would be ending it. "Not meeting a chick, but I can't stand here and argue with you. Have a nice night."

I walked past her, letting the curses and names she spat as I retreated bounce off me. Ignoring her and knowing that probably pissed her off more than if I'd just fought with her. Whatever. Women like her—quick hookups and quicker getaways—were part of my past life. I was working toward a new future.

One the man before me stood squarely in the way of. "Friend of yours?"

"She came to one of Edge's parties," I said as I took the seat across from him.

"Seems feisty."

I snorted a laugh at that one. "Try addicted to coke and willing to do anything to get it."

He nodded, looking over my shoulder toward where the girl

had been sitting before taking a sip of his coffee. "Sounds like what I expect from Edge."

What we all expected from him at that point.

"Why do you keep him on?" I sat back as the waitress stopped by, giving her another damn smile when she set a cup of coffee down in front of me, relaxing once more when she left. "He's a total fuckup and will drive that house into the ground. Why do you allow it?"

"What we do at the national level is our business. And speaking of business..."

He purposely let that trail, knowing why I'd come. Knowing what I owed him. I pulled my phone from my jacket pocket and unlocked the screen, flipping through pictures to show him exactly what he wanted. To prove the completion of the mission he'd sent me on.

"Here." I tossed the phone on the table, the image of two dead Soul Suckers in a trunk filling the screen. "Happy now?"

He looked at the phone for a long time before pushing the device back my way. "Quite."

That was it. We'd killed two men, and I got a one-word response. That wouldn't be enough.

"So, she's free, right? Jinx is no longer property of the Soul Suckers or the Black Angels."

"I'm a man of my word. I'll send directives out that the girl is not to be touched again."

Which was about the best I could do. "Good. And one more thing."

"What's that?"

Time to play my last hand. "I'm leaving the Vegas club."

Cartel's smile turned icy, his expression flattening. A man fighting for control. "Try me again."

"I earned my nomad patch, and I'm taking advantage of it."

To be free from the chains tying one to a particular city or house, to give up the family vibe of a specific crew to stand alone. To begin a new life right there in Justice. All things I didn't need to tell him. "I don't want to be in Vegas anymore."

But Cartel hadn't risen to the power that he had by backing down easily. If ever. "I need you to keep an eye on that Vegas crew."

"And I need you to respect the nomad life." I tapped the patch over my name, the one declaring me a nomad—a free member of the club. "I earned this fucker, and you know it. The national prez knows it. Fuck, Edge knows it. I'm done babysitting him for you. Find someone else."

Cartel sat back, staring at me. Likely waiting for me to crack. I wasn't about to. It took him way too long to figure that out, though. "I'll consider it, but I need one more thing from you."

He could consider my dick—my nomad patch meant I was not just allowed to leave a particular house, I was expected to—but I held my tongue on that. "Like you haven't gotten enough from me over the years?"

"You are my favorite little workhorse." His lips kicked up into that serpentine grin, the one I hated. The one that meant he was about to put my ass in a sling. "Tomorrow morning, there's a shipment coming into Rock Falls. Edge and his team are meant to handle it, but I want you there."

"Why?"

"You said it yourself—Edge is a total fuckup."

At least he wasn't blind to that. "What's in the shipment?"

He stabbed me with a look. "You know what's in the shipment."

Drugs. Guns. Toys for Edge to play with. But that didn't quite fit if he wanted me there. "For use or for sale?"

"For sale. This Rock Falls thing has become quite expensive

for us, so the Soul Suckers are yielding a small part of their territory while we're here so we can earn back what we've spent."

Translation—the shipment contained drugs the guys would be expected to make money on. "I'm not selling shit."

"I didn't ask you to. I just want you there to oversee the delivery. Make sure no one gets an itchy trigger finger."

"Why isn't Tiny handling that?" Since it would technically be his job and all.

Cartel shrugged. "I want you on it."

One job—one delivery—and then I could go back to my nomad lifestyle. No home club, no church meetings on Sundays, no allegiance to anyone other than the national prez. I could stay in Justice. I could show Mercy and Beckett the kind of man I really was. I could have a shot at a different life.

Yeah. One delivery was worth it.

"Fine. I'll take that on, but then I'm out. No more Vegas."

"Agreed." Cartel shook my hand, his grin making me uncomfortable. "Meet up with the Black Angels at the truck stop at six tomorrow morning. Tiny'll be riding out from the campground."

"Where's the drop happening?"

"He'll tell you."

"How long will it take?"

"From what I understand, most of the day."

Fuck. I needed to get back to my girl, but I also needed to tie up this loose end. To pull myself from the bullshit Vegas club so I had the freedom to be where I wanted to be. Which was at Mercy's side. Another day wouldn't kill me...I hoped.

"I'll be there."

Cartel grinned. "Good man."

I didn't feel good.

In fact, hours later as I finally made it back to the motel and was able to strip off the clothes I'd been wearing, I noticed I didn't look good either. Pale, drawn, tired...I looked older than my forty-some-odd years, weary in a way few people could understand. Things didn't get better when I saw the rest of my body. The stab wound Tiny had given me looked gnarly—all deep purple and blue and yellow bruises spreading halfway up my rib cage with a violent little slash in the center. He'd hit harder than necessary but hadn't sliced at all, which was good. If he'd gotten the angle right and aimed a little lower, he could have killed me.

He'd likely try again when he learned I was leaving Vegas.

"One more time," I said to the old man staring back at me in the mirror. One more mission, one more day away from the people I wanted to protect, before I could take my spot in Justice. I itched to call Mercy, to hear her sweet voice, but I didn't. Couldn't. That woman and her son didn't need to be sullied by the shit I still had to do. They didn't need to be pulled into this world. One more mission, and I could step back. Not leave but put some distance between them and the bullshit club stuff.

One more day, and I could start a new life.

<h1 style="text-align: center; font-style: italic;">Chapter Seventeen</h1>

MERCY

I'd never been one to let my anger get the better of me, not even after Beckett's dad had taken off on us. I'd justified his decisions instead, while hiding my own rage at how unfair life was. I might have simmered under the surface for a lot of years—might still have been slightly ticked that he'd walk away like that —but I'd never exploded on him.

Parris leaving us with nothing but some donuts and a few pretty words ignited my temper like nothing else.

Maybe because Beckett liked him, because I'd started to see an opportunity I hadn't been open to before. Maybe because I'd let the man not just into my life but into my bed. Maybe because the guy was an asshole and deserved my wrath.

Whatever. I was pissed. It had been almost two days since Parris had walked away from us, and I hadn't heard a word from him. Thirty-six hours of silence after such an intimate night.

After breaking his promise to Beckett. After walking away with my heart.

"Can I ride my bike when we get home?" Beckett caught my eye in the rearview mirror, his smile hopeful. Yeah, he'd picked out a bike—a really nice one. He'd also gotten an upgraded seat, a helmet, and a GPS tracker installed so that I could follow him with an app on my phone. All on Parris' dime. I wasn't complaining—the gift was kind, thoughtful, and ridiculously excessive—but time was so much more valuable than stuff.

I pasted on a smile, hoping he couldn't sense my irritation. "Sure, buddy. We'll ride over to the restaurant. Show Uncle Gage and Aunt Katie your new bike."

Beckett stared out the window for a minute, seemingly happy with my response. But then he said, "I hope Mister Parris comes back soon. I want him to see my bike."

I gripped the steering wheel a little tighter. "I hope so too."

I made a turn off the highway, heading for the mountains. Sam—my glassblower—had sent me a text that he was finished with a few more pieces and asked if I wanted to come out to see them. The drive, the trek through late fall in the hills, should have been good for us. My mood, though, seemed permanently soured by Parris. I'd even gone looking for him—showing up at The Jury Room that afternoon and questioning Deacon about where the man had disappeared to. I'd gotten nothing but a "you've been on his mind" line of BS. Not on it enough for him to actually call or text or...show up.

"That tree looks like a dragon," Beckett said, dragging my attention away from my angry thoughts.

I glanced out the passenger side window. The late afternoon sun had cast deep shadows along the roadside, and the golden glow of the coming sunset gave the perfect backdrop for a tree stump that absolutely looked dragon-ish.

"You're right. It really does."

"We should take a picture with it."

But night would be falling soon, and these mountain roads got a little dicey since there weren't any streetlamps.

"Maybe on the way back, okay? I don't want Mr. Sam having to wait on us. And only if the light holds. It's going to get dark fast out here once the sun starts setting."

"Okay. I'll remind you."

Of that, I had no doubt.

A truck in my rearview caught my attention. Odd—I was pretty sure I'd seen a red pickup in town as we'd left. That seemed awfully...well, odd. I rarely saw other cars in the mountains, let alone ones I sort of recognized.

Quit making something out of nothing.

I took a deep breath and refocused on the road. There had to be a bunch of red pickups in Justice and the surrounding area—everyone drove big vehicles, and red was a popular color. It wasn't a motorcycle. Besides, so long as they didn't try to roll up on my bumper, they were not my concern. Not today.

I slowed as we came to the final hill before Sam's place. Turning carefully into his driveway. The little farm in the woods sat still and silent, doors to the barn open and smoke coming from the chimney on the house. Nothing unusual about the scene, but something in the air felt off. Out of place. Of course, I'd been feeling off since Parris had left, so it was likely just me.

"Come on, buddy," I said as I unbuckled my seat belt and cut the engine, leaving the keys in the ignition. "Let's go do some business. Mr. Sam is likely waiting for us—he texted me over an hour ago."

Beckett cheered. "Yay. Mister Sam learned to text."

"What?"

"Mister Sam doesn't text, remember? You say that all the

time. He calls, but you don't like to use your phone for that. You complain that he needs to learn to text."

He wasn't wrong—Sam didn't text. Never had. He called or emailed. But today, his message had come as a text. Odd for sure, and something that made the hairs on the back of my neck rise. The texting and the red truck following me... I had a sudden urge to grab Beckett and run. To haul butt back down the mountain to the safety of Justice. But that was ridiculous. Sam wasn't anyone to be afraid of.

Besides, I had a job to do. "Texts or calls or emails, there's still work to be done, so let's get to it."

"Then we'll take pictures with dragons."

"Then we can take pictures with dragons, yes."

Beckett practically skipped around the front of the truck, chattering on about all the trees and the land and the view. Me, I still had a sick feeling in my stomach. Sam hadn't come out to meet me. Not super unusual—he was often busy in his workshop and missed my arrival—but that little detail along with the text and the truck bugged me. I gripped Beckett's hand as we approached the open barn doors, keeping him right beside me just in case.

Just in case ended up being a mountain of a man standing in the shadows. I barely had time to make a sound—only caught a glimpse of him—before he was on us, shoving me to the ground and snatching Beckett away.

He took my son.

"No," I cried on some instinct, pushing myself back to my feet and running those few steps toward the man who held my baby. Who was a threat to both of us. "Give him back to me."

But the man didn't look as if he was going to drop my shaking son anytime soon. And when he moved, when he angled himself just right, my world went completely gray. He had a knife to Beckett's throat.

This was bad. This was so very bad.

"You must be Parris' girl," the guy said, which turned my stomach to lead. "Fitting that I kill you with a knife stained with his blood."

Oh shit. No, no, no.

"I don't know what you're talking about." I edged closer, wanting to reach for Beckett. Fighting hard to keep my heart from beating right out of my chest. "Just hang on, buddy. Everything will be fine."

"See, I don't think lying to your kids is a good idea. And I especially don't think lying to me is either. Your Parris' girl—he nearly jumped out of his skin yesterday when I mentioned coming to see you." The man glanced down at Beckett and grinned. "I found the fucker's weakness."

"Mommy." Beckett wriggled in the man's arms and started to cry. Breaking my heart and sending more adrenaline shooting through my veins.

"Please," I whispered, trying so hard not to scream. "He's just a little boy, and he's scared. Just put him down."

But the guy didn't let Beckett go. Instead, he tugged him in tighter, making my son squeak in what sounded like pain. "Quit being such a baby. I'm not hurting you."

Beckett sobbed a little louder, and my temper that had been burning all day because of Parris turned into an inferno. Fuck this guy—he was not hurting my son. I'd kill him myself.

"Give me back my son," I said, trying my hardest to keep my voice level. "We can figure out some other way to get you what you want."

"What I want is Parris' head on a platter."

The guy took one giant step toward me, dropping Beckett into my arms and shoving me forward. There was no time for relief—no chance to celebrate. I clung to my baby and followed this man's directions, hoping like hell I could figure a way out of this. I didn't have anything useful on me—just my phone. If I could get enough signal to call for help or make it to the truck where I'd left my keys, I might be able to get help. Unlikely, but maybe.

But as soon as my feet hit the porch of the house, the man stopped me with a heavy hand to the shoulder.

"Give me your phone."

"Mommy," Beckett whispered, clinging to me.

Opportunity—lost. "It's okay, baby. We're going to be okay."

But I doubted—I doubted so hard.

"Phone," the guy said, sounding far more menacing this time. "Now."

With a shaking hand, I did as he asked, tugging my phone from my back pocket and setting it in his hand. I had nothing—no way to call for help and no possibility of an easy escape. I could try to walk out with Beckett, but if the man didn't stop us, the mountains would. Especially at night, which was quickly falling. It was dangerous out here. In a lot of ways.

"Inside." The guy pushed me into the house, forcing me down a hallway. I held Beckett to me, thankful to have him in my arms but also kicking myself for bringing him. I should have left him with someone else, should have dropped him off at the restaurant to play with Katie and Gage. I should have done anything but expose him to this insanity.

The man directed us into what looked like a storeroom, shoving me by the shoulder when I paused at the door. I stumbled forward, one hand reaching for the shelves across the way and the other still clinging to my son. Before I could even truly regain my balance, the door slammed behind us, the click of some sort of enforcement locking us inside. But that wasn't the worst of it—Sam lay on the floor in the corner, bloody and bruised. Raspy, shallow breaths coming slowly, the only sound in an otherwise silent room.

And we had no way out.

The roar of a bike starting had me tucking myself into the corner, trying to shield Beckett as much as possible. The bike wasn't coming, though—it was going. The man who'd locked us in here was leaving. Were we alone?

"What are we going to do?" Beckett whispered into my ear, shaking in my arms.

I patted his back, looking for something. For some possibility of finding safety. For anything I could use as a weapon or a battering ram on the door. A tool to take apart the handle set so I could release us.

There wasn't much in the way of options, but I refused to go down without a fight. "We're going to get out of here."

"How?"

I shook my head, wishing Parris were with us. He'd know what to do. But Parris wasn't there, didn't even know we were in trouble or missing, and therefore wasn't about to be the knight on the noble steed coming to save the day. I was going to have to figure out how to get us out of there alive. On my own. As usual.

My kingdom for a damn screwdriver.

"I don't know yet. But we'll think of something."

Chapter Eighteen

PARRIS

Thirty-six hours. I'd been missing my girl and my little man for a full day and a half, much of which had been spent dealing with other people's bullshit. All day, I'd put up with Ravel and his mouth, following him out to who-the-fuck-knew-where to pick up this delivery that was so important to Cartel. He'd finally left once we had our hands on the goods, giving me a blessed hour of silence before I'd hit the road myself. Guns and drugs received—job completed. I'd spent over ten hours between being on the road and waiting for the shit. I wanted to be done. My new life was right there, totally within reach. I could see the finish line.

I wasn't done with Vegas yet, though. I still had a couple of things to do to pull myself away from one life and lean into a new one, to stop being a spy for Cartel and move fully into the nomad status I deserved. One of those things was telling Edge he could go fuck himself. I really didn't think I had too much to worry about in terms of retaliation. It should have been a relatively easy—though slightly dangerous—conversation, so long as the bastard was even the slightest bit sober.

At least, that's what I thought until I rolled into camp and saw the chaos the place had descended into.

Tents had been flattened, left on the ground with garbage strewn around them. Campers and bikes were gone or going, everyone trying to get on the road. Trying to leave. And as much as I liked the sight—anything to get these fuckers out of town and away from my girl—the scene chilled me to the bone. Something had gone very, very wrong here.

"Yo," I yelled to a younger rider—Knuckles—as he stood in the bed of his truck, strapping his bike into place. "What the fuck is going on?"

"Someone hit camp."

Which could mean guns, bombs, or...anything, really. "What are you talking about?"

Knuckles jumped out of the bed of his truck, his face grim. Not stopping for a single second as he headed for the driver's door. "Edge and Ravel are dead—gunshot wounds. We're leaving."

"Tiny make that call?" He was next in line with the president and VP down. No one should have been making a single move without his say-so.

But Knuckles shook his head. "We can't find Tiny. Look, we know it's not procedure and all that, but no one really expects to find their president and VP shot to death, you know? We made the decision as a crew—we're out." He hopped into his truck, slamming the door closed before rolling down his window. "I don't know where we're all going—"

"Vegas." I shot him a strong look as his jaw snapped shut. "It's time to say fuck this. Spread the word—with our executive board unable to convene, I'm making the call. Go the fuck home."

The kid almost smiled. "Thanks, man. I'll let everyone know. See you in Vegas."

Yeah...that wouldn't be happening. But I didn't need to tell him that. In fact, the only man I should really be seeing, considering Edge and Ravel were dead, was Tiny. And fuck my life, that made things harder. The man had stabbed me only the day before.

I rolled through camp, heading straight to Edge's trailer. Assuming that would be where the bodies were. Edge had always been a man of his habits—both good and bad ones. He would have been in his trailer tonight, popping pills and fucking women. No doubt about that.

When I pulled up at the RV, I didn't even need to worry about how to find the bodies. They'd been set up in metal lawn chairs right at the front of the vehicle. Both men seemed to be relaxing in the night air, save for the fact that they were covered in blood. Their own, I had to assume. Pills, powders, and syringes created a druggie's wonderland on the ground around them, spreading what looked to be six feet in diameter. Someone had had a little fun with this.

I had a feeling Deacon Mann was involved, and I was going to wring his neck for fucking up my escape.

"Parris," someone yelled, forcing me to push down my ire. Another younger rider—Nash—hurried over. "Cash says we have to get this shit cleaned up."

Cash. Of course. The little fucker always had thought he was in charge.

"Cash isn't boss."

Nash frowned, glancing at the two bodies behind me. "Uh, yeah, but...the bosses are dead."

"There's a hierarchy in clubs, son. Cash isn't the next in line. Anyone on the executive board make a decision on what to do as a club?"

"I don't know. We found the bodies, couldn't get in touch with Tiny, and people started running. Cash sort of took over and said deal with this." He looked behind me again, likely seeing the same thing I did—prison sentences if the cops decided to pin any of the death or drugs on one of us. "I've never been on cleanup before."

"And you're not now." I stalked back to my bike, knowing exactly how to play this one. "Pack up and get to Vegas. Tell everyone you see to do the same."

"You're pulling us out?"

"The fucking Soul Suckers come walking into camp and slaughter our prez and VP? Yeah, kid—I'm protecting my crew. Everyone needs to go home. Now."

He almost looked excited. "Understood. I'll spread the word."

As would I. But first, I had a few things to do.

I waited for Nash to leave before slipping into the trailer. No sign of anyone else around, though the party that had been raging for days had definitely been continuing in my absence. I hurried to the back, sliding on my gloves as an extra precaution. Every drawer, closet, and cubby, I opened. Every possible nook to hide something in, I investigated. Anything that looked to link Jinx or her mom to this crew, I stuffed into my pockets. One last gift to the girl I couldn't protect—a relatively clean slate to start over with.

It was in the glove box that I found a little black book sitting under Edge's wallet. Inside was a list of names and numbers, contact information for the Black Angels. My info—legal name included—sat toward the front. I found Wolf's in the middle, but what caught my attention was another name. One I'd been hunting for as well. Coyote. That was good info to have, and definitely not something to be left for the cops. I pocketed the book before walking outside.

A couple of riders I didn't really recognize caught me as I was about to roll out of camp, giving matching chin nods toward the RV Edge had been staying in.

"Nash said you pulled the retreat flag," the darker-haired one said as soon as I'd cut the engine on my bike.

"I did." And no way was I backing down on that order.

"Cool. Anything you need us to do here before we go?" The one elbowed the other. "We're pretty good with gasoline and matches."

Perfect. "Do it. I don't want evidence left behind."

"You know who killed them?"

Definitely, but that wasn't the question I answered. Mine was more for a question of *Do you know who you're going to pin this on*? "Absolutely. And I'll be taking care of that."

"We'll light it up, then." The bigger guy held up his fist, bumping knuckles with me and reminding me so much of Beckett that my chest ached. Time to tie up all these loose ends.

I left them to their work, starting my bike and tugging my face shield into place before rolling toward the driveway. I needed to get to Justice, to tell Deacon and Zane that the Black Angels were leaving, and to figure out the most advantageous way to spin this. I also needed to set a couple of small-town soldiers straight on when to murder a biker. If anyone had seen them, if anyone even suspected Deacon or Alder or whoever from Justice had been the ones to kill the prez, the Black Angels would have burned their entire town to ash.

And there would have been nothing I could have done to stop them.

But the Black Angels were gone, Edge was dead, and my ties to that house were completely severed. All because someone decided to grab a gun and solve a few problems. Ones that lined up with mine and therefore might end up good for me.

Sometimes blessings came in the strangest fucking packages.

———

I rolled into The Jury Room parking lot in way less time than I should have, having driven well over the speed limit to try to catch up with Deacon and whoever he'd taken with him on his mission. No cars were parked in the lot, though. The motel sat empty as well. That was fine—no way would everyone just up and disappear. They'd end up here eventually tonight, and I'd be ready. So I parked my bike, took a spot near the door, and I waited.

Not long, though.

Deacon's truck rolled into the lot, the shadows of the people inside too dark for me to distinguish. That was fine too. I didn't mind laying a smackdown in front of witnesses.

The sniper stepped out along with a man I didn't recognize but who had to be a Kennard, then Finn and Jinx came out of the back. Jinx looked wrecked—wobbly and almost half asleep or something. Finn picked her up to carry her, and my mind went red with rage. As if that girl hadn't been through enough, now she had to deal with...whatever had happened? No fucking way.

Finn was the first one to open his mouth. "You got something to say?"

Plenty, but I was starting with the conversation I wanted to have. "You shouldn't have gone in there hot."

Deacon took a spot beside Finn, backing up the Kennard. "There was no other way."

I pushed off the wall and moved into the sniper's face, staring him down. "I've been working them for two years, been selling my soul to the devil for weeks now to figure out how to get them the fuck away from your little pissant town, and you go in guns blazing to take out the prez and his VP? For what?"

"For *what*?" Finn's obvious rage took me by surprise. He set Jinx on her feet, pulling her behind his body as the other man—definitely a Kennard—slipped into place behind her. Creating a wall of man against anything coming toward her. "They had Jinx, and we weren't leaving her there to be tortured."

That made no sense, though. Cartel had accepted the killings as payment. No Black Angel would have touched her after that. "They didn't have orders to bring in Jinx. I would have let you know."

"They didn't bring her in," Finn said, still obviously pissed as hell. "She went there to make a deal with them."

"She went there." Voluntarily. The fuck? The girl had always been a handful, but my god, that was the most ridiculous idea ever. I couldn't hold my tongue. "You stupid or something, girl?"

"Fuck you," Jinx said, though her voice didn't have the strength it should have. "I thought I could get them to leave."

This girl. "Yeah, well, you might have just set off a club war. What were you thinking?"

"It was my fault," Finn said, ever the white knight. "She went there to protect the town because we had a misunderstanding."

"That's quite the misunderstanding. You know they'd likely kill you, right, Luckless?"

"Stop calling her that." Finn flexed, his entire upper body leaning just a little bit closer. Enough for me to notice and understand the movement. That was a threat if I'd ever seen one.

I was impressed. "You grow a backbone or something, kid?"

The other Kennard—another version of Finn now that I got

a good look at him, which meant he must have been the twin brother—huffed. "He always had one. He just never had a reason to use it. He does now."

So the Kennards and their team had basically taken care of the Black Angels, had secured Jinx, and were totally backing each other up. I liked them more and more. They were making my job easier.

"Okay then," I said, just before refocusing my attention on Jinx. "You look like shit, though."

Little Luckless never had been one to let me get away with talking shit. "Is that what you used to say to my mom when she'd come home high? Because I have to tell you, I've got more of a temper than she did."

Damn. I really did need to clean up her misunderstanding about me and her mom, as well as let her know the fate of the men responsible for her death. This wasn't the time, though. Not with mixed company. "You don't know anything about your mom and me."

"I know enough." Jinx disappeared behind Finn, letting out a small moan. "I don't feel so good."

"We're done here," Finn said, his expression set and unchangeable. His mind obviously made up. "She's had enough. You want to fight about this, fight with me."

"And me," the brother said. Elijah, if I remembered right. Lawyer in Denver. Finn's twin. What he was doing in Justice, I had no idea, but he must have been needed to show up.

Two against one, both fighting on behalf of the same woman. Good goddamn.

"You Kennards are all pussy-whipped." I sighed and scratched at my head, trying to loosen up my tired brain so I could think my next steps through. Trying to give them what little information they needed without supplying them with anything that could come back to bite them in the end. And if they thought I was still on the club's side in all this? So be it. "Fine. I'm sorry I didn't think about Jinx's safety before I blew up. I'll deal with the fucking upheaval of two dead Black Angels."

"You think the other guys will leave town?" Deacon asked, his eyes locked on mine. His understanding much deeper than the rest of the guys around us.

I could have told him they already were. Could have given him the full story

"I'll definitely plant the seed that they should. Maybe sow a little discord with their current partners. Make them think the Soul Suckers could have had a hand in this." Which I'd already done, along with removing every trace of Jinx from that site. But she still wasn't safe, because if Finn broke...if the brother couldn't keep his mouth shut, she'd be in danger again. Which I couldn't let happen. I caught Finn's eye, keeping my voice level as I asked, "You strong enough to keep your mouth shut about what happened tonight? Confident Deacon, Jinx, and Elijah will be as well? Forever?"

"Yeah. I am." Finn sounded sure as could be, which was good enough for me.

"Good. Then I'll deal with the fallout. You take care of Jinx."

"I can take care of myself," she said, though she certainly didn't speak with the same conviction as her man.

"Anything you need us to do?" Deacon asked.

"Yeah. Quit murdering people."

"We make no promises." Elijah smirked my way, looking far cockier than his brother.

I had to make sure who he was. "You the twin?"

"Yeah."

"You're a defense attorney in Denver, right?"

Elijah shrugged. "Among other things."

I nodded, liking him already. "A lawyer breaking laws. Guess I've seen everything now."

"Lawyers break laws all the time—we're just experienced enough to know how not to get caught. And if that fails, we know how to work the legal system to minimize the trouble."

"You'd better. Because murder isn't going to get you a mere seven years like your brother got for selling drugs."

"No, it won't," Elijah said, suddenly looking more like Alder than I'd ever seen another Kennard. This wasn't a man to fuck with...ever. "I'm solid, though."

Solid. Strong. Ready to fight. Of that, I had no doubt. "Good. I need to get back to camp and deal with your mess. Keep out of trouble, would you?" I headed for my bike, calculating the time needed to drive to Rock Falls and check in on the fire. Once done, I could make my way to Sterling. Maybe deal with Cartel and finish this. Maybe be able to be back in Justice before breakfast. Maybe have time to stop at Katie's and pick up some donuts for Beckett since he liked them so much. Yeah. That sounded like a pipe dream, but it was a goal. I still had shit to do before I could reach it, favors to call in, which reminded me of the little black book in my pocket. "Oh, and Finn?"

"Yeah?"

"Does our deal still stand?"

He froze for a second as if he didn't remember our conversation. Our agreement for info on Coyote in exchange for a favor. But realization soon shone on his face, and he nodded once. "Definitely."

Good. I'd go above and beyond, though. I'd get him more than info. I'd bring the mark right to him. "Expect a text from me."

I rode out and turned toward town, needing a fix of a drive-by before I headed back to Rock Falls. Just a quick pass to make sure Mercy and Beckett were okay. Not that I'd actually stop, but even seeing a light on in their windows would give me the strength to get through another night without sleep. Would give me the energy to tie up these loose ends and get ready to come home.

Sadly, I never made it to Main Street. My phone buzzed in my pocket. I ignored it at first, having not turned on the Bluetooth in my helmet so the phone could read them to me. But the buzzing didn't end. Once, twice, five more times before I stopped and pulled over. Text messages lined my home screen, all from Deacon.

RED ALERT

Zane says Mercy and Beckett are in trouble.

He followed them into the mountains.

There's a Black Angel holding them hostage.

Get your ass here.

The last text contained a map pin. One that looked awfully familiar.

"Fuck, Mercy. Why'd you have to go to the glassblower's place tonight?" I tucked my phone away, my heart ready to beat out of my chest. Mercy *and* Beckett. No. No fucking way. I wasn't losing them both when I'd only just found them. I wasn't letting anything happen to my family.

I roared up the mountain, not giving a single fuck for speed limits or rules of safe driving. All I could think about, all I could focus on, was how scared Mercy had to be. How worried not just for herself but for her son. And how much of an asshole I was for leaving them alone for even a minute. I'd known Zane couldn't keep them as safe as I could have. I should have listened to my gut. Should have hidden them away somewhere or something. Should have—

What I should have done was be honest with her and tell her the danger this entire town represented. I had failed her, but that wouldn't happen again.

Just as I'd expected, about a mile before the glassblower's house, I spotted a little convoy of Justice friends. Elijah, Deacon, and Zane all stood together, looking grim as fuck.

"Anything new?" I asked the second I turned off my bike.

"Nothing yet," Deacon said. "We were waiting for you to go in."

"Got a plan yet?"

Deacon looked to Zane, who shook his head. "Not yet."

I walked up, smacking fists with Deacon and grabbing Elijah's hand when he offered it. "Didn't you two already kill a couple of people today?"

Zane raised an eyebrow as he grasped my hand for a shake. "Anyone I need to know about?"

Deacon shook his head, obviously fighting hard to keep a straight face. "Nope."

And that was the extent of law enforcement involvement in our day.

The four of us took off through the woods, heading up the mountain a ways to the far side of Sam's property. The night was dark as hell, but there was enough moonlight to make good headway through the pines. Still, it took longer than I would have liked. And once we could see the house, we had to stop because someone seemed to be patrolling the property.

Someone I recognized.

"Motherfucking Tiny," I said, my whisper growly and rough. "That's the enforcer of the Vegas Black Angels crew."

"He took the woman and kid into the house," Zane said, sounding much calmer than I felt. "That was when I realized something was wrong. She was clinging to that little boy."

His words might as well have been a knife to the heart for all the pain they caused, but that wasn't all. There was also rage. That man—a fellow Black Angel—had dared to put my girl in danger. Had taken her and her son and likely scared the shit out of them. He knew they were mine—even without meaning to, I'd made that plenty fucking clear yesterday after killing the two Soul Suckers for Cartel. He knew, and he'd pulled this shit? That was a direct attack on me.

I was going to snap Tiny's thick fucking neck.

"What's he doing?" Elijah asked as Tiny made another pass from the house to the barn.

I didn't have a complete answer for him. "Preparing."

Tiny reappeared, carrying something that looked like a toolbox. Something I couldn't quite make out. At least not until he walked into the circle of light cast from the porch lamp.

Not a toolbox...a gas can.

My entire world might as well have slid right down the mountain. A gas can meant fire, which meant death. Which meant Mercy and Beckett were suddenly in so much more danger.

"Son of a—"

Deacon grabbed my arm, tugging me back to a crouch. I hadn't even realized I'd stood up.

"What do you know about him?" Deacon asked, holding me in place and pinning me with a serious look. His sniper expression in place. "What's his aggressive kink?"

I'd never thought about anything like an aggressive kink, but

I still immediately knew what he meant. "He's not the burning type. He prefers hand-to-hand stuff. Show of strength and all that."

"Maybe Tiny picked up new skills," Elijah said, but I shook my head. Fire wasn't his thing and never had been. Even with the blaze likely burning down in the valley below, it wouldn't have been his first choice for anything. That gas can didn't make any sense.

The reason for the tank slammed into me, though, as the rumble of another bike coming up the mountain buzzed in the distance. My blood chilled, and I had to fight the urge to run down that hill. To run for my family.

"He's not the one setting the fire," I said. "And he's not going to be alone for long."

My first thought was that it could be Coyote coming to help Tiny out. That option would have made sense—the guy liked to play with fire from what I understood, and he was a Soul Sucker. Tiny had shown up at the cabin where Grudge and Bama had been living; he was obviously working with them. He'd known who was local and could be counted on for a little light it and run. But when the biker pulled to a stop and took off his helmet, it wasn't Coyote. It was a face I recognized, though. One I'd been hunting for years. One that made my blood run cold.

"Who's that?" Zane asked, peering down at the newcomer.

It took all my energy to choke out his name. "Wolf."

Chapter Nineteen

PARRIS

Motherfucking Wolf.

The man who'd killed my sister.

The one I'd been chasing for years.

The one Cartel had kept as a carrot on a stick, leading me through this double-agent life, all the while having to know exactly where he was. If Wolf was working with Tiny and Tiny was working for Cartel, that meant Wolf was working for Cartel as well.

Motherfucker, I'd been double-crossed.

I wanted to kill all of them—Wolf, Tiny, and Cartel—more than I'd ever wanted anything.

Except Mercy and Beckett alive and safe.

A thought that stopped me from racing down the mountain with guns blazing.

"Who's Wolf?" Elijah asked, having no idea the battle raging inside of me.

I swallowed hard, fighting for every ounce of control I'd ever learned. "The man who killed my sister. I've been hunting him for years."

"Ah, fuck." Elijah grabbed my shoulder. "Don't lose it now, man."

I wouldn't. Not yet. I needed to get Mercy and Beckett out before I dealt with anything else. No way could I blow this because of that fucker.

And man, did I feel like an idiot for not seeing this coming. "I've been focusing on Edge and Ravel, but Tiny—he's the one. He's the Black Angel running the show with Cartel, and I never noticed it."

Deacon frowned. "How can you know that?"

"Because Wolf? I've been looking for him for years, and Cartel knew it. I let that fucker keep me on a leash because I was promised that guy, but Cartel played me. He's working with Tiny, who's working with Wolf. They're all tied together."

Zane huffed. "Aren't you bikers supposed to be all *brotherhood above all else?*"

Unless the *all else* suddenly becomes worth more than anything else in your life. "Yeah. We are."

"And you're both in the same crew."

"Mostly. I'm a nomad so have no home club to speak of, but we're all Black Angels."

Zane nodded. "And Tiny just betrayed you."

"Yeah. He did. In a lot of ways." As had his boss, Cartel. Something else I was going to have to deal with. After I got Mercy and Beckett off this mountain.

"Well, he seems like an asshole. And not at all Tiny." Zane nodded toward Deacon. "What's the plan?"

The sniper looked my way. "Want me to get my long-range?"

I had to shake my head. "Not enough time. We're going to have to take them down up close and personal."

"How?" Zane asked.

How indeed. The only way I knew to. The only way that would get the job done and keep my family from being burned alive. The only way that would settle the beast within me.

"Like this." I rose to my feet and started running, gun in hand and prayers in my mind. No way. They were not burning Mercy and Beckett. It wasn't happening. I'd do anything to save them, including sacrificing myself so the guys behind me could take out the two bastards who deserved to die. Anything for my family. Including death.

A couple of gunshots popped, but nothing hit me so I kept running. Kept my gun gripped tight as I focused on the path leading me to that pool of light. To the two shadows firing at me. As I reached a slightly steeper part of the hill, I dropped and rolled, coming back up in a kneel and raising my gun. One shot was all it took to drop Tiny. Wolf, on the other hand, had the self-preservation instincts to run. To try to escape me once again. *Not today. Not again. Not my family.*

But Wolf made it to his bike. He started that engine and gunned the motor, throwing gravel from under the rear tire as he pulled a tight turn. No way could I make it in time. No way would I be able to hit that target. I was losing him, and as much as one side of my brain said I needed to chase him down, the other refused to let me. Mercy and Beckett were in that house. They had to be my priority, which meant Wolf would escape again.

And, for once, I was okay with that.

"Fuck," I said, breathing hard. Coming to a stop before Wolf even made it up the driveway. But I had angels on my side —or at least a really good shot in the form of a vigilante sheriff's deputy. Zane jumped up onto a rock and took a shooter's stance —legs spread and braced, both arms holding one hell of a pistol, and eyes locked on his target. Three shots fired in quick succession sounded through the night, but his mark fell. Wolf was down.

That fact didn't bring me the joy or relief it should have.

Elijah strolled up behind us, clapping. "That was an excellent show."

Zane took a bow from his spot on the rock. "Better than *Hamilton*?"

"Nothing is better than *Hamilton*."

Jesus, those two were another Deacon and Alder. And I didn't have time for any of this. "You two finished now? Because there are people trapped inside that house who are likely scared."

"Right." Zane hopped down and hurried over to the rest of us. "Plan?"

"He's your mark," Deacon said, nodding toward Wolf. "You make the call."

But I was already moving in the opposite direction. "Someone else deal with them. I want to get my family out of there."

I stalked into the cabin, throwing open the door and letting it slam into the wall behind it. I didn't even think to holler for Mercy, just immediately began searching her out. Hunting through the space like a dog on a scent. Single-minded in my task.

The cabin was a bit of that open concept thing I saw on television—big living spaces linked together without walls. Not the kind of place to hold someone prisoner. One door off the back hallway sat closed, which was the one I headed for. They had to be in there. *Had* to be. The door was locked when I reached it, but that certainly wasn't going to stop me. I took a step back then rushed forward, growling through my shouldering of the door. Thankful as fuck when the thing gave beneath my weight.

And then falling to the floor as something hard and heavy slammed into the side of my head.

"Run, Beckett."

Mercy's sweet voice kept me conscious, and I reached out a hand into the dark. "Beauty. Wait."

There was a pause, then a shuffling of feet before light stabbed me right in the eye sockets. Motherfucker, that hurt.

"Parris?" My beauty appeared above me, looking pale and so damn scared that I wanted to rage against the world for putting that expression on her face. Once my head stopped pounding. "Oh my God, I thought you were that guy."

"Mister Parris!" Beckett jumped on me, not helping my head but easing something inside my chest. Making the perfect object to hug to my body. "I prayed that you'd show up."

"Then I'm glad I made it, little man." I sat up, taking Beckett with me, bringing a hand to my head and pulling it away to find blood on my fingertips. "What the hell hit me?"

Mercy shrugged, holding up a cast iron skillet. "I did."

Okay. That actually made sense. "You've got a good arm."

"Yeah, well...I wasn't staying in the house a second longer."

"Brave woman." I rose to my feet, wobbly but still holding Beckett in my arms. Gripping her hand and tugging her along behind me as I led the way through the hall. "Let's get you out of here."

Mercy resisted, though. "Sam's in there,"

The glassblower. Her friend and someone she worked with. Yup, he needed saving too. Just not by me.

"Someone else will get him. I want you two out of here. Now." There was no way I was stopping. No way I was letting her spend another second more than absolutely necessary in that house. Gas cans and fires and what could have happened had I been just an hour later swirled through my mind, bringing out my protective side even more than usual. No, we weren't sticking around. I didn't care who was still inside.

Mercy squeezed my hand and stopped trying to hold me back, keeping close to my side. "Good plan."

Yeah, it was. Escaping alive was always a good plan.

I carried out Beckett with my arm firmly wrapped around Mercy as well. I couldn't let go of either of them, couldn't put an inch of space between us. Tiny and Wolf—they had been prepared to burn my family. If Zane hadn't been there, if Deacon and I hadn't been close, if anything had gone wrong... I would have lost them both. I really wished I could kill those fuckers all over again.

"Zane," I hollered before I even left the porch. "There's a man inside—looks like he needs medical care."

The lawman took a solid look from me to Beckett and then to Mercy, his face expressionless, his reaction unreadable. "I'll take care of him."

Mercy's gait stuttered, but I pushed her along, leaning down to whisper, "He means he'll take Sam to the hospital. Not any other kind of *take care of*."

She nodded, silent, her steps fast and her body trembling. I needed to get her out of here, needed to take her home. Sadly, I had a crew of men who were unwittingly in my way.

"You two okay?" Deacon asked as he came up beside me, not putting himself in our path.

Mercy huddled against my chest, still not speaking. I gave Deacon a look that I really hoped said *Leave them the fuck alone*, one he apparently recognized because he nodded once then slowed down. No longer keeping pace with us.

"I'll be calling in Gage for cleanup," he said, before raising his voice. "Hey, Elijah, you know how to ride a motorcycle?"

Elijah walked closer, frowning. "Yeah, I do. Why?"

"Parris needs to take his family back to town."

My heart jumped, and something close to a primal urge to mark territory and protect my den surged through me. My family—damn right, it was, and I would do anything to protect them. Including leave my bike up in the woods and let the fucker rot. Let Elijah drive it down to Justice—it didn't even matter at the moment.

"I can take care of it," Elijah responded.

"Anything else, Parris?" Deacon asked.

If I weren't so torn up inside, my emotions roiling from rage to relief to terror again, I would have laughed. "Do you really think we need to take care of more stuff today?"

Deacon chuckled. "Nope. I think we've covered just about everything."

Elijah nodded, suddenly looking a number of years older than even me. "It's been a long fucking day."

It had, and there was always more to do. Like telling Cartel to fuck off. Like walking away from not just the Vegas chapter of the Black Angels, but the entire club. Fuck my nomad patch. They'd tried to take out my girl and her son, two innocents. Two people who deserved so much better than espionage and drugs and being targeted just because they were important to me. They deserved to get all of me, not just the part left over after what the club took.

Yeah, there was a lot of shit to do still. Just not tonight.

Mercy's SUV sat under the glow of a large halogen light, looking like pure heaven after the last few hours. I led us straight there, helping her into the passenger seat before buckling Beckett into his booster seat. That didn't work, though, because Beckett whimpered and reached for his mom, which had Mercy turning in her seat as she tried to soothe her son. Fuck, I couldn't separate them. I yanked open Mercy's door and pulled her out of the seat, racing her around the vehicle without a word. Not caring that she seemed even more upset at being farther away from Beckett. That was fine—it was temporary. Within seconds, I had her on the other side of the car and was popping her into the back seat so she could stay close to Beckett.

"You good?" I asked, leaning into the cab and looking from one to the other. "You need anything else before we go?"

Mercy shook her head, clinging to Beckett's hand as he appeared to doze. That kid was about to knock out. Good. Sleep off the bad stuff and start tomorrow fresh.

"All right, then." I tapped the roof of the SUV and shut the door, ready to drive them home, but Deacon stood in my way. "What?"

"They okay?" he asked, his voice restrained. Quiet. Not wanting anyone inside to hear him.

"They will be."

He nodded, glancing over my shoulder. "Keys are still in the ignition. Zane will follow you into town. Gage is already sweeping Main Street to make sure you're clear to get them inside. Once you're secure, we'll move on medical for Sam and clean up."

"The glassblower going to be okay?"

"Yeah," he said with a nod. "A little dehydrated, a little beat-up, but he's a tough old coot. He'll be just fine."

"Good." I grabbed the handle of the driver's door, ready to end this. Unable to calm my racing heart. Not yet. Not until I had Mercy and Beckett back home. Until I had locked doors between them and the outside world. Maybe then I could breathe again.

"Hey, Parris?" Deacon stepped closer, keeping me from

opening the door. "It wasn't a kill shot."

One of our two targets hadn't died from his wounds. Not yet.

I clenched my hand into a fist. "Which one?"

But I knew...of course, I knew. No way could it not be the man I'd been hunting for so long. No way could my past not be coming to bite my ass when I needed to focus on Mercy and Beckett. No way had killing the man who'd murdered my sister been that easy.

"Wolf," Deacon said, confirming my assumption. "Zane didn't get the kill shot. He's incapacitated, but he's technically not dead yet." The sniper ran a hand over this face, looking tired beyond reason. "Do you want to handle him? He seemed awfully important to you."

He had been. I'd chased the man for years, had been hunting him for almost as long as Beckett had been alive. I'd gone to jail because of him. Lost the last member of my biological family because of him. I was about to answer, but Mercy's drawn face turned toward the door, her red-rimmed eyes meeting mine through the glass. The woman looked exhausted and in need of something we wouldn't find on that mountain, something I couldn't give her if I were out there torturing Wolf.

She needed me to be better than my past, which meant putting her and her son first.

"Just take care of him," I said, knowing this was the most anti-climactic ending to my story possible. But that didn't mean it was the wrong ending. "So long as he's dead, I'm good."

"Understood." Deacon stepped back, giving me plenty of room to hop into the driver's seat. "Drive safely."

I glanced into the back seat, taking in a sleeping Beckett and an exhausted Mercy. Understanding my role in this moment.

"I will. I've got precious cargo."

Chapter Twenty

MERCY

Parris drove us down the mountain, another truck following close enough behind us for me to see his lights the entire way. I still couldn't believe what had happened, couldn't wrap my head around what we'd been through. From that first moment of fear at seeing the knife at Beckett's throat—which was an image I'd never be able to scrub from my brain—to finding Sam inside the room and being clueless as to how to help him. To waiting in the dark for something, anything, to happen so I could take my shot at getting us out of there. To whacking Parris upside the head with a pan. This whole day had been shit, and I just wanted it to end.

I wanted all of this to end. Justice—the bikers—the fear and constant being on guard. None of this was normal. None of this was what Beckett should have been exposed to. He wasn't safe, especially not around the man at the wheel.

"So, this is it?" I asked, keeping my voice low so as not to wake my boy. "Is the whole battle with the Soul Suckers thing over?"

Parris didn't take his eyes off the road. "What do you mean?"

"You said you wouldn't be back until you'd cleaned a few things up. Are you done?"

He sighed, giving me his answer before he opened his mouth. "No. But I got rid of the Black Angels, at least. They won't be hanging around Justice anymore."

I closed my eyes, my heart sinking. "That's your club."

"Yeah."

"You got rid of all but one."

"One what?"

I opened my eyes and met his in the rearview for a brief moment before he refocused on the road ahead and I turned to look out the window. "The man who put a knife to Beckett's throat wore the same jacket you do. So you got rid of them... except for one."

Parris stayed silent, gripping the wheel a little tighter. Not like I'd expected him to say anything—what could he do? Say sorry he missed one? Whoops, I forgot about that one guy who decided to come after Beckett and me because of him? The Black Angels were his crew, his brothers from how I understood those biker gangs. They were him.

And one had put a *knife* to Beckett's *throat*.

"Look." I pointed out the window as we made another turn, the lights of the vehicle behind us illuminating a large tree trunk. "Beckett said that tree looked like a dragon."

I'd promised to take pictures with it if there would have been daylight. So many hours later, it was too late and too dark and too scary to even pause. After everything, maybe Beckett wouldn't even remember. Maybe he wouldn't care that I hadn't been able to keep my word. But I would.

Parris grunted at my comment but didn't reply, driving faster as he hit pavement. Taking us back home to Justice, where we still weren't safe.

"Two Black Angels left," I said, not looking at him. Keeping my eyes firmly staring out the window. "The guy who locked us up—and you."

His club. His guys. Him.

A battle brewed inside of me, one I already knew the ending to. As much as I wanted Parris, as much as he made my heart jump and my body sing, he was a biker. A Black Angel. His so-called brother had put a knife to Beckett's throat. The man was dangerous, and no matter how much I may have wanted him, I couldn't have him. I couldn't risk my baby again.

The rest of the trip was made in silence, him driving and me fighting to stay awake. When we reached the alley behind the hardware store, Gage stood at the back door, looking all sorts of dark and terrifying as he practically bled from the shadows. I'd never seen a more welcome sight.

"All good?" he asked, not even glancing my way but staring hard at Parris. Looking mean and mad and ready to go to battle if needed. I really hoped all that rage wasn't needed.

"Yup." Parris moved around the truck to grab Beckett as I slipped out my side, practically bumping into a silent and sneaky Gage. The mechanic stared down at me, those almost-black eyes of his seeing all the way down to my soul, it seemed.

"The question was for you, too," he said, keeping his voice low. "Are you all good?"

All good with what had happened, what I'd seen, with Parris coming home with me, with life in general. No, I wasn't all good with any of it. But there wasn't much I could do at that moment.

"I'm fine."

He looked over my shoulder before dropping his gaze to mine

once more. "That changes or you need anything, you let me know."

"I will." But I was too distracted to say any more. Parris had just rounded the back of the SUV with Beckett in his arms, my little boy looking almost toddler-like in the big man's arms. I didn't want to be away from my baby again, not for a minute, so I followed Parris to the door, slipping in front of him to unlock it before holding it wide. "Thanks, Gage."

"Anything you need, Mercy."

"I've got them," Parris said, sounding far angrier than he had any right to be. "Thanks for your help."

Gage didn't answer, just stood and watched as the door closed behind me. As the metal seemed to slam so hard into the frame and close out the rest of the world. As I locked my son and myself in with *one of them*.

I trailed behind Parris down the short hallway and up the stairs, slipping around him again to open the door to my apartment. Letting him lead the way to Beckett's bedroom. He tucked my son into bed, giving him a sweet kiss on the forehead before moving out of the way. I couldn't help it—I crawled into bed and clung to Beckett. Needing a moment or two of peace and calm before I dealt with the storm inside of me. Needing to know he was here and okay before I walked out of that room. My baby kept sleeping, his warm body curling around mine the way it always had. His breath blowing across my face as I simply stared at him.

I could have lost this.

Parris disappeared into the hall, leaving us alone. Giving us space. I could sense him close, though. He hadn't even left the hallway. I didn't care. I had my son with me, which was all I needed.

Time passed—maybe minutes, maybe more like an hour—

but I didn't move. At least not until Beckett sighed and rolled over, chattering in his sleep the way he did sometimes. Talking to himself in gibberish I would never understand. The move released something inside of me, gave me the strength to leave his bed and rise to my feet once more. To face the imposing man still standing just outside the door like some sort of sentinel.

Or at least, that's what I'd assumed he'd be doing. Instead, Parris stood hunched over just outside of my bedroom, looking about as worn-out and exhausted as I felt. Looking shattered. I understood that look—I probably wore the same one.

Parris pinned me with his light gaze as soon as I stepped foot into the hallway. "Mercy, I—"

"No." Just his voice ratcheted up my emotions, turning anger into rage and fear into panic. I pushed past him, tearing at my clothes. Heading right for my bathroom so I could shower. Needing every inch of this day off my body. "I don't want to hear sorry or you have to go or whatever bullshit line you're about to give me."

"No bullshit lines."

"Then, what?" I ripped my shirt over my head, tossing it toward the laundry basket. Knowing I'd likely never be able to wear it again without feeling sick and worried about Beckett. "What could possibly be so important that you just have to say it right now?"

He didn't say anything, of course, so I yanked off the rest of my clothing and stepped into my shower, letting the water pelt my shoulders for a second as I caught my breath. Needing the sting of the too-hot water to feel something other than the emotional popcorn inside of me. I couldn't handle this, couldn't deal with how much this man put me through. I'd been yanked through both emotional highs and lows in only the handful of days I'd even known him—had been raised up and dropped flat on my face so quickly, I hadn't been prepared. Hadn't been able to recover. Any more time on this ride would be too much. Would create a pressure I might not be able to escape from.

Would break my heart into a million pieces, ones that would never find their way back together again.

"Mercy." Parris placed his hand against the glass of the shower door, not looking at me. Not making a move to enter. Looking like he needed to unburden himself but didn't know how.

"Say it," I said, giving him permission. Readying myself for all sorts of words that meant nothing to fall from his lips. "Whatever it is, just say it."

"I thought I was going to lose you and Beckett." He broke, his eyes going bright red and watery. Taking a couple of deep breaths as if to collect himself while looking like a man ready to completely fall apart.

Parris was about to cry.

My heart broke for him. I hadn't been expecting that. Hadn't been prepared for the upheaval seeing his fear and pain so plainly laid out would bring me. I couldn't even think of what I had been expecting other than *not that*. This man, this beast of a human male, looked and sounded so unsure of himself. So fearful. Terrified. As if we truly meant something to him.

My heart slammed into the walls of my chest and made its demands known. I couldn't hold it back from what it wanted, what it needed. So I opened the shower door and exited—slowly and with intention—before grabbing a towel to dry myself. All while keeping my eyes on Parris, who had moved across the small room to lean against the vanity. Still looking so lost.

I had to be sure, though. "The man who took us was one of your brothers."

Parris shook his head. "No. True brothers wouldn't do that.

He knew you were important to me—he shouldn't have gone near you or Beckett."

"But he did."

He looked up, a fierce sort of rage burning in his eyes. "And he died for doing that."

Oh. "So, he won't be coming back?"

My voice broke, all the fear inside of me still pounding through my veins but at a slower pace. At a little less pressure.

Parris ran a hand over his face and sighed. "No, beauty. He's not coming back. None of the Black Angels are. I accomplished that, at least."

"Are you sure?"

"Positive. And if they do, they'll end up in a hole in the ground just like the one who put his hands on you and Beckett." He stabbed me with his cold gaze, his lip curling as he said, "I fucking swear it."

Calm. It blanketed me, warming me from the inside. This man would kill for me, for us. He likely already had. As much as some part of me knew that wasn't the way the world should work —that there were laws and rules and procedures—I couldn't help but be happy that Parris looked past them to take care of Beckett and me. Because when that man had put a knife to my baby's throat, I'd wanted to kill him. I'd wanted him dead.

And now he was.

"Good." And then I ran for Parris, hopping into his arms and kissing him with everything I had. All the fear of the day, the terror and the agony and the sick of knowing how much trouble we were in—it all coalesced into something close to need. Close to desire. It created a burning want to live, and being in this man's arms was about the most living-est thing I could have possibly done. It wasn't smart or right or what I should be doing, but I didn't care. I needed to feel something other than fear, and I wanted Parris to help me do that.

"Beauty." He didn't miss a beat, grabbing the backs of my thighs to lift me against him and walking me to my bed. "I was so terrified I'd be too late. I would have done anything to get you off that mountain. Anything at all."

I couldn't even answer him, couldn't offer him the solace of my words, but I could hold him. I could steal comfort from him with my body and maybe give him a little of what he needed, too. So I gripped him tightly, clinging to his shoulders as he laid me down. Digging my nails in as he covered me with his weight. Wrapping my legs around him before thrusting upward to knock him off. He rolled to the side, looking at me in confusion until I grabbed at the fastenings of his jeans, keeping my eyes on his as I freed his hefty erection. Parris grunted when my hand gripped his hot, hard flesh, rocking once into my hold before standing from the bed. He stripped himself as bare as I was, his jeans and shirt dropping to the floor at the side of the bed. Never looking away from me. Never breaking our connection. But then—

"What happened to you?" I reached for him, my eyes locked on his side. On the damage done.

Fitting that I kill you with a knife stained with his blood

Holy shit. "Were you stabbed?"

He flinched, his arm coming up to cover the giant bruise just under his ribs. As if he could hide it. "It's nothing."

"That's an awfully big nothing."

"It's fine, really. Tiny got a hit on me but not enough to do any damage." He shot me that arrogant smile and crawled over top of me, pinning my body to the mattress. "Besides, it's not that the bruise is that big—it's that I'm an awfully big guy."

He was. He really was. Not too big, though. Our bodies fitting together in the way they were meant to. The feel of him against me, the pressure of his weight on me, it put a few of my pieces back together. His warmth finally soothing something sharp and achy loose inside of me. Smoothing out the chill that had settled over my body the second that man had gotten his hands on my son and—

A knife to Beckett's throat.

I squeezed my eyes closed and rocked against Parris, seeking some sort of pleasure. Some sort of way to forget, even if only for a moment. Chasing the unattainable one last time because I needed it. Needed this memory. Needed this distraction.

"Beauty, wait." Parris pulled away, lifting onto one arm to stare down at me with regret in his eyes. "I didn't get to the store."

I reached behind me, fumbling with the nightstand drawer. Sliding it open. Reaching inside to grab the box he'd promised to provide.

"Good thing I did."

Parris froze, his weight still pinning me in place, his hand on mine with the box between us. Breathing hard and heavy. More warmth worked its way through my system, a feeling of right that had a tactility to it. A sensation all its own. This was our moment, our time to connect. Even if it never happened again.

"I'm only going to ask you this one time if you're sure," Parris said, practically trembling above me. Looking like a man who *needed.*

"Good, because I'm only going to tell you this once that I am." I tightened my legs around his waist and tugged him forward, sighing as all that manly scent enveloped me. As the force of his collapse pushed me into the mattress. I was surrounded by him—the feel and sound of him, the way he smelled and his breath in my ear. Everything. This—the sensory overload of sex with another person—was what I'd been missing.

Sure, I had toys and fantasies and could get off when I needed to, but this connection, the physicality of the act, that was something you couldn't replace with silicone and batteries. That was what I'd been craving. To be overwhelmed by another person's very being.

Looking about as frantic as I felt, Parris leaned down, slipping the box from my hand and pressing his lips to mine. Completely covering my body before rocking against me. Caressing my pussy. And just like the last time, the feel of him there—the tease of it—drove me half out of my mind. To the point that I arched up, letting the tip of him slide inside. Trembling as the man groaned all low and deep before stilling.

"Fuck, beauty. I can't go slow tonight." He growled low in his throat, breathing into my neck as he murmured, "I just want to fuck you so bad."

"Then do it." I pushed him away, trailing my fingers back to that box he'd never let go of. "I want you inside me. I need it. I'm so wet for you."

His groan filled the room, and his body jerked forward. Within seconds, he'd ripped open the box, freed a condom from its wrapper, and sheathed himself. All without stopping the motion of his hips. All without easing a single pound of his weight from me. I responded to his movements, following them along. Making sure our bodies were lined up just enough for him to feel me. For him to know I hadn't been kidding when I'd said I was wet. And when he finally notched himself at my entrance and pushed inside, when he breached what he'd avoided the last time he'd been in my bed, there was no holding back.

Just this once.

"Good goddamn, you're so tight." He thrust into me, grunting with every push. Not holding back or being gentle at all. He'd wanted to fuck me, and that was exactly what he did. He filled me up and never let me go, purposely rolling those hips to put pressure on my clit. Pressing deeper than any man had been before. And my god, was it good. So good. I was a shivering, quaking mess in mere minutes. Ready to let go and crash before he could even move us into a second position. This was it—all I'd needed. All I'd craved right there. Me, Parris, and him inside of me. Perfection.

"Parris," I gasped as he angled his hips a little more and hit something inside of me that sparked a flame I knew would soon burn out of control. "Parris, I'm going to come."

"I know, beauty. I know." He lifted my leg onto his shoulder and slid impossibly deeper, pulling a moan from me that bore more weight than a sound should have. Pressing a thumb against my clit to give me the added friction I hadn't even known I'd needed. "I want to come, too. I *need* to come. Let me get you off first, though. I want to feel you squeezing my cock. I need to know how much wetter you get when you come nice and strong."

I made a mewing sound, unable not to. Unable to control myself enough to hold back for a single second longer. I came with a shout and a gripping of Parris' shoulders that likely left marks, splintered and flew through the air before slamming back together as he followed along behind me. Holding me close. Chanting my name as he slowed his movements and shallowed out again. As he came.

So good. This man was so, so good for me. And so bad for us.

"I'm sorry," he whispered as he kissed up and down my neck, still inside of me. Still rocking slightly. "I'm so sorry for today."

His words stabbed me in the heart, making what I knew needed to be done that much harder. Making me want to put it off, but I couldn't. This had to be like ripping off a Band-Aid. Quick. Painful—but over in a second.

"Me too," I replied, giving him one final kiss before I held his face in both hands and pushed him away. Before I inched my body up the mattress so he could slide out of me. "And I think it's time for you to go."

He jerked back, that heavy brow pulling tight. "What?"

"Go." I rolled out from under him, grabbing my robe from where I'd left it that morning and covering myself as I rose to my feet. "Leave. Again."

"Beauty, no—"

"I'm not your beauty, and I said it's time to go. So, please, I need you to get your stuff and walk right out that door like you did last time." I crossed my arms over my chest, locking down everything inside of me because it hurt. Kicking Parris out hurt so much, but this was what needed to happen. This was what was best for Beckett and for me.

Parris wasn't one to give up without a fight, though, at least not this time. "Fuck that."

"Parris—"

"My name is Chase." He hopped to his feet and grabbed his jeans, yanking them up over his legs. "The man you just fucked and are now kicking out of your life—he has a real name."

That brought me up short. "What?"

"Parris is my road name because I was in the Marines. My name is Chase. Chase Fowler."

And my God, didn't his admission just make everything that much harder? That simple statement—that single truth—should have made me feel like a true connection had been formed. Made me bask in the intimacy of the moment. But all I could feel was fear, all I could see were the shadows in Beckett's eyes when that man who'd worn the same patch on his jacket that this one did had put a knife to his throat. And all I wanted was to go back to that one single moment and make it all go away.

I couldn't do that, but Parris was my connection to those people, so he needed to go. Which meant the nice side of me with the soft heart that wanted him to stick around needed to shut the hell up and my inner bitch needed to come out to play.

"Well, *Parris*," I started, trying hard to ignore his flinch when I used his Black Angels name instead of his real one. "While that's all fine and good, I still think it's time for you to go."

His face hardened, and he looked away for a moment before pinning me with a look. "You don't mean that."

"I do." I retreated when he reached for me, glaring hard. Spitting my words out. "He could have killed my son. Do you get that? Not because of me or anything I'd done, but because of you. Because of the club you love so much. So, thanks for saving us, but I don't want this life. I don't want any of this."

He jerked as if I'd slapped him. "You don't want me?"

There was no way for me to lie to him. Not about that. It would only add fuel to his fire, make him think there was a weakness in my armor.

"No, I want you—" *bad enough for the need, the craving, to make my eyes water* "—but the bikes, the criminal stuff, and the danger? Biker life? Mystery bruises you won't tell me about? I don't want any of that."

He sighed, clenching his hand into a fist against the counter as if wanting to reach for me but holding himself back. "Beauty, I'm trying—"

"Your trying isn't enough. You and the biker lifestyle are a package deal, and I've made my decision. I don't want it." I headed for the door, fighting to hold myself together for just a few more minutes. Needing to put something physical between us before I could break. "You need to go."

Parris still wasn't giving up, though. He took me by the shoulder and spun me around, tugging me in tight to his body.

"I'll walk away from it. All of it. Tell me that might be enough, and I'll do it."

"No." Too little, too late. I pulled away, the scratching, aching pain of loss heavy in my chest. The residual fear of the day clogging my throat. "I'm saying no, Parris. I can't risk my son."

Stricken. The man looked absolutely stricken. "I'd never put Beckett in danger."

And yet, he already had.

"That man could have killed him today!" I yelled, unable to hold back. Unable to control the anger and the fear and the hurt. "That biker wearing your colors had a knife against his—"

I choked, gasping for air. Hating myself a little because I couldn't even say the words, couldn't stop the pictures from playing out behind my eyes. My baby boy had been so close to death. That had been the scariest moment of my life. Bar none. And then being trapped inside that house, not knowing what would happen next. So afraid that I wouldn't be able to get Beckett to safety. The entire day had been an exercise in living out some of my worst fears, but Parris didn't seem to get that.

And I was tired of trying to make him understand. "I could have lost my son, and it would have been because of my connection to you. I won't make that mistake again."

I yanked open the door and stepped back, giving him all the room he needed. Letting him go live the life he wanted to so I could go back to the quiet and security of my pre-Parris days. To being alone but safe.

"Goodbye, Parris."

He paused, breathing hard for a moment before striding out the door and into the hallway. But before he left, before I could slam the piece of wood and put that physical barrier between us, he lobbed one final bomb my way.

"The name's Chase, and you're going to be saying it a hell of a lot before we're through, Mercy."

I shook my head, refusing to even look at him. Keeping my eyes trained on the floor at his feet. "Are you trying to say I'll be screaming it like I did Parris?"

"Nah, beauty. Sex is easy—I'm not settling for that." He placed a single finger under my chin, forcing my head up. Refusing to surrender until I met his eyes. "This time, I'm going to hear you say it in some vows."

I practically shivered under the intensity of his gaze. "Excuse me?"

"You heard me." He backed away, giving me my space once more. "Now get inside and lock up. I'm not leaving until I know you're safe."

"Parris, there's no way—"

"It's Chase. Say it."

But I wasn't giving in to him. "No."

"Then I'll try again another day." He turned and moved toward the stairs, giving me one final look over his shoulder. "Good night, Mercy. Lock the fucking door."

I did as I was told, shutting and locking the apartment door. Listening through the wood slab to the sound of his retreating footsteps. Cringing as the metal door leading into the alley slammed closed.

And with that, he was gone, and I was a much bigger mess than I'd ever thought I would be.

I'm going to hear you say it in some vows.

Such a pipe dream.

Chapter Twenty-One

PARRIS

Three fucking days without her, and my world had stopped. Just...stopped. I hadn't left my motel room, hadn't made any plans in regard to Cartel. All I could do was mope. I had become the mopiest fucker on the planet, all because some little woman had kicked me out.

A woman I was pretty sure I was in love with.

One I'd been convinced would love me eventually, too.

Instead, she'd ended things. Abruptly. After what had been some seriously intense sex. My confusion over that ran pretty deep, I had to admit. And still, I couldn't be mad at her. She'd been protecting her child, had gone full momma bear on me and cut me out of her life. Like one of those trapped animals in the woods that chewed off their own leg, except it sure hadn't seemed as difficult as chewing off one's leg would likely be. I mean, she'd turned on a dime, and I'd been gone within minutes. Removing a limb had to take longer than that.

Which was how I ended up lying on my shitty motel bed watching videos on my phone of animals stuck in traps and how they reacted.

I was a sad, sorry fucker for sure.

A knock on my door interrupted my watching time, so I refused to answer it. On the second knock, I yelled out, "Go the fuck away."

There wasn't a third knock—instead, Deacon Manns came strolling inside, his motel keychain in hand.

"Did you really just break in to my room?" I asked, not removing my eyes from the screen. There was a fox in a cage, and she looked ready to spit nails at anyone who came near her. She sort of reminded me of my Mercy, and I really wanted the little vixen to figure out a way to escape. Or bite the hand of the man who'd trapped her clear off.

Deacon had other plans. "Let's go."

Going meant leaving, which wasn't on my agenda. "Go where?"

"Katie's."

Town. Main Street. The Baker's Cottage. All too close to Bell's Hardware for me to resist, and yet I had to. Mercy didn't want me there. "Why are you going to Katie's?"

"Not me, motherfucker. We. And we're going because it's Thursday. Cream of chicken soup day."

The fox had somehow managed to grab the top bars and pull herself up, contorting her body as she attempted her escape. *Come on, girl. You can do it.*

"Did you hear me?" Deacon said, coming to rattle the bed with a solid kick. "Cream of chicken fucking soup day. You don't miss that in Justice."

"The fox is almost out."

"Is that code for something? Am I watching you watching

porn?"

Yeah, that pulled a laugh from me. "Is my dick in my hand?"

"Can't say that I looked."

Fair enough. I turned the phone enough for him to see the phenomenal escape happening. "There's a fox. In a cage. And she's almost out."

He moved closer, leaning a hand again the headboard of the bed so he could get a better angle. As the two of us watched, that little vixen somehow twisted her body almost all the way around and pulled her hips through the bars, practically danced across the top of the cage before jumping into the brush. Disappearing from the frame. Safe.

I wanted to give the beast a high five for that one. "Damn, that was amazing."

"Smart fox," Deacon said. "You through now? Because I really want some soup, and you need to get out of this room. You're moping."

He was right. I was a mopey motherfucker. A hungry one. So I rose to my feet, not fighting him but still not really up for anything other than moping. Soup sounded good, though. As did busting his balls a little. "I'm not moping."

He laughed. "Sure you're not."

I grabbed my jacket off the chair, the one with the Black Angels patch on the back. The one I'd been ignoring for days. Deacon wrinkled his nose at it.

"You don't need that."

I stuttered but slipped it on, the weight of it rubbing my shoulders the wrong way. "It's chilly."

"Not chilly enough for that." He grunted and held open the door, waiting for me to pass him. "Come on, Romeo. We've got soup to eat and people to say hi to."

"What sorts of people?"

Because Mercy didn't want to see me, and I wasn't ready to see her again. Not if she looked at me the way she had the other night. Flat eyes, dead inside, no heat. No spark. I couldn't handle that again. Not right then. I already felt flayed open—seeing her look at me with that expression would completely gut me. There would be entrails, which Deacon liked to say was me being dramatic. No way could I deal with entrails today.

But Deacon had to know where my mind went because he intentionally avoided the land mine of the Bell family. "Katie and Gage, obviously. Plus, Finn and Jinx will likely be there. I miss the cranky Kennard, and she's way cooler than anyone else in this town. I need my fix of her spirit."

Jinx. My former ward. Yeah, she was cool—her mom had been too. Smart and full of life, a real joy to be around. At least until the drugs had taken hold of her. Then...well, she'd been a junkie. I'd tried real damn hard to get her to kick them, to loosen their hold on her throat, but that Vegas crew had worked against me. Had fed her more whenever my back had been turned, all because she was club pussy. The woman hadn't deserved that. She hadn't deserved me failing her the way I had.

And I was about to come face-to-face with her daughter, whom I'd also failed. Jesus, I never got anything right anymore. Not since the day I'd walked into that Vegas club, my nomad patch firmly affixed, to set up a couple of years of residency. Not since the day I'd started working for Cartel.

As Deacon turned onto Main Street, I couldn't help but look toward the hardware store. The lights looked to be off, the closed sign in the front window. No one home.

No way could I not ask the question. "Bell's is closed. Is Mercy okay?"

Deacon glanced my way before refocusing on the road. "She's fine. Just no longer open for business without an appointment."

That was smart, but not what she'd wanted to do. "What made her lock the store down like that?"

He pulled into a spot, throwing the truck into park and cutting the ignition before sighing. "She's scared. Tiny getting his hands on Beckett really got to her."

It had gotten to me, too. Every time I tried to sleep, I had nightmares of what could have happened if we'd been too late. If Zane hadn't followed Mercy out of town that day. If Tiny had decided to act the second she'd shown up instead of waiting for Wolf. All the what-ifs haunted me. I'd bet they just about killed her.

And there was nothing I could do to help her because she didn't want my shadow darkening her doorstep anymore.

Without further conversation, we walked inside The Baker's Cottage and headed for the bar, both of us taking a seat facing the single television on the back wall. The thing was only ever on for lunchtime, and it was tuned to the nearest news channel. A pretty woman with long, dark hair and pale, pale skin pointed at a map of the Front, talking about weather patterns and upcoming snowfall. I'd be needing to change out my bike for my truck again before that hit.

"Snow coming," I said, unable not to comment on the obvious. "How do you all deal with clearing roads?"

Deacon stared at the screen, looking way too interested in the weather. "Alder has equipment up at the mill. He and his team handle it."

"Hi, guys," Shye said, practically bouncing across the restaurant with two glasses of ice water on a tray. "I assume you want the cream of chicken. Anything else I can get you?"

"No thanks, Shye." Deacon grabbed his water and smiled her way. "Just the soup for today."

"I'll have Katie serve it up. Gimme just a minute." She

pranced away, her ponytail bouncing, her joy a palpable force. Not that it could break through the cage of despair locked around my chest, but still—it was nice to see the girl happy. She'd be marrying Alder soon enough. The man deserved a good woman like that. He hadn't failed everything he'd touched.

"It's going to get cold for a few days," Deacon said, still staring at the television. I watched him watching the news, paying attention to the tic at the corner of his jaw. Noticed how he sat back and relaxed once that woman was off the screen. How very not Deacon-ish.

"You know that weather chick or something?"

Deacon glanced my way, looking almost uncertain for the first time ever. "Yeah. I dated her."

I took a sip of my water, raising my eyebrows. "Dated. Past tense."

"Past fucking tense, yeah." He tapped his fingers on the bar top and huffed, not looking at me. "Killing bikers at all hours and being called away to rescue people while not being able to tell her a lick of it all sort of put a damper on our relationship."

Yeah, that couldn't have been easy. "Sorry to hear it."

"Eh, it's fine." He shrugged off the melancholy, grabbing his water and taking a drink before continuing, "She was way too fucking young for me, anyway."

"How old is she?"

"Just about to turn thirty."

"That's not young, man."

"I said too young for me."

"How old are you, anyway?"

"Coming up hard on thirty-seven."

"That's not old."

"Too old for a thirty-year-old woman."

Doubtful, but I wasn't going to argue. I knew enough about

Mercy to know there was about a ten-year gap between us. I never would have said I was too old for her or she was too young for me—the connection had been there, bright and solid and true. If Deacon couldn't look past the age thing, then that girl wasn't meant to be his.

Thankfully, Shye interrupted our age discussion with a bright smile and two steaming bowls of soup. She placed a bread basket between them, giving Deacon a wink as she said, "I brought extra. I know how much you love Katie's homemade bread."

Deacon grinned, turning on the charm. "You're too good, woman. When are you going to stop messing around with my best friend and come home to me?"

Shye's cheeks flushed, and her grin deepened. "Sorry, Deacon. My heart belongs to Alder."

"He's a lucky man."

She shook her head, turning to return to the kitchen. "I'm the lucky one for sure. Holler if you need anything."

Shye wasn't gone ten seconds—not even enough time to take my first bite of soup—when Deacon decided to get all Deacony on me.

"So," he said as he grabbed a hunk of bread and slathered it in soft butter. The weight of that one word far exceeding the two letters that made it up. "When are you going to pull your head out of your ass and go get that girl?"

As if things were that easy. "I'm no good for her. Besides, she doesn't want me."

"Well, you're mostly right."

I grabbed some bread, holding it up as if to throw it at him. Not that I would—that shit was too damn delicious to waste. I buttered it instead and simply growled a low, "Fuck you."

Deacon chuckled, dipping his bread in his bowl and taking a

bite. Looking like a man in the middle of some sort of blissful experience as he groaned. "Damn, that's good."

"I swear, Katie puts crack in this soup. How else could it be so good?"

"She's a genius with food." He nodded, grabbing his water for a sip before going in for the kill. "Back to Mercy."

"Or not."

"I never let anyone off easy, son. You'll figure that out soon enough."

"I'm older than you, therefore not your son."

"You're acting like a lovesick teenager. *Therefore* I get to call you son, son." He waved a hand in the air, indicating me. As in all of me. "Mercy doesn't want this you. She wants the man underneath all that."

Underneath what? The club jacket, jeans, tee, and boots? Funny—she'd had that man. Had me straight-up naked. And she'd still kicked me out. "They're one and the same."

"Not even close." Deacon cocked his head, giving me a side-eye that held a metric fuckton of weight. "But if you haven't figured that out yet, I don't really know how to show you the differences."

How many differences could there be? I was who I was—Marine, ex-con, badass. Biker.

It was the last word that didn't sit well with me. I'd been in the club life for decades at that point. Had gone to jail for them, had killed for them, had almost died for them. And though I'd known since the whole Mercy thing had kicked off that I needed to get the fuck out of my Vegas assignment, leaving the club altogether had never crossed my mind...until my so-called brothers had come for my girl.

But it wasn't just her that I needed to consider. Justice had been terrorized by the Soul Suckers. The colors on a man's back wouldn't matter to them—all they'd see was biker. Criminal. Danger. Townspeople would always associate me with them if I wore my colors even as a nomad. Leave the Angels? That had never been an option before. But for my girl? For the chance at a *family*? I'd do it in a heartbeat, a thought that might as well have been a load of bricks slamming into my brain. I'd realized the need to break my connection to the Black Angels on that mountain when we'd saved Mercy and Beckett, but I hadn't given it any further thought. Hadn't made a move to do so because I'd been moping.

That shit needed to stop.

I was still stuck in my head, still thinking about the club and the crews and the brotherhood—and how I'd be walking away from all of it for a single shot at getting Mercy back if I decided to do this crazy thing—when Jinx and Finn came in. They looked happy—happier than I'd ever seen the girl, for sure. I envied them that. I sort of hated them for it, too. Jinx was snuggled into Finn's side, smiling and laughing with him. The two obviously in love with one another. And man, while I was so glad she'd found herself a good man like Finn Kennard, I just couldn't deal with watching that. Not while my Mercy sat a few doors down alone and unwilling to see me.

"I'm out." I tossed my napkin over my bowl and threw a twenty on the counter. "Lunch is on me."

"Don't you need a ride back?"

"Nah, I'm going to grab my truck from the storage garage. Gotta be ready for snow and all that." Gotta start rebuilding my reputation as more than just a biker, though I didn't say that.

Deacon eyed me as if he knew, though. "I'll be at the bar tonight for some heavy cleaning. Come on by and grab a drink."

"Fine, but I'm not cleaning."

"I didn't ask you to." He held out his fist for a bump,

accepting mine with goddamn firework fingers. "Oh, and by the way, Saturday night there's a joint bachelor and bachelorette party here for Alder and Shye. You're coming."

"The fuck I am."

"The fuck you are. You can be my date." He blew me a kiss, laughing the entire time. "Go be your sparkly, sunshine self, Parris."

And man, asking him to call me by my real name sat right there on the tip of my tongue. Wanting to come out. Needing to. I bit it back, though. I wasn't ready for that level of commitment to this retire-from-the-Black-Angels idea just yet. I still needed to be Parris for a little while longer.

That didn't mean I couldn't put out feelers. "Hey, Deacon?"

"Yeah." The man turned in his seat, eyeing me with a smirk that said he knew I wouldn't make it out without saying something.

Jackass. "You up for one more mission with me?"

He cocked his head and leaned against the bar, practically sprawling right there on that stool. "I thought you'd never ask."

"I'm not asking, just...thinking things through."

"You think, I'll get some supplies together, and we'll make shit happen. Any time, any way. So long as we don't miss the party Saturday."

Answers like that made him the perfect partner to pull off something as stupid as I was contemplating. "You're a good man, Deacon."

"No shit. You should tell more people that." He spun back around, mumbling something about not getting enough respect. Flapping his jaws, really. I'd gotten what I needed from him, though. It was time to get the hell out of Dodge.

But Deacon's words refused to stop rebounding through my head as I strode outside. Mercy didn't want Parris, but she might want Chase. She might be willing to give me a shot if I was fully untangled from the Black Angels. That wouldn't be easy—biker gangs didn't take well to men walking away. Someone in my position didn't really quit them. But I'd spent a lot of time inside, a ton of time getting to know the good and the bad of everyone. And I had a few chips I could play. A few favors I could call in.

One big one that I'd never even considered...before now.

As I drove past the hardware store, I saw a shadow move in the window above it. Someone in the apartment going about their day. I wanted to be there, be one of those shadows. Wanted to pick up Beckett from school at the end of the day and find out what he'd learned. Wanted to take advantage of those kid-free hours with Mercy's hot little body wrapped around mine. I wanted lots of time with her, just talking and touching and being a couple. I wanted everything.

And fuck any past promises, but I was going to get it.

Chapter Twenty-Two

MERCY

Planning a wedding that wasn't yours while trying to deal with the heartache of walking away from the first man I'd felt anything even close to romantic for in a lot of years was practically some form of torture. One I inflicted on myself with a single-minded focus and dedication no one could have argued about.

"So, the florist will be here at two tomorrow to deliver the wildflowers, and Katie's made space in the walk-in for them to sit while we decorate the dining area." I added a bullet to my to-do list to call the florist in the morning just in case, then handed Shye the photograph we'd used to place our order. "I've confirmed the color palette is the same as what you see here."

Shye nodded, glancing over her shoulder to where Alder stood with Beckett. "That is just too darn cute."

The eldest Kennard was working with my son on his bike riding, having set up a small ramp to teach him how to handle bumps on the trails. You couldn't grow up in Justice without mountain biking, even if you were barely finished with training wheels.

"Cute but dangerous." I clipped the photo back into my planning binder and flipped to the food and beverage section. "Katie's confirmed the menu and has everything on hand to complete the dishes. We received most of the wine yesterday, and I'm expecting another shipment today. I'll send you a text once it arrives so you don't have to worry."

Shye giggled. "Mercy, I'm not worried at all. You've run this party planning like a military operation. Even Alder—Mr. Plan All the Things—is seriously impressed."

Her words eased a little of the tension that had been sitting between my shoulders all week. "You asked me to handle the planning, and I wanted to make sure I gave you what you'd expected."

"You've given me a lot more than what I expected. Honestly, you've made everything so much easier on me."

"Good. That's what I'd hoped for." I looked up again as Beckett laughed, the sound warming my heart. "Alder is so good with kids."

"He is."

I knew that breathy tone, that look of love and desire on her face. The woman's ovaries were howling at her to get busy with the baby-making. Not that I could blame them. "So, should we expect a little Alder sometime in the not-too-far-off future?"

Shye smiled wider, laughing softly again. "Maybe. We don't have any specific plans yet, but..."

Yeah. *But.* That sort of but had made many a woman a mother. "Just let me know when it's baby shower planning time. I love all those stupid games people play."

She shot me a sarcastic glance. "Like taste the baby food?"

"Yeah, but I'd only pick sweet ones like blueberry buckle or that orange-banana stuff. Nobody wants to eat pureed meat."

Shye made a noise as if she were gagging. "Nothing about pureed meat sounds appealing."

"It isn't, which is why Beckett never had any of it."

Shye hummed, watching Alder and Beckett some more. Smiling broadly when her man shot her an amused look. Those two were such a matched set—completely in love and happy together, even with all the drama going on around town. Not that there'd been much—everything had been quiet for the last few days. Not a biker in sight. Not even Parris.

Something that secretly bothered me.

"Hey, Beckett," Finn said, appearing through the back entrance with his girlfriend Jinx in tow. "You don't need lessons from Alder. He's an old man. Let me teach you a thing or two."

Jinx headed our way, leaving the men to trash-talk each other good-naturedly while my son stood watching on with a grin on his face. He'd handled everything so well these last few days—a nightmare now and again, but otherwise, it seemed as if his evening trapped in a cabin in the mountains had been just another adventure. I, on the other hand, was still a wreck. I'd sat outside his school that first day, too afraid to leave him. Too worried he'd need me and I'd be in Justice. Terrified that men on bikes would storm the school and take him from me. I'd done better the second day, though. I was sure I'd eventually stop panicking whenever he was out of my sight.

Maybe.

Hopefully.

"That's an explosion of cuteness," Jinx said, pointing toward where the males were all huddled together. "Pretty sure there's some hormone overload going on right now."

I pointed my pen at Shye. "Yeah, with this one."

"Not surprising." Jinx flopped into a chair, keeping her eyes on the boys. "Alder looks pleased as punch."

"He is." Shye leaned back, turning her body to address us both. "He got word last night that the Black Angels are definitely gone."

All the air in the room seemed to disappear, and a hollow sort of ache appeared in my chest. "They're...gone?"

She nodded. "Apparently. Sherriff Grogan called to talk to him about the investigation into Sherriff Baker's death, and then told him the Black Angels had disappeared as well. Guess they'd been gone from Rock Falls for a few days already."

A few days. Parris hadn't been by in a few days either. Four, to be exact. I'd kicked him out, but I hadn't expected him to leave town. Not really. Not completely. Not without at least saying goodbye.

My heart...it actually *hurt*.

Meanwhile, Jinx sat there staring at me, an inscrutable expression on her face. One I wasn't comfortable with.

"What?" I asked her, unable to sit there and take her stare a moment longer.

She shrugged. "Finn saw Parris this morning."

Oh. That... I should not have felt as relieved as I did. "Here?"

"No, out at the motel. Finn ran out there to help Deacon with something and said he saw Parris out back." She didn't relax that hard stare for a single second. "I don't know what you did to that man, but I'm glad you did."

"I didn't do anything."

She raised an eyebrow—just one. "He was burning his colors."

That didn't make any sense, though. "I don't know what you're talking about."

Shye jumped in on that answer. "His club jacket—the symbol of him being a Black Angel. They're called colors."

"Right," Jinx said. "And he's destroyed his."

I was still not putting the pieces of the puzzle they were obviously building together. "So?"

"So, in two years, I've never seen him without that vest or coat on. He always wore his Black Angels gear. All bikers do. It's a sign of their connection to the club."

And he'd burned his—removed the biker part of himself from the equation. Maybe. Bikers didn't just walk away from their clubs, though. At least, not that I knew of. "I'm not sure why you're telling me this."

The other eyebrow joined the first in its raised status. "He wouldn't have destroyed his colors without a good reason. Seems to me a woman and child he's chasing after might be considered a good reason."

Doubt was a brat who refused to let go once she got her claws in you, and I doubted. I doubted hard. Parris hadn't even mentioned sticking around Justice, hadn't ever talked about the possibility of leaving the club for good. He'd never talked about any of that. I knew almost nothing of him except his real name. Chase Fowler.

A name I'd refused to use.

No, Jinx had to be wrong. Parris hadn't set that fire. There'd be no reason to because I'd given him no hope. I'd kicked him out like trash. A man like Parris likely wouldn't come back for more of that.

"I haven't even seen him in days." Which was true but didn't really stand as an argument to Jinx's statement. And she knew it.

"Look, you can keep fooling yourself all you want, but this is a big deal. Huge. Monstrous." She rose from her seat, focusing her attention on Finn once more. "Men don't make big changes like this often. And if you think that's not important, maybe you're not the woman I thought you were."

Shye glanced at me, looking almost embarrassed on my behalf. Not that I could blame her—I'd just been scolded by a young woman who didn't really know me. She knew my attraction to Parris, though.

Chase. His name is Chase.

Not that it mattered. I still had a son to take care of, to protect. And whether he was Parris or Chase, he didn't add into that future. Not when he kept walking away so easily. Not when he could bring danger back to our doorstep. Not when his life was so entangled in a group like the Black Angels.

I'm going to hear you say it in some vows

Vows, he'd said. Promises. Things I couldn't depend on when he was involved. There would be no happily ever after with Parris. No wedding and talk of babies like with Shye and Alder. There couldn't be, and that had to be okay. I had other commitments to fulfill, other priorities besides my own heart. I had a son I loved more than life, and I'd been raising him alone just fine. I could keep doing that. Dating could be put on hold, not becoming a possibility for me until Beckett went to college or something.

I was good at being alone. Just because I'd gotten a taste of a possibility didn't mean anything. I could ignore the craving for more.

I had to.

Chapter Twenty-Three

PARRIS

Saturday morning rolled in like a beast, bringing a sense of apprehension with it. It was party day, but there was more to it as well. Stuff to do before that evening event. The mission I wanted Deacon with me for? Today was the day.

Time to kill off Parris for good.

"You ready?"

Deacon had asked me that question six times already, and every time I'd given him a halfhearted sort of affirmative answer. Was I ready to completely walk away from my old life and start a new one? Yes. Definitely. I'd destroyed both my vest and my jacket with the Black Angels colors days ago, saving one patch for today, for this last mission. I also hadn't bothered answering Cartel's messages or any from the Vegas crew. That wouldn't be enough, though. Not by a long shot. If I disappeared, they'd come looking for me, which wasn't an option. Not if I wanted a life with Mercy. Leaving the club would require more than ghosting. I needed freedom, and there was only one way to escape—I was going to have to fight my way out. And Deacon was going to help me.

"Hell yeah, I'm ready." I grabbed the last of the guns Deacon had brought—the man was quite literally an armory of all things dangerous—and tucked it into my shoulder harness. Ready and armed.

"That's what I've been waiting to hear." The sniper smacked me on the shoulder before he walked out of the motel where we'd spent the previous evening strategizing. "Let's go fuck up a warlord and get you evicted from the Black Angels."

If only it were going to be that easy.

Deacon took the job of driving us to Sterling, where I'd learned Cartel was still hanging out. Not the diner this time, though. Apparently, he'd moved on from there to some bar that had been closed for a couple of years. Hiding like a rat in an abandoned hole. Typical. That info had cost me three favors, ones I was happy to trade in. I likely wouldn't need any more after today. At least, I hoped. Once I'd known where the man had taken up residence, I'd sent him a text. A quick *We need to meet*. No sense trying to take him down blind—let him know we were coming. Let him think he had a shot at regaining control over me. Besides, subterfuge required time, and that was a luxury I definitely did not have. I wanted this done. Today.

We spent the ride in silence, both of us quiet. Contemplative. Preparing in our own ways. I knew what was coming at the end of this ride—blood. Mine or Cartel's, death or not quite. You had to shed blood to leave a club, and though I'd already been stabbed this week, that wouldn't be enough. Cartel might kill me. He might kill Deacon, too. This wasn't going to be easy.

Pulling up outside a bar on the edge of town, I could see why Cartel had chosen it. No way would anyone come bother him there—it was too much of a dump. An abandoned shack with holes in the roof and boarded-up windows. This would be the place where Parris died.

"One last chance, man. You sure you're ready?" Deacon asked, staring straight ahead at the door. The hardest, meanest look I'd ever seen the man wear on his face. "We can't go in there half-cocked."

"I'm ready." I checked out the building again, the sag to the doors, the general feeling of abandonment and disrepair. This was as good a place to die as any. "Mercy and Beckett deserve better than all this."

Deacon cut the engine. "So do you, Parris. You deserve better, too."

But that wasn't true. I'd chosen this life. I'd lived it, loved it, and relished the brutality of it. I wasn't an innocent man by any stretch. Mercy and Beckett? Totally innocent, and no way was I fouling up their goodness with this shit. I had a lot of repenting to do once I left Parris behind.

We hopped out of the truck and sauntered for the door. Both of us wary and watchful. I noticed Deacon's hand resting awfully close to the pistol on his hip. I also couldn't help but keep my own tucked under my jacket—my non-Black Angels leather coat —for easy access to what was in my shoulder harness. My left hand hovered over the pocket where I kept my blade. I totally believed in taking a knife to a gunfight so long as that wasn't the *only* weapon you brought. I liked to use my blade as a scare tactic, a little reminder of how bad things could get. How slow death could come. Bullets were hella faster and often less painful if the shooter hit the right spot. Sometimes, you needed to make a point.

"Roof's clear," Deacon said, just before we walked under the awning over the door. "Doesn't look like a man on the door either."

I noticed the same thing. "Low security."

"Or not and we're about to find out."

As he reached for the door, I slipped my fingers over the handle of my pistol and nodded once, prepared to pull and fire if necessary. We were ready for an ambush. We didn't get one.

Instead, we walked into the bar as if nothing bad were about to happen, made it all the way inside without issue. Either Cartel was too confident in his ability to control me or he was stupid. I'd never called the warlord anything other than cunning, so this whole bar scene with no real security? An act. A play he was putting on. Nothing but a show.

Two Black Angels sat at the bar, both angled just right so they could keep an eye on the door and still have the man of the hour in their periphery. Ever the showman, Cartel sat at the back in what looked like a dark, pleather-upholstered booth. Like some sort of movie mob boss, alone under a pendant lamp, the golden glow almost making him appear softer than I knew him to be. I wouldn't fall for that, though. There were shadows surrounding him, seeping inside at every moment. The man was a demon wearing a halo, and that was something I couldn't forget.

"Is he putting on a show?" Deacon asked in a whisper as we moved toward the ridiculous booth.

"Seems like it."

He grunted. "At least he's got style."

And a bad attitude. Cartel did not look happy.

"Where are Edge and Ravel?" the warlord asked right away, not even giving us time to sit down.

That was fine. I had his answer ready.

"Dead. But you know that." I slid into the booth, Deacon doing the same but across from me. Cartel's frown deepened as he watched us, and he suddenly seemed to realize his needing to be the center of attention—therefore sitting in the literal center of the booth—had ended with him being surrounded. I was on one side of the booth and Deacon on the other. The man had no way out except over or under the table.

He kept the act up, though. Kept that superior tone in his voice as he chastised me. Or tried to. "I want to know what happened in Rock Falls. No one gave the Vegas crew the okay to retreat. Their leaving caused every chapter we'd brought to follow suit. All my Angels are gone."

"I gave the order to leave." I sat back, throwing my arm over the back of the booth. Intentionally casual. "What else do you want to know?"

"On whose authority?"

"Mine. The prez and his VP were dead in an obvious ambush, and their warlord was missing. I sent the crew back to their Vegas house to save some lives."

Cartel's sneer peeked out, his anger still a palpable thing. "And the warlord—Tiny, I believe?"

As if he didn't know everything about the man, likely including shoe size and favorite brand of underwear. "He's dead too."

"How?"

I couldn't answer the man because Deacon made a sound like a laugh and grinned. The motherfucker *grinned*—all toothy and white and...what the fuck?

Cartel even seemed to notice that look. "You got something to say, Sniper?"

"Not really, no. Well, maybe that your friend Tiny's dead. That's all." Deacon smiled wider, showing more teeth. Looking almost...dangerously happy. "He made the mistake of taking some locals hostage, so we killed him."

True, though obviously not what Cartel wanted to hear. He turned that viper gaze on me. "You murdered your brother?"

Yeah. That whole family line worked unless the man using it had assigned you to spy on your so-called siblings for the past few years. "He wasn't my brother. Besides, he took hostages specifically to hurt me, people from Justice he targeted because of me, so we took him out. It was that simple."

Cartel sat back, looking way too cocky for the situation. "He went for the hardware girl, so you threw a tantrum."

Motherfucker. "That woman and her son are protected by the people in Justice. Tiny knew the danger he was getting into messing with them, and not just from me. You go for Justice, and you'll have a full war on your hands."

Again. Just like when my sister had been murdered because of the club war he'd started. This carousel never seemed to stop.

Deacon didn't seem to be grinning anymore. He'd even stopped paying attention to what was going on in the booth, instead watching the guys at the bar with particular interest and his back almost fully to Cartel. Something even Cartel noticed.

"What say you, Sniper?" the national warlord asked, demanding Deacon's attention to come back to him. He even waited until Deacon turned to look at him before giving the sniper his snake-oil smile. "You think it's okay for Parris here to turn his back on his family and kill his own for something as simple as pussy?"

I wanted to tear the man apart for the implication and that pussy comment, but I didn't. I stayed in my seat with one hand on the table and the other resting against the top of the booth. Kept myself as relaxed as possible. I'd rip Cartel's throat out later —right now, we still had business to do. And part of that business was letting Deacon say whatever the fuck he wanted to say.

"Pussy is never simple," the sniper said, sounding far too sage for the man I knew him to be. "And your idea of family is fucked up. Tiny deserved to die, so he's dead. It was as simple as that."

Cartel did *not* look happy with that answer. "We take care of our own in the Black Angels."

"Bullshit," I said, barging my way back into the conversation before Deacon—the former Special Forces soldier—could light the man up about what taking care of your own actually meant. "You left those men you call *brother* to hang in the wind with a shit leader and a lot of fucking danger on their heels. You don't get to call them your family. And I'm done calling you mine." I dropped the Black Angels patch I'd been holding, my last official club item, on the tabletop and pushed it to the center, right underneath that damned pendant light, for Cartel to see. Never say he was the only showman in the club. "I'm done with the Black Angels. For good."

"You think you can walk away?" Cartel asked, his voice rising and growing shrill. "No one just leaves the family. I know you've been banging that chick at the hardware store—"

I grabbed the knife from my pocket and thumbed it open, stabbing the man in the hand and basically pinning him in place at the table. Deacon moved right along with me, almost in concert. As if we'd planned this out—which we actually had. He hopped to his feet, letting me deal with Cartel while he focused on the two guards, firing off three shots and, hopefully, hitting the two men who'd been at the bar with kill shots. I wasn't done with Cartel yet, though, so I couldn't be bothered to check on his success. Instead, I dove across the table and grabbed the warlord by the throat, yanking him closer. Getting right up in his face so he couldn't even see past me to know what the fuck was happening across the room.

"I'm going to tell you one time," I said, making sure each

word I spoke was imbued with my rage. "You go anywhere near that girl, you send anyone to Justice, you step one foot into Colorado ever again, and I won't just kill you. I'll fucking gut you and make you eat your own entrails."

Cartel's face had grown awfully red, and he seemed to have trouble breathing. Poor guy.

I tightened my grip on his neck. "Don't bother talking because I'm through listening to you. I spent five years in prison for this club. For you. My sister died because of a club war you started. You disrespected the brotherhood, the nomad patch I earned, and the club as a whole, but asked for more. I am done. I have given enough *to you*."

Cartel coughed, spitting on me as he choked and forcing me to loosen my hold just a bit. "You will live to regret this."

The man never had been smart about self-preservation, and I wasn't about to start a new life with my old one throwing such huge shadows. "Then I guess you won't live at all."

I shoved him back into the booth and pulled my gun, pointing it straight at Cartel's head. But I didn't shoot. That man had been a huge, negative part of my life for so long, it almost felt wrong to give him such an easy way out. To let him die a quick death.

"He won't ever stop," Deacon said, coming to stand behind me as I stared at the cowering warlord across the table. As if my pause were born of indecision. "You let him walk, and he'll be back."

"I know. I was just thinking this is too easy for him. He deserves to suffer more."

Deacon reclaimed his seat, frowning Cartel's way. "You think? Because we've got plans tonight, and I really would hate to be late."

True, and at the end of the day, the how didn't matter. Just like with Wolf, no matter who pulled the trigger or how they died, all that mattered was they were gone for good. "You're right. Say goodbye, Cartel."

His eyes widened. "Parris, don't—"

A single gunshot quieted him right down.

Deacon moved to stand beside me, looking over the table as Cartel's blood spread. Watching the same macabre sight I was. Finally, he sighed.

"We just invited a shitshow, didn't we?"

I shook my head. "Nope. I've got an out."

"An out?"

"Yeah. The national prez owes me a favor, and I'm calling it in."

Deacon didn't seem convinced. "Must be some big fucking favor."

"I stopped his assassination—so yeah, big."

"Well, okay then." He blew out a breath and cracked his neck. "Might as well tell his boss he was in on the whole selling kids thing as well. Make it real easy to cut ties with him."

Motherfucker, this man was brilliant. "Are you serious?"

"Cartel said it himself—trafficking kids isn't an approved activity for the club. Once your prez hears that not only was Cartel doing business with Soul Suckers who were in that sick shit, but also bringing legal attention on the club for it?" He tsked and shook his head, exaggerating the sound and motion for my benefit. "He'll be glad to be rid of the bastard."

Yeah. I had no doubt about that. "You are one smart SOB, you know that?"

"I do. Tell Alder—he needs to remember to bask in my greatness sometimes."

"I wouldn't go that far."

Deacon and I worked side by side to clean up our mess,

which involved a fuckton of accelerant, a broken propane cylinder, and what was essentially a Molotov cocktail made from a bottle of Jack Daniel's we killed to celebrate the end of what we considered a successful mission. We changed out of our clothes, piling the dirty ones in the middle of the floor and dousing them in gasoline. Left the guns behind too. No sense having that particular trail leading to either of us. It took long enough to finish setting the bar up to burn that the sun was just starting to bathe the sky in the golden tone of sunset as we stepped outside. Deacon took the honor of actually lighting the place up, tossing the cocktail in through the window before hauling ass across the parking lot for his truck. It didn't take long for smoke to pour out as the fire really began to build. We just had to wait for the place to go boom.

I leaned against the truck, watching the sky darken over the bar. Looking out across all that dead lumber in the distance. "Should we be worried about a forest fire?"

"It's handled."

That, I hadn't known. "Handled how?"

"I know people." Deacon shrugged, as if having people to come deal with a fire where bodies burned inside was totally normal. "They'll be here in a few to keep the fire contained."

"Sounds like loose threads that could come back to tangle us up."

"They're Zane's guys. They can be trusted."

Zane, the sheriff who'd help us save Mercy and Beckett from Tiny. Yeah. They could be trusted, all right.

Just then, a loud boom came from within the bar, the entire building seeming to expand and then collapse back in on itself. I almost wanted to applaud with how well that whole thing had gone.

"Looks like we're done."

"Yup." Deacon slid into the driver's seat of his truck and waited until I got in on my side to start the engine. "By the way, again with the entrails?"

"I like to be consistent."

"You like to be dramatic." He rolled out of the lot, leaving the burning building behind us. Leaving my past there, too.

Parris of the Black Angels had died in that fire, right along with Cartel and his two guards. And I was going to prove it. "Yeah, well...you want to see drama, just wait."

"For what?"

"I'm getting my girl back."

Deacon's smile grew slowly, as if he were fighting it. "How you going to do that?"

That was the question of the day. "Don't know exactly, but first things first—I gotta get a fucking suit for this wedding."

"You got a week, son." He pressed on the gas, speeding down the highway toward Justice. "Speaking of which, we're late. If there's one thing I am loath to do, it is break my word. I promised Shye I'd be there to keep Alder in line. I can't let her down."

For Alder and Shye's joint bachelor/bachelorette party at Katie's restaurant. The one I'd only found out about the day before yesterday. The one Deacon had basically demanded I attend...as his date. Where Mercy would definitely be and likely Beckett, too.

Oh hell, why the fuck not?

"Let's go, then." But Deacon's little comment about keeping his word struck something inside of me, a deal I'd almost forgotten about. A bit of information in a little black book I'd snapped a picture of for safekeeping. I had one more thing I needed to do as Parris, one more promise to fulfill. One more favor to put in my pocket for later. I sent the picture in question to a friend, asking if he had any information on the man. I had the last known location of the Soul Sucker named Coyote who Finn Kennard had been chasing and had traded in some larger favors to have him redirected—I just needed to confirm that plan was in play.

I didn't expect an answer right away, so I tucked my phone into my pocket and hoped to make it to the party in time. I had a new life to begin, starting right then.

"By the way—my name's Chase. Chase Fowler."

Deacon glanced my way, not at all surprised by that particular subject change. "Nice to meet you, Chase. Welcome to Justice."

Yeah, that sounded good.

Chapter Twenty-Four

MERCY

Bachelor and bachelorette parties had never been my thing. Not that I'd gone to many of them, but there had been a few drunken nights with friends celebrating upcoming nuptials before Beckett had come along. The whole wearing penises and watching strange men strip for money had never appealed, though. Thankfully, that wasn't anything like what Alder and Shye were doing. In fact, this might have been the only bachelor/bachelorette party I would have ever felt comfortable taking Beckett to. He'd even gotten his own invitation.

"Beckett," I yelled as I clipped my earrings into place. "Are you ready to go?"

"Mommy." My buddy came racing into the bathroom with a huge smile on his face. "Mister Gage came to walk us to the party. Can I go downstairs to show him my ramp-jumping skills?"

One bike, and my kid had somehow become a BMX champion in his mind. "Sure. But don't get dirty, okay?"

"Okay." He took off, disappearing down the hall in a blur of motion and stomping feet.

"And stay with Mister Gage!" I yelled, the idea of him being out of my sight not sitting well with me. I still wasn't over the incident at Sam's house, still couldn't stand to be away from Beckett for more than his school hours, and even those were spent with my worrying. In fact, I had no intention of letting him out of my sight for long tonight. I needed to finish getting ready and join him in the alley.

I applied a little extra pink lipstick and took one last look in the mirror. Good enough. It wasn't as if I were going to find some sort of sexy Prince Charming at the party anyway. A thought that stabbed a little in all sorts of places I didn't want to think about.

"Could be worse," I said to my reflection, tidying up the counter before turning for the door. "You could be forced to wear a tiara covered in dicks tonight."

Feet in painful heels that I'd likely kick off at some point in the evening and keys in hand, I headed downstairs. The wrap dress I wore was one of my favorites because it showed off my figure without being too revealing. If I were being honest, I'd have to admit that I'd picked it in the hope Parris would show up at Katie's tonight. Not that I was about to be honest with myself. My pretty dress had nothing to do with that man.

And I was a damn liar.

I also was *not* prepared to see the man in question when I made it to the alley.

And—oh, my heart—he was working with Beckett on his ramp jump.

"Mommy," Beckett yelled, his smile lighting up the entire alley. "Mister Parris came to visit me."

"I see that." I crossed my arms over my chest, covering myself as if that could keep the man from affecting my heart. "How about we head down to the party, buddy? We're already late, and Uncle Alder will be waiting for you."

"Okay." He jumped off his bike and bumped knuckles with Parris. "Thanks for the help. I'm getting good, right?"

"You totally are, little man. You'll be tearing up the trails come spring." Parris rose to his feet, watching with me as Beckett practically skipped down the alley. Inching closer, too. "He looks good."

God, his voice made everything inside of me clench. "He is."

"No nightmares or anything?"

"Only for a night or two. He seems to be back to his normal self now."

"Good, that's good." Parris led the way toward the rear entrance to The Baker's Cottage, his steps slow and measured. Not pushing me to go any faster than I planned to. "And how are you, Mercy?"

Mercy. Not beauty. I had no idea his using my real name could hurt, but it did.

"I'm fine."

He chuckled. "Woman, I am not so ignorant as to believe you mean fine when you say *fine.*"

I laughed along with him, unable to argue the point. But the moment passed, the lightheartedness dissipating in the chilly October night. Left in its wake? An emptiness that I'd been battling all week.

One I was tired of fighting. "I thought you'd left."

"Nope."

One word. That was all he gave me. Which would never be enough.

"What are you doing here?"

"I made your boy a promise, and I'm keeping it." He gave me

that look—the one that sizzled, the one that made my pulse quicken and my breaths come faster. "I made you one, too."

Oh, my heart. He was going to steal it if I wasn't careful enough to hide it.

"Parris, I—"

"Don't tell me no just yet. I know I need to do some apologizing, maybe even some groveling." He bumped my shoulder softly, releasing me from his gaze. "But that's going to have to wait for a few more hours. Tonight isn't about my fuckups and all the things I'm going to do to fix them. It's about Alder and Shye, and I respect that. I'll start on you tomorrow."

He walked me the rest of the way to the restaurant in silence. Not really together. Not at all apart. He never pushed for more, though. Never demanded anything I wasn't already giving him, which at that point was nothing more than my time. And when we reached the door, he held it open for me before circling my arm as he moved past. His warm hand massaging my flesh, the touch half tease, half demand, and altogether confusing. And then he used his other hand to tuck a lock of hair behind my ear, and I almost swooned. *This man.*

"I know you're going to be helping Katie tonight, so I'll leave you alone. But you look good, Mercy. Damn good." He gave my traitorous arm—the one that liked his touch far too much—another squeeze. "Grab me if you need anything. I'll be walking you home."

Then he was gone, and I was left to pull myself together. To watch him walk away while the scent of him still lingered around me. Damn that man and his smell and touch and heat. His stupid charming nature. He could get under my skin like no other, but nothing had really changed, had it? He was still Parris, and I was still a mom who couldn't let my son be around someone so dangerous.

Nothing had changed. Not even my feelings for the man.

I did not have time to worry about all that.

"Okay, Katie," I said, lifting my chin and striding into the work area of the kitchen, shoving all thoughts of Parris and bikers and lost chances out of my mind. "We've got half an hour before this thing truly starts. Let's get this show on the road."

Chapter Twenty-Five

PARRIS

Mercy Bell wearing that dress and those shoes was going to be the death of me. No fucking doubt about it. She looked good. Too good. I was going to be fighting a hard-on all night long, not exactly what I'd planned for the evening.

"Parris," Gage said as he sidled up beside me and handed me a beer. "What's doing?"

"Not much, man." I nodded my thanks and took a swig, looking over the room. "Katie's done a great job here tonight."

"She always does. You planning on sticking around now that the Black Angels are gone?"

Direct. To the point. No bullshit. I liked that. "Yup."

He nodded. "Good. Because that kid is like family."

I got his point. Quite clearly, in fact. "I'm not going anywhere."

His dark eyes locked on to Katie as she appeared from the

kitchen, a dog following along behind her as if on guard duty. Which he likely was, knowing Gage.

"Any worries about tonight?" I looked over the room, finding Beckett quickly enough but not Mercy. "Anything I need to watch out for?"

"Just the usual." Gage sighed and shook his head. "I told her not to carry those big trays. Her hand is still healing."

I followed his gaze, spotting Katie and the big tray in question. She looked capable enough, but that didn't mean much with a man like Gage. Not that I could blame him—if it had been Mercy carrying something that large, I'd have been rushing across the room to help her.

"Go on," I said, nodding toward the woman. "You know you want to."

"She's cranky with me right now." He settled back, the tension around him almost a physical thing. "Says I've been too helpful, as if that's a thing."

"She's healing, you said."

"Yeah, from a nasty burn. Her hand still gets tired."

I shrugged. "I'll go in your place."

Gage whipped his head in my direction, that near-black stare deadly. "She won't want you to help her."

"So? Then she gets cranky with me instead of you. I see that as a win on your part. Besides, I owe you for taking care of Mercy and Beckett while I've been—"

"Stuck with your head up your ass?"

Okay. I deserved that one. "Something like that."

He nodded, then seemed to chew on my idea for a moment. "Okay. Just...don't let her carry anything heavy."

"Done." I took a couple steps in Katie's direction before turning back around. "Thanks for the beer, and the name's Chase."

If the beard movement was any indication, the man smiled. "Good to know you, Chase. Don't fuck up around my girl."

Direct again. I headed across the room, nodding and saying hello when greeted but not stopping. I had a woman to rescue from herself. One who definitely should not have been carrying a tray that looked to weigh about half as much as she did.

As soon as I reached Katie, I lifted the tray from her hands. Smiling. "Let me."

"Oh," she said, looking perplexed. "Parris, hi. You don't have to do that."

"This tray is almost as big as you. Let me help."

She glanced over my shoulder. "Did Gage send you?"

See, this was where being a skilled liar could have come into play. Could have, but I chose the truth just this once. "Yes, but don't be mad at him. He's worried about your hand."

She smiled just enough for me to know she wasn't really mad. "He's always worried about me."

"Good men take care of the women they love. He can't help himself."

I caught a glimpse of Mercy for just a second before she disappeared into the crowd again. Something Katie seemed to notice.

"You can't take care of her if you're disappearing." She shrugged when I whipped around in her direction. "Just calling it like I see it."

"I have no plans to disappear again."

"Good. Because she deserves more than being left behind to protect her. Not all of us need that sort of protection—we've gotten pretty good at taking care of ourselves over the years." She turned her hand over, the burns Gage had mentioned obvious. The placement and shape clearly that of a handle of some sort. Knowing her job and the story about the explosion in the restaurant, my guess would be a heavy pan that had gotten awfully hot. Not a mistake many professional chefs would make.

My respect level for the bubbly brunette skyrocketed. "I hear you loud and clear, miss."

"Good. Now don't tell Gage, but my hand is really starting to cramp. Think you could haul a couple more things for me?"

"As you wish." And with that, I was put to work as a pack mule, hefting trays and stocking the bar for her. With every passing minute, the restaurant filled up a little more, seemingly everyone from this small town showing up to wish the couple luck in their upcoming marriage. No Deacon, though. I'd left him back at the motel to get ready, so I had no idea why he'd be so late. I just hoped he hadn't run into trouble.

I had pulled my phone out to see if the man had texted me, when an incoming message alert lit up the screen. I quickly swiped through, the name one I hadn't expected to hear from today. The information something I'd been waiting on.

"Someone sending you nudes?" Deacon strolled up beside me, looking pale but awake.

"Only one person I want nudes from, but she'd better not be taking any. You never know who's going to hack in to your phone and see what they shouldn't." I typed out a quick response. "Seen Finn?"

"No, but I just got here. Snuck in through the back."

"You hiding from someone?"

"Not really. Just..." He sighed, his shoulders hunching slightly. "It's been a long fucking week."

The man had never spoken a single word that held more truth than that. "We did it, though. Got rid of the Black Angels."

"And the kiddie traffickers."

"And those fuckers."

Deacon nodded. "We're rock stars at this. We should be winning awards and shit."

"And the winner of the best sniper of the year is…" I chuckled, typing out a message to Finn. Fulfilling my side of our arrangement.

"Why do you want Finn, anyway?"

"I found someone he's been looking for."

"This have to do with the fire at Camden's?"

It was my turn to nod. "From what I understand, yeah."

"You find the guy who set it?"

"Sure did."

"We taking him out?"

I glanced at the sniper, having hit send. "This is a Finn project. I don't know why, but he's got a hard-on for this Coyote guy."

"Camden is Finn's best friend."

Yeah, okay. That made a fuckton of sense. "I think we should leave this up to those two. Let them know we're here to help but not take it over."

Deacon looked around the room, his expression pensive. "They're just kids. They might fuck it all up."

"Or they might not and find the closure they need."

"You getting all Dr. Phil on me?"

As if. "No, fucker. I'm just—"

I spotted Jinx and Finn across the room talking to Alder. My internal checklist practically sang, seeing Jinx reminding me that I had a mess with her to clean up. A conversation that needed to happen. If I was going to stay in this town where Jinx had quite obviously also chosen to be, I needed to put some shit behind me.

"Everything okay?" Deacon asked.

"Yeah. I just need to talk to Jinx."

"You had to text Finn, and now you need to talk to Jinx. Next thing, you'll be wanting to get Mercy alone."

I shot him a raised eyebrow. "Don't I always?"

His laugh exploded out of him, startling a few people nearby and gaining some serious attention. Specifically from the future groom.

"You better watch it," I said, tilting my head in Alder's direction. "Looks like he's coming for you."

Deacon sobered up, adopting an easy smirk. One that almost hid the dark circles under his eyes. "Go on, Chase. Go find Jinx and have your conversation. I'll distract this jackass."

"I thought he was your best friend?"

"He is. Doesn't make him any less of a jackass."

Alder picked that moment to reach us. "It's about time you got here."

But Deacon wasn't taking the bait. "Alder, this is Chase. Chase, Alder."

Alder looked from me to him and back again, his brow tight. "What the fuck are you talking about?"

I smacked Deacon on the shoulder. "You're on your own. Good to see you, Alder. Shye."

I took off before anyone could stop me, heading toward the front of the restaurant. I tucked myself into a corner and waited, keeping my eyes on Jinx and Finn. Giving them time to talk to Finn's brother Bishop while I kept a surreptitious watch on Mercy. She had joined Beckett at the bar where he was playing with some sort of tractor toy. The two of them shared a few laughs and a hug, making me miss them even more. Making my heart hurt in ways I wasn't prepared for.

List. Focus on the list.

Lots of shit to get done still. Lots of things to do before Mercy would even think of taking me back. And first up on that list was talking to Jinx, who had just walked away from the people she'd been talking to with Finn at her side. Jackpot.

"Hey," I said as soon as I reached the couple, giving Finn a handshake. "You got my text."

He nodded once. "Yeah. Thanks. Whatever you need in return—"

"Nah," I said, holding up my hand. "This one's on me."

Jinx frowned. "You never give up being owed a favor."

I caught Mercy's eye for just a second, spotted her looking at me. That moment, that slight connection, gave me hope for more. And more meant staying. And staying meant being friendly with the neighbors, including Finn Kennard. "This one, I will. Consider it a gift."

The tattooed girl's smile fell when she caught my eye, and those walls she'd put up to protect herself from me locked into place. Jinx always had been a hard nut to crack, and apparently today would be no different. "What is it you want?"

Nothing, but that wasn't the question I wanted to answer. Not anymore. With Mercy and Beckett firmly on my mind, I opened my mouth and let loose the secrets that technically weren't mine to tell. That were the Black Angels' and would be seen as a betrayal to them if it was ever discovered I'd blabbed. The ones that mattered most to the girl before me.

"Ravel killed your mom." I waited as her eyes widened, as she jerked back and grabbed Finn's hand. Gave her a second to take that in before I spilled the rest even though my neck felt about a hundred degrees too hot. "She was a good woman so I tried to get her off the drugs, but the guys would feed her more every time my back was turned. Her addiction got worse and worse, but she was smart, you know? She paid attention. She caught Edge with a girl way too young to be legal, and she didn't like it. She made sure he knew she didn't like it, so he ordered her death. I don't know where her body is, but I know they killed her. And I'm real fucking sorry I couldn't tell you that before."

She took a deep breath, her eyes growing red. Tears building in the corners. "You're an asshole for not telling me."

"I know, and though I don't deserve your forgiveness, I'm sorry." I nodded to Finn, feeling like shit for ruining their evening, before heading for the kitchen to hide out so she could process all that without me in the way.

But before I could reach the door, Jinx hurried up behind me and grabbed my arm. Stopping me in my tracks.

"Thank you," the little gray-eyed beauty said, looking so much like a younger, healthier version of her mom that it made my breath catch. "I needed to know what happened to her."

"I know you did, and I'm so sorry I didn't tell you sooner. That was a club secret, but it wasn't worth honoring anymore."

She nodded, squeezing my arm one last time before returning to Finn. I watched them come together—watched him wrap his arms around her little frame and tug her in close. Watched him protect her. She would be fine with him. I'd broken through her last connection to the Black Angels. Her prison sentence was over.

And mine was somehow just beginning—my prison sentence of being surrounded by men like Deacon Manns.

"Hey, my date is here." Deacon held up a glass filled with dark liquid and grinned, Alder standing at his side. "Good to see you, Chase. Where you been?"

As if I hadn't just left his side a whole five minutes ago. "Deacon. Alder. It really hasn't been that long."

But the eldest Kennard wasn't paying any attention to me. "Who the fuck is Chase?"

Deacon tilted his glass in my direction. "This big lug."

"You going by your real name now?"

I gave myself a second to take a breath, to prepare for any feelings of loss or anxiety over using the name my parents had given me as a baby. Over losing the identity I'd built with the Black Angels.

Nope. No feelings about all that whatsoever. "Yeah, I am."

He nodded, almost frowning. "Mercy know this?"

"She's—" *gorgeous, stunning, killing me, ignoring me, angry, everything I have ever wanted in a woman, and totally not giving me the time of day* "—not really calling me anything right now."

Alder's smirk snuck up on his face, and he lifted his own glass of dark liquid to his lips. "Should we expect some groveling?"

I grabbed a beer from a passing waitress, taking a swig before throwing a grin his way. "Probably not tonight, but yeah. Definitely."

I just hoped it worked.

Chapter Twenty-Six

MERCY

Parris kept his promise. Two of them, actually. First, he didn't even attempt to make amends or hog my attention at the party. He mingled instead, hanging out with Alder and Deacon mostly. But his eyes—they stayed on me. There were moments when I could practically feel the weight of his stare. I'd look around, and there he'd be—watching. Keeping watch. I caught him playing with Beckett and helping Katie, too. Entertaining my son and running food back and forth while I kept the party flowing. Being quite the good neighbor and friend, to be honest.

The second promise he kept was to walk me and Beckett home that night. He didn't push me then either, simply asked how the party had gone for me and if I'd had a good time. And when we'd gotten to my door? Still no pressure. A simple goodnight, a hug for Beckett, and a kiss on the cheek for me before he shooed us up the stairs.

The non-forceful Parris was going to take some getting used to.

Which was the main thought in my head the next morning as I stood in my kitchen, clutching that first, blissful cup of coffee. Beckett hadn't even woken up yet, and the silence felt downright luxurious. Even the quiet buzzing of my phone vibrating in the other room couldn't annoy me. Work could wait.

I finished my coffee and rinsed out my mug before heading into the bedroom to retrieve my phone. But when I brought the device to life, it wasn't all email notifications on the lock screen. Most were, but there were also a couple of text messages. From Parris.

I was hoping to take Beckett on a bike ride today. Let me know if that's okay with you and what time.

I stared at those words for a long time, not sure what I was feeling. What I should do. The next message only added to my confusion.

You're welcome to come too, of course. I thought you might want to get some work done.

And then...

I can ask Gage or Deacon to hang with us in case you don't want Beckett alone with me.

That one stole my breath. Did I want Beckett alone with Parris? I bit my lip, thinking over my plans for the day. It really would be helpful to be able to focus for an hour or so, but the danger...the possibility of bikers coming into town and snatching him from me. I just didn't know.

Parris texted again before I answered.

I promise to keep him safe.

That one. That text did it, gave me the ability to take a deep breath and type out a response.

Sure. Sounds good. How about after lunch?

Perfect. See you then.

And just like that, I'd put at least a little bit of faith back in the man. Not a lot—I wasn't about to let him back in my bed, but he could hang with Beckett for an hour or so. Close by. Where I could keep an eye on them.

Because I may have been able to breathe, but I wasn't yet willing to trust.

———

Beckett liked to scream as he rode over the little jump ramps Gage and Alder had built for him. I hadn't even realized how much that sound soothed me as I worked, how hearing him yelling and laughing from the alley kept me calm. At least not until I stopped hearing it.

It took me a minute to understand why my anxiety had started creeping up, why that fight-or-flight sensation had begun taking over my body. The silence grated on my nerves until I couldn't take it anymore, so I got up and headed toward the alley door. Just one glance, one moment to check in on Beckett. To make sure everything was okay.

What I was met with was more than just okay.

Parris had my son across his lap and Beckett's sleeve pulled up to expose a scraped elbow. My baby's cheeks were pink with tearstains, but that wasn't what gutted me. It was the words I could just barely hear Parris whispering.

"It's okay, little man. There's nothing wrong with crying."

Beckett sniffled, not even noticing me standing ten feet away. "The kids at school say boys don't cry."

"Well, they may be right. *Boys* don't cry—but men do. And you're a little man, right?"

"Yeah."

"So then, it's okay for you to cry. Don't bottle that up. If something hurts, you cry."

My son, my beautiful, kind, happy boy looked up at the big man holding him. "Do you ever cry?"

"Yeah, I do. When something hurts, I cry." Parris looked up, catching my eye and giving me a wink. "All better yet? Think you're ready to get back to it?"

"What if I fall again?"

"Then you fall. And you get up and try again. A good man doesn't just give up."

Words for my son and yet somehow, I felt they were for me, too. I crept back inside as Parris set Beckett on his feet, giving them their time together. Letting Beckett have his little independence from me. But I found myself thinking of that moment a lot, enough so that I couldn't get any work done. In fact, I was sitting and staring at my computer screen when the two busted in through the alley door, creating chaos around me.

"I'm starving," Beckett yelled, jumping at me. "Feed me, Mommy."

Parris shrugged, his grin slightly sheepish. "Sorry about that. Apparently, riding his bike gives him an appetite."

Beckett used both hands to grab my face and pulled me close enough for our noses to touch as he got super serious. "Starving. Need food."

A jangling noise caught my attention, and I pulled away from Beckett to see Parris standing across the room. His keys were in his hand. That fact had my stomach plummeting.

"Going somewhere?"

His lips twitched as if he wanted to smile, like he'd heard the unhappiness in that question of mine.

"I was thinking it might be fun to head to the truck stop for dinner." He fidgeted with his keys, looking suddenly uneasy. Not at all like the confident man I was used to. "I'd like to take you two out."

Beckett looked at me, his eyebrows raised. "Can we go, Mommy?"

I shrugged, still watching Parris. Still wondering what he was up to. "Sure. I didn't want to cook anyway."

But as soon as Beckett was far enough away not to hear me, I took advantage of the privacy.

"Is it safe?" To be so far from Justice. To basically be in Rock Falls. To hit up a place where there might be bikers to deal with.

"Definitely. I won't let anything happen to you or him." He met my gaze, his eyes burning into mine. "Ever. I promise you that."

Well then. "Okay."

———

Dinner went well, better than I could have imagined. Parris had focused on Beckett while still involving me in the conversation, and man—my kid was funny. The night was filled with good laughs and good food and a sweet kiss on the cheek before Parris left us at the alley door. The man was holding back, not pushing me, and being the most respectful gentleman I'd ever encountered.

I was ready to climb that big body like a tree.

Not that I would any time soon.

The next morning, I woke up to a number of text messages. All from Parris.

I currently live in the motel attached to The Jury Room. I don't consider it a home, but I'm on the hunt for something more suitable for my plans. Maybe something up in the mountains a bit.

Something about that message pinged at a memory, but it wasn't strong enough for me to grasp. I didn't respond—unsure how to or what to say to that. It didn't help that I had a lot to do anyway. Mondays meant school drop-off and work and pickup and all the things that kept busy moms busy. And while Parris didn't interrupt any of that, he kept sending me messages. Ones that made me think he had a plan.

I've mostly done security work as a way to make a living for the past few years, but I'm retiring from that. I'm not sure what I'm going to do going forward. Need a stock boy?

I stared at that one, my memory pinging louder. Something about an argument and Parris leaving. Something about—

And by security work, I mean being a soldier for hire. I just want to make sure I answer all your questions as honestly as I can.

My questions. The memory of our fight, of me throwing questions at him rapid fire, of not getting answers—he was actually answering me. He'd remembered. I didn't know what to do with that.

All through the day and into the dinner hour, he sent me answers to the things I'd asked.

I didn't wear a city patch because I'd earned a nomad patch by saving the life of the Black Angels' national president. It meant I could ride anywhere and not be tied to a home club. When I came to Justice. I'd been with the Vegas crew for two years.

Even after dinner.

My real name is Chase Fowler, as I told you. I was given the road name of Parris because of being a Marine— Parris Island is where I attended basic training.

And one last message before bed.

I intend to stay in Justice as long as you don't kick me out. Forever, if you'll have me. This place offers the same sort of brotherhood I'd been missing since leaving the military, but it's not home. That honor sits with you. So, wherever you go, expect me to follow.

Sweet words. And yet, I couldn't respond.
Not for many hours.

Not until I woke up in the middle of the night, unable to fall back asleep. My mind repeatedly circling on all he'd told me. All he'd said.

So I grabbed my phone, and I sent him a text.

Thank you for all of that.

It didn't feel like enough, but it was all I could handle. His response came within seconds.

You're welcome. Get some sleep, beauty.

And all was right with the world...for the moment.

———

The day of the wedding dawned bright and warm—the perfect fall day to say I do. I was up early to deal with all the little details I needed to check off to make sure the day went off without a hitch. Even after a night of girl time with Shye, Anabeth, and Katie, I couldn't have slept in. Good thing there was coffee.

"Come on, buddy," I said, travel mug and clipboard in hand. "We should get to the restaurant to check in with Aunt Katie."

"Will Aunt Lainie be there?"

The youngest Kennard, the only girl in the family, and one of my best friends from high school. Also, the person who'd jumped at the chance to stay with Beckett at my place so I could party it up with the bride. Why she hadn't wanted to go... Well, I knew the reason. She had deep issues with her older brothers, Bishop and Alder, particularly. Hopefully, she'd get to know Shye, who was about as sweet as a person could be. I doubted, though. Lainie was good at holding grudges.

"Yeah, she'll be there." She'd told me so just that morning when I'd come slipping into the apartment at the butt-crack of dawn to get ready. "Hurry up—Shye is going to be taking over the apartment next door soon, and we don't want to be in her way."

We found Parris sitting at the bottom of the stairs by the alley door. Looking to all the world like a bodyguard at a club or something.

"What are you doing here?" I asked, too focused on all that needed to be done to hide my surprise.

"The bride is getting ready in Katie's old apartment today. I'm on guard duty." He looked me up and down, smiling slowly. "You look amazing, Mercy."

"Thanks. You look good in a suit."

He grinned. "I try."

Beckett high-fived the man, practically jumping to reach Parris' hand. "Hey, Mister Parris. You want to watch me ride my bike?"

Parris frowned. "I'm sorry, Beckett, but I can't play today. I've got to work."

"Oh." Beckett's smile faded, making my heart hurt. "That's okay. Maybe later."

"Definitely." Parris knelt before Beckett, leaning close. "I'll make you a deal—once the actual wedding shindig is over, I'll come to the reception. We can share some cake."

Beckett's eyes went super wide. "There's going to be cake?"

Parris' chuckle brought a smile to my face. "Little man, it's a wedding—there's always cake."

Beckett ran off, heading for the restaurant. Not going too far for my comfort, though. Still, I had one last thing to say.

"Thank you."

Parris frowned. "For what?"

"For being so kind to him. You've really made Beckett feel special these last few days."

"He should feel special. He's a really special kid."

He was, and knowing Parris saw that only made me like him that much more. "Well, thanks again, Parris."

I was halfway down the alley when he hollered, "It's Chase."

I spun, cocking my head. He didn't wait for me to reply, though.

"My name is Chase, and I'd really like to hear you say it sometime, beauty."

Much like the Grinch from my childhood, my heart grew three sizes. Or at least that's what it felt like inside of my chest. "Thank you, Chase."

He grinned, nodding once. "See you at the wedding."

"Yeah. Okay."

———

The good thing about weddings was that they eventually ended with people full and happy and in a great mood. Usually. At least, that's what happened with Alder and Shye's nuptials. Everyone seemed to be happy as could be when we shut the party down. Everyone except Beckett.

He was fast asleep.

"I've got this," Parris—no, Chase, though that would take me a long time to remember—said, stepping in front of me to pick up my sleeping son. The man had been pretty scarce all night, not partaking of any of the usual wedding traditions like the garter toss—caught by Gage—and dancing. I had actually missed him for that. The idea of Chase holding me against him for a slow dance or two had been something I'd been looking forward to.

Alas, the man had been asked to keep watch just in case, and I could understand that.

I could also be thankful that nothing bad had happened.

Parris carried my son into the alley, holding the door for me so I could follow.

"I can take him," I said, reaching for Beckett.

"It's fine. I was going to walk you home anyway."

"You don't have to do that. It's been a long day for you."

"I know I don't have to, but I want you two safe, so I will. Now walk, beauty. Or do you need to take off those shoes first?"

I glanced down at my heels. "I'm good."

"Then lead the way."

So I walked, all the while remembering the last few days with Parris—no, Chase. Thinking over every moment, every sweet gesture. Every second of wanting to give in and bring him back into my life. But I couldn't just do that—couldn't just break and give in. Not without getting a few answers.

So when he offered to carry Beckett up the stairs, I let him. And when he came back from tucking my boy in, I was ready.

Mostly.

"Why are you doing this?"

The man froze, looking as if he might be expecting a firing squad all of a sudden. "Doing what?"

"This. Spending all this time with us. Why are you doing it?"

He shrugged. "I promised Beckett."

"You promised to teach him to ride a bike. He knows how now."

He sighed, leaning against the doorway. "I'm trying to let you get to know me."

"I know you."

"No. You know Parris the biker. I want you to know Chase. The man."

Parris versus Chase. Something that reminded me of an earlier conversation. "Jinx said you gave up your club colors."

"I did."

No reason, no excuse. Just...done. "I assumed when you were texting me about your nomad patch that you'd go back to that life."

"Past tense."

"What?"

He shot me a steely gaze. "Those messages were in past tense—I was a nomad, I was allowed to ride wherever with no house affiliation. Was. Not anymore."

"I'm sorry you lost your...lifestyle."

He inched closer, stalking me like a predator, not letting up for a second. "The possibility of what I could gain is worth a fuckton more."

That wasn't enough. I needed more—details. Confirmation. "You gave them up—stopped riding with the Black Angels—for us?"

"Yeah. I did."

No excuses or hedging that truth. He'd changed his entire life, given up his place in a group he'd been part of for years and years. All for me. Well, me and my son. For our little family. He made it so hard to resist him.

"Beckett deserves to be loved," I said, no longer wanting to fight the feelings building within me.

Parris—no, Chase—didn't even hesitate. "I love that kid."

"He deserves stability."

"I'm stable as fuck."

I stepped closer, unable to hold back. Needing to feel him and soon. "He deserves—"

"What about you?"

"What about me?"

Par—*Chase*—closed the gap between us, towering over me. Enveloping me in his scent and his heat and just…him. "Beckett deserves the world, but what about you, beauty? What do you deserve?"

I couldn't hold back. I rose onto the balls of my feet and pressed a soft, sweet kiss to his lips. "I deserve a man who will fight the world for me then draw me a bath."

"I'm not afraid of a tub."

Of course he wasn't. He also wasn't afraid to grab my hips and tug me into his body. "I deserve someone who will break the arms of other men trying to grab my ass—"

"Done."

"I wasn't finished."

He slipped his hands down my hips and gave my butt a squeeze. "Sorry. You distracted me with talk of your ass. What else can I do for you, beauty?"

Good lord, I was about to melt. "I deserve a man who will stand up and fight for me but also let me do my thing, who will respect me and my boundaries, who won't cheat or lie or walk away."

He bent closer, shaking his head slowly. "Never again, Mercy. If you let me back in, I'll never leave you again. And I'd never cheat."

"How can I know that?"

"Because I swear it. On my life. This is me, groveling. Whatever you need to forgive me and let me try to build back that trust, I'll give it to you. I'll do it."

The claws of doubt lessened, the bloom of hope growing bigger and brighter, taking up so much room in my chest. "I deserve a man who is a good father to Beckett and a good protector of my heart."

"I am that man." Chase bent me over backward, leaning in to

kiss up the length of my neck. "Jesus fuck, beauty. I will be that man and more for you."

"Will you?"

"Yes. That's what I want. To prove to you that I'll be the man who shows up, who doesn't leave, and who will take care of you the way you deserve to be cared for." He pulled back, keeping hold of me but moving so he could look me in the eyes. "I know I've screwed up, but I'm done. Done with the lifestyle, with the clubs, and with walking away from my deepest desires. I want you and Beckett in my life. Every single day of my life. So if you let me, I'll do everything I can to be the man you both deserve. I'll try really fucking hard, beauty."

And really, what more could I ask for but for him to try? Words could sometimes have magic healing properties. The right apology, the correct phrase to ease an ache, the promises you had to take a leap of faith to believe.

Thankfully, I'd never been afraid of falling. So I leaped.

"You know what else I deserve?"

Chase hummed. "What's that?"

I ran my nose along his jaw and up so I could bite his earlobe before whispering, "A man who will make me scream his name."

He hoisted me up the length of him with a growl, pressing his hard cock right where I wanted him to be. Heading straight for my bedroom.

"That I can definitely do. But only under one condition."

"What's that?"

He set me down at the end of my bed, stripping me of my dress before shucking his shirt and pulling us back together. "The name you'll be screaming had better be Chase."

I reached between us, unfastening his suit pants. Pushing the fabric down his legs so I could cup him over his boxer briefs. "And if I forget?"

"We'll just have to start again." He picked me up and tossed me onto the bed, crawling up my body with a hungry expression on his handsome face. Thrusting inside and beginning those long, slow pulses that drove me absolutely out of my mind. Filling me with every inch of himself. Making me want to come so very quickly.

"We need a condom," I said, biting my lip as he angled himself to bump my clit. "Fuck, Parris."

He pulled out, growling as he bit my neck. Reaching for his discarded pants as he glared at me. "What's my name again?"

"Parris."

Head shaking, he sheathed himself before plunging back inside me. Fucking me hard and fast, virtually pounding me up the bed.

"Try again, Mercy," he said, gritting out his words. "What's my name."

But I wasn't brainless enough yet not to be willing to play with him. "Parris."

He grabbed my legs and pulled them up onto his shoulders, changing the angle and making me grip the bedsheets so I didn't go flying into the ether. My god, this man knew how to play my body. Every note, every stanza, was exactly what I needed. If I weren't so happy to have him back, I might have been embarrassed by how fast he could make me come.

"Try again," he said, slowing down and dragging his cock almost all the way out of me. "I want to hear it, beauty. I need it."

I shook my head, still playing. "You're going to have to earn that."

He tugged my legs onto one shoulder and twisted my hips, changing the position again to something even better. Something where he could slide deeper. The pressure of my closed legs teasing my clit in the best way.

"Oh, Ch—"

"Not now," he said. Still breathless. "If you say it now, I'm going to come."

Jackpot. "Oh, Chase. Come for me, Chase. I want to feel you, Chase."

He had to stop thrusting, he was laughing so hard, his face going red. "That was exceptionally not sexy. Are you ever going to take this seriously?"

I reached for his shoulders, pulling him down to kiss me. Groaning as the movement brought him deeper inside of me. "I will. I promise. Just...not tonight."

He nodded, moving his hips once more. Fucking into me as he released my legs so I could wrap them around him. "Okay. Not tonight. I can be patient."

"You can?"

"Sure. You'll get it right eventually. Besides." He slid a hand between us and rubbed his thumb against my clit, making me arch into him as I tried not to scream. "Messing up is going to be so much fun."

I had a feeling he was very, very right about that.

Epilogue

CHASE

Christmas had never been a big deal to me. When I'd been in the club, I'd spent it drinking with all the other single guys, enjoying a dinner usually provided by one of the old ladies, and basically trying to ignore the holiday since I didn't have a true family to celebrate with. I'd paid my dues that way.

This year, the very idea of Christmas morning might have been the most exciting thing I'd ever had to look forward to.

I stood in the kitchen in a house I owned, one that sat within the Justice city limits. One I'd moved both Mercy and Beckett in to less than a month before. It had been a fight to get her out of that apartment over the hardware store—Mercy was one hell of an independent woman—but I'd managed to make enough promises for her to take the risk, and I was planning on living up to each and every one. Starting with making sure I treated Beckett to the best Christmas possible.

"He's finally asleep." My beauty walked into the kitchen,

looking radiant and excited. So fucking beautiful, it hurt. I may have started our relationship being cocky as hell and saying she'd fall in love with me one day, but it still surprised me that she had. I would never, ever, take that woman for granted.

"You ready for this?"

She slipped into my arms, rising onto the balls of her feet to give me a kiss as I grabbed hold of her perfect ass. "You're going to help me, right?"

As if I wouldn't. "Of course."

"Then I'm ready."

I smacked that ass a little harder than just for play, a little lighter than I would later in bed. Much later. We had shit to do. "Let's go."

We headed out to the attached garage where I'd hidden Beckett's Christmas gift. A four-wheeler completely decked out that included lots of safety features and things to keep him protected, because no way would I ever be responsible for that kid getting hurt. It would gut me.

"I still think he's too young." Mercy scrunched her nose, looking over the big machine I'd bought for the boy.

"We'll start him off slow. He can ride around the backyard before we go into the woods."

"He hasn't even taken his bike onto the trails, and now he has a machine to drive on them."

"Two different skill sets. He'll have fun with both."

"And the other one?"

She meant the matching one I'd picked up for us to go out on the trails with him. More me than her, I figured. "We'll have fun with him."

"I think it's a big toy for you."

I shrugged, unable to deny that one. "Someone needs to be with him when he's out in the woods."

She shook her head, a smile defying that motion. She smiled a lot lately—more than she had before I'd made her move in with me. Not enough for me, though. I vowed to keep that look on her face, to make her happy every second I possibly could. I'd waited long enough for her to come into my life—I was willing to put in the work to deserve her.

"Come on, beauty. Let's get this set up in front of the tree."

We rolled the machine into the house, moving furniture and likely scratching some walls along the way. Not that we'd had any other choice—there was almost three feet of snow outside. Winter had hit the Front hard, and Justice was a quiet, almost unreachable town at the moment. Which was good—we'd had enough trouble with strangers on our roads and in our businesses. Hell, Mercy no longer opened the store without getting a call from a local or someone setting up a delivery. Her online business had far surpassed her hardware sales, though with me making deliveries for the store, that could change. Whatever —so long as she was safe and happy, we'd make it work. In store or online. It was why this house had appealed to me so much. There was a big pole barn in the back that we could use to stock and ship her artisan products. We'd even started experimenting with drop-shipping items direct from manufacturers around the world. Mercy thought up ideas, and I provided funding—mostly money I'd saved up during my biker days—and whatever support she needed. Win-win for both of us.

"Okay," she said as she finished attaching the giant bow to the front of the four-wheeler. "Now for Santa's gift."

I headed back out to the garage and unlocked the cabinet where I'd been storing the gifts. Mercy had been pretty adamant that any big gifts came from us, while Santa's gift had to be something small. It had taken us a bit to track down the perfect present for Beckett from Santa, but we had. And I'd been dying for him to open it ever since it had shown up at Deacon's house the week before. The man had mocked me, but I didn't care. Beckett would love it.

"Ho, ho, ho." I grinned, popping a Santa hat on my head before walking back into the family room. "You want to wrap this one or something?"

Mercy took the BMX biking teddy bear from my hands, giving it a squeeze. "I think I'll just put a bow on the bear like the four-wheeler. He's got enough presents to unwrap."

No doubt. The whole damn town had sent the kid presents. There weren't many young ones in Justice, though the population would be expanding soon enough. Bishop Kennard and his wife Anabeth had a baby due in the coming year, and I had a feeling Alder would be making a similar announcement soon enough. He'd been even more protective of Shye than usual. As had Gage with Katie. Which got me wondering.

"You think Katie's pregnant?"

Mercy blinked, looking surprised by my sudden question. "What makes you think that?"

"Gage seems super protective lately. So does Alder, actually. Maybe Katie and Shye are."

"Is that how you think men act when their wives are pregnant? Overprotective?"

I shrugged. "It's how I would act."

She nodded, looking thoughtful as she said, "It's past midnight."

That sudden subject change felt intentional, so I went with it. "Merry Christmas to us. Do you want your present now, beauty?"

"Only if I get to give you yours as well."

"Deal."

I grabbed her hand and tugged her to the couch,

straightening the Santa hat I wore along the way. "I'm going to admit this is more a present for me than for you."

"Really?"

"Yeah." I pulled the box I'd been carrying for days out of my pocket and took a deep breath. I suddenly felt more anxious than all the times I'd gone into battle. But just like then, this was life or death for me. And like those times, I'd do anything to make it out alive...with my girl at my side. "I love you, Mercy, and I love Beckett. Both of you bring so much joy to my life, and I want to be selfish. I want to hoard that happiness and never share it with anyone else. I want the two of you to be mine and mine alone. A real family. So selfishly, I'm asking you to marry me. I'll get you a better Christmas gift, too."

She started to cry, her hands shaking as she reached for mine. "You're such a beast."

"I know. But I'm your beast." I leaned closer. "At least, I hope I can be."

"Yes."

One word, and my heart went soaring. The woman had just given me the best gift, the ability to call her mine. Legally. I couldn't help but smile. And clarify. "Yes, I can be your beast?"

"Yes, I'll marry you, you asshole."

I grabbed her chin and laid a kiss on those lips I loved so much, feeling far too happy to speak. Far too grateful to put into words how much her answer meant to me. But I'd show her for sure, as soon as I got her naked.

"My turn," Mercy said, pulling away from me. Still dressed.

"Beauty," I said, sounding a lot like Beckett when he didn't get his way. "I have plans for us."

Her giggle only made me want her more, but she pushed me away. Again. "We'll get to them, but I have a present for you first."

"You are the best present I could ever ask for. You and Beckett. I couldn't ask for more."

She bit her lip, giving me a sly sort of smile. "Just us two?"

I didn't get a chance to ask about that because she handed me an envelope. Forced it into my hands, really.

An envelope. For Christmas. "What is it?"

She looked ready to roll her eyes. "A plane. Quit asking silly questions and open the card."

"Yes, ma'am." I ripped the top of the envelope, watching as her smile turned worried. As her eyes locked on my face. "Beauty?"

"Read it."

So I did.

"To the world's greatest dad." I had to cough a little, the tickling in my throat something that took me by surprise. "I love that fucking kid."

"It's not from Beckett."

"No?"

"Nope." She tapped the front of the card. "Read the inside."

With shaking hands, I pulled the card open. Inside, was a little note that said "can't wait to meet you" with a date. A date seven months away.

A ton of bricks was a weak metaphor for what I felt hit by.

"Are you..." Fuck, I had to wipe my eyes. I'd never been a man who cried, but this seemed like a good time to change that. "Are you serious?"

"Yeah." She laughed, her tears falling freely. "I told you we shouldn't do anything without protection."

"Beauty." I couldn't hold back another second. I grabbed her and rolled her underneath me, being careful not to hurt her. Knowing there was too much to say for such a moment, but needing to make a few things real fucking clear. "I will never not be there for you."

Her smile gutted me. "I know."

"I'm not going anywhere."

"I know that too."

"Beckett is going to be thrilled."

"For both things."

Marriage and a baby. I had no idea what I'd done to deserve such blessings, but I would never turn my back on them. This was what I'd wanted, what I'd hoped for. And it was better than I could have dreamed it to be. "Our first Christmas as a family."

"Yeah." My beauty ran her fingers over my face, the softest, sexiest smile in the world beaming up at me. "The first of many."

The first of forever. I'd finally been blessed with a real family, and nothing—absolutely nothing—would ever get in the way of that.

"Come on, beauty." I helped her off the couch, tugging her with me as I led the way to the bedroom. "Let's go celebrate Christmas our way."

"By our way, you mean naked?"

"Yes." I spun her into the room, grinning at her giggle. So fucking happy, I might never get over it. "I promised you a non-selfish present. I intend to deliver."

"You going to make me scream, Chase?"

I would never grow tired of hearing my name on her lips. "Not tonight. Tonight, I'm going to make you beg."

Not that she needed to. I was hers, and I'd do absolutely anything she wanted me to just to make her happy.

Forever.

Kristin Harte started off as a chemistry major in college but somehow ended up writing romances featuring ex-military heroes and the women who knock them to their knees...literally and figuratively. She likes drinking in the shade, snuggling under a warm blanket on a cold evening, and researching how to blow things up. Her children know nothing of what she writes, and her husband just hopes he's not at their Chicago-ish home the day the government shows up to confront Kristin about her Google search history.

When not writing good men doing bad things, Kristin can be found writing paranormal romance as Ellis Leigh, co-writing naughty novellas as London Hale, or taking her signature style into the mystery realm as Mille Thorne.

www.kristinharte.com
Kristin@KristinHarte.com